The Ballad of Wrath and Death

H.T. Mejia

The Ballad of Wrath and Death

Copyright © 2024 by H.T. Mejia
Cover and internal design by H.T. Mejia

All rights reserved. No part of this publication may be reproduced, stored or transmitted in any form or by any means, electronic, mechanical, photocopying, recording, scanning, or otherwise without written permission from the publisher. It is illegal to copy this book, post it to a website, or distribute it by any other means without permission.

This novel is entirely a work of fiction. The names, characters and incidents portrayed in it are the work of the author's imagination. Any resemblance to actual persons, living or dead, events or localities is entirely coincidental.

Self published in 2024 by H.T. Mejia

To my husband,
Thank you for believing in me.
I never could have made the leap without you.

The Ballad of Wrath and Death

H.T. Mejia

The Ballad of Wrath and Death

…

PROLOGUE

We're taught the rules from a young age: don't go outside at night, don't go into the woods alone, don't acknowledge a black dog when you see it. And never, under any circumstances, utter the names of the Gods.

Wrath grows like a pomegranate tree. It starts like a small seed, growing quietly beneath the surface, unbeknownst to those walking around it. When it first breaks through the crust of the earth it's soft and unsuspecting. With a little nurturing it becomes unyielding. It bears fruits to fuel those around it. Some would say wrath alone is not sustainable enough to get you through life, but I beg to differ. I have come to not only accept mine, but to love it.

My grandmother taught me to be kind, to be selfless. She taught me *'The Meek Shall Inherit The Earth'*. I smiled, bowed my head, and shut my mouth. I followed her word as law, all the while my anger and my fury grew deep within me. It blossomed, sharp teeth exposed, as its petals unfurled. It begged to devour the weak. My grandmother was wrong, the meek will not inherit the earth.

I will.

ONE

Red and gold leaves crunched under my boots as I walked through the woods. It was my favorite time of year, when the full moon was a deep orange and the sky was a blanket of darkness. It was a harvest moon sitting high in the sky, reminding us it was time to prepare for winter. I would be canning the bounty of my garden soon.

I inhaled the crisp air, the smell of autumn inundating me. My head craned back, more stars than I could ever hope to count glistened above me. A breeze kissed my face and whipped my hair around. I pulled my cloak tighter, tucking copper curls behind my ear. The chill cut through my linen shirt and breeches with ease, causing me to shiver against the cold.

Unease washed over me. The trees were bare, leaving the branches creaking in the wind. It didn't matter how many times I walked the same path, the quiet of the woods at night was uncomfortable. There was never another soul out, especially after dark. Stories of Gods and death lingered in my mind, even so many years after my childhood.

A twig snapped and I whirled around towards the sound. Panic settled in my stomach and I stood, holding my breath, staring at the darkness between trees. Seconds felt like minutes as I remained frozen.

"You're being watched," a voice inside me whispered.

A wave of regret flooded me. I was foolish for tempting fate by making such a trip so often; foolish and stubborn to break the rules of our village.

Something brushed my hand from behind. A scream ripped through my throat before I could even think, and panic became terror as I turned, every instinct I had told me to run. Pain shot through my hands and back as I fell to the ground, rocks scraping my palms. I expected to see a looming figure. Some God wreathed in power, ready to cleave the soul from my body.

Terror quickly melted to relief as a familiar canine stood before me. She was a large, black dog with shaggy fur and intelligent eyes. She dove on me, licking my face, her tail wagging. A sound escaped my mouth, half laughter, half sob. I wrapped my arms around her, petting her softly. Her brown eyes met mine, then glanced up over my shoulder. As she stared into the trees her face became serious. I paused. She was looking exactly where I had heard the twig snap earlier. Bile rose in my throat. Her erect ears twitched, and she turned the other way, looking towards my destination. Her face relaxed, tongue lolling out of the side of her mouth, and her tail began wagging again. She took several strides to the cabin I was heading to and turned back, looking at me expectantly.

"Yes, yes. I'm coming, you mangy hound!" My voice was barely above a whisper, shaking from adrenaline.

I pushed myself onto my feet. With a groan, I wiped blood and dirt on my trousers. Wrath crept around inside me like a hungry beast at the sight of my bleeding hands. I kept her reigned most of the time but she yanked on her chain often, the slightest thing setting her off. The urge to look over my shoulder was strong, but fear mingled with my anger and kept my eyes straight ahead.

As I walked on, my grandmother's voice dripped into my mind. *'The Gods are evil, child. You mustn't go out at night. The God of Death waits in the shadows, preying on the unsuspecting. The Witch Queen drinks the blood of maidens for their youth.'* I shivered, the hair on my arms raising.

Calm down, Kora. They're stories, nothing more.

I followed the dog down the worn path, my hands still bleeding. The cabin came into view as we rounded a bend. It looked ancient. The wood was worn and splintered. I had asked how old her home was several times but my question was always avoided. Dark, heavy curtains hung in the windows, blocking any candlelight that might be burning inside. Smoke billowed from the chimney– my only sign she was home. There was a small garden in the front yard, full of a variety of herbs. Large pots littered the porch. *'Poisonous plants,'* I had been told previously. I had questioned the safety of growing both herbs and toxins so close together and she had only laughed.

I couldn't explain how I had come to know the old woman, she had to have been 60 years my senior. *'Fate'* she had called it. I didn't believe in fate, it felt more like a fable to me than the Gods did. Some sort of justification for the awful things that happened to people, or a way to explain the good things without giving credit to any sort of God. I thought it was a childish idea.

I enjoyed my time with her, though, seeking her out whenever I could slip away from my responsibilities. She preferred nighttime visits, which was how I ended up wandering through the woods at night a few times a week. She had assured me many times that it was safe, contrary to the belief of everyone else in our village. She let Hecuba, her black dog, out on nights she expected me so that she could accompany me to the cabin. The villagers called the old woman a witch, averting their eyes and scurrying away when she came to town. I called her Hellen. My most beloved friend.

Hecuba bounded up to the porch as I approached the steps. The smell of a fire burning mingled with something else… My steps quickened as I registered the aroma as apple pie. The wood groaned and creaked as I ascended. Hecuba was scratching at the door, whining impatiently. As I reached the top another twig snapped somewhere in the trees behind me. Hecuba's attention shot to the woods and she stared, growling. Her lips peeled back, teeth bared, and her hair stood on end. Fear washed over me again and I bolted to the door. Something was in those woods and I was not eager to find out what it was.

I reached for the knob, but before I could grab it the door swung open. The old woman looked at me with shock, her eyes wide. She turned to whatever Hecuba was growling at and her face paled. Her brown eyes met mine and she grabbed my arm, yanking me inside. She beckoned her dog to come in after us. I jumped as she slammed the door loudly.

Her face was full of confusion and concern. Her gray hair was pulled into a loose braid that reached the bottom of her back. The collar of her black dress covered her neck, the sleeves met her wrists and the hem nearly dragged the floor. She was thin and taller than me. Her tan skin was wrinkled with the life she had lived.

"What the *Hells* are you doing here? It's not your usual night to come."

Her voice was laced with annoyance, which was not unlike her. It was one of the many things I liked about her. She was blunt and said whatever crossed her mind. She did not keep her emotions on a short leash, as I was always expected to.

"I could smell your delicious pie from my house, Hellen! How could I stay home after that? It would be torture." I smiled softly, knowing she hated to be buttered up.

Amusement did not reach her eyes as she smiled back at me. She looked to the door, as if she could see straight through it, and shook her head.

"It's a full moon, Kora. The season is thick and the veil is thin. You should not be out at night this time of year." Despite her words, she motioned me to follow her to the kitchen.

Her home was quaint, her decor mostly consisted of dried herbs, bottles, and jars. Candles crowded every surface imaginable, lighting her home enough to see. Her walls were painted shades of dark purple and black. All of her furniture appeared to be as old as the cabin.

She had a large pie already sitting on the table, and a pot of tea brewing over her small wood stove. Two cups sat on the counter. My curiosity was piqued at the sight, her comment about not expecting me repeated in my head. If I was not the company she was waiting on, who else was coming? I pulled a chair out and took a seat at Hellen's table. She poured a cup of tea and set it down in front of me. I reached for the cup and she grabbed my wrist, startling me.

"You're bleeding," she noted, turning my palm up to inspect it.

"It's nothing. I fell and scraped my hands on the way here."

I pulled my hand back, glancing up at her. Her eyebrows knitted together as if she were examining my words for a lie. She turned and opened a small drawer, pulling out some dried herbs and strips of cloth.

"Foolish. Out walking in the woods amid a thin veil. And bleeding, no less!" I couldn't tell if she was talking to me or just grumbling to herself.

She took both my hands and roughly crammed the dried herbs into my cuts. I winced, sucking air in through my teeth. Her eyes flicked to mine and she gave me a disapproving look, shaking her head. She wrapped the herbs to my palms, her touch a little more gentle this time.

I opened my mouth to ask about the pie, but I thought again of her mystery visitor and changed my mind. "Who else were you expecting tonight?" I mused instead.

Her eyes locked onto mine, boring into my soul. She sat quietly for a moment as if she were considering whether or not to tell me.

"Curiosity killed the cat, girl." I could tell by her tone that I was not going to get an answer. She had a way of avoiding most of my questions, or just flat-out refusing to answer them. I hated the way she hid things from me. Her deceit poked my anger, causing it to stir inside me.

She glanced back to the front door. "Drink your tea and head home quickly. You can stop by tomorrow before dark if you would like."

"Very well, then." I quipped.

I picked up the cup and took a drink of the bitter tea. I wanted to stay, to meet whoever she was waiting for. I ran through everyone in the village, pondering who might be coming to see her. She was good with herbs, perhaps someone coming to purchase some sort of medicine or tonic?

"Or poison," the voice inside me whispered. There was a middle-aged woman in the village who could always be found complaining about her husband. He drank often and her face was usually peppered with bruises. Everyone pretended not to notice. Or the young girl who was locked in an arranged marriage? Maybe she wanted

to free herself of a lifetime with the old man she was promised to. Who could blame her?

As I finished the last of my tea I noticed Hellen wringing her hands. She seemed nervous, eager for me to go. I set the empty cup back down on the table, rising to my feet.

"Tomorrow," I said, my voice laced with frustration.

"Tomorrow," she echoed, fake sweetness coating her tongue in response. It was a familiar dance between us, one we had done many times. She took anything I threw her way and gave it back to me. It was refreshing.

She led me to the door, opened it, and stepped out onto the porch. Her eyes scanned around the tree line, searching. With a curt nod, she stepped aside and waved me out. I gave the inside of her cabin one more look, smiling as I saw Hecuba sleeping in front of the fireplace.

"Go on, then. Be careful going home. Don't speak to anyone. Don't stray from the path."

As she spoke, I felt uneasy. She had never spoken like that before. She had always laughed at the way everyone held so tightly to their superstitions. I wanted to ask her what had changed but I felt certain she wouldn't answer me anyway, so I turned to leave.

The wind started picking up as I descended the stairs. I pulled my cloak together, looking over my shoulder at Hellen. She was still standing on the porch, arms folded, watching me as I walked into the tree line. I thought of the Gods again as I looked ahead. The woods were much darker than when I had come through earlier. The darkness felt tangible.

My skin started to crawl as I walked deeper into the shadows. The feeling of being watched came over me again. My eyes threatened to look around, but fear of actually seeing something stopped me. I cursed under my breath, wishing she had just let me stay the night. That voice inside me raged, threatening to burst my composure.

The trail through the woods was not a long way from the village, but time seemed to pass slowly. I had walked too long to see no progress. I glanced around, wondering if I had somehow stepped away from my normal path through the woods and gotten myself lost.

Leaves crunched to my right, causing a pit to sit heavily in my stomach. My body froze, but my legs screamed for me to run. The woods were eerily silent, the sound of my breathing drowned out by a rush in my ears. *It's just an animal.* I forced my head to turn, to look for what I hoped was a fox. I saw nothing but darkness. No. It was more than that. It was a living shadow, blocking everything behind it. My body started to shake as my eyes trailed up the void. Finally, about a foot taller than any person I had ever seen, I locked onto a set of eyes peering at me. They glowed a soft red, unblinking. The smell of smoke and iron filled my nose.

Run. I thought. *Run!*

My body refused to move. I could only stand there, staring into the red eyes. I wondered if it was some monster who would tear the flesh from my bones. My lips trembled. As Hellen's warning filled my head, I spoke.

"I'm just going home." My voice was quiet, barely audible.

'*Don't speak to anyone*', she had told me. A wave of nausea hit me as I waited to see what the shadow would do. I thought of the whole life I had ahead of me. I had only lived twenty and five years; I was not ready to die.

It continued to stand there, staring at me. Curiosity overpowered my fear, and I strained my eyes, trying to see anything within the darkness. The red eyes blinked and then they vanished, the shadows going with them. As soon as the entity was gone the wind blew again and the sounds of the woods resumed. I shuddered, closing my eyes and breathing the cool air in deeply.

It was probably just your eyes playing tricks on you.

The thought fell flat in my mind, the image of those red eyes resurfacing. When I opened my eyes, I started running, my body finally able to move again. My heart was pounding in my chest and my legs burned. My breath fogged the air with every exhale and my cloak billowed behind me.

I didn't look back.

TWO

I woke up the next morning, my body ached and exhaustion weighed me down. The sun was out, filling my room with bright light. It had taken me a long while to finally drift off to sleep. Red eyes haunted me as I tossed and turned. I groaned, blocking the sun out with my hands. A soft breeze washed over me, kissing me sweetly.

My eyes snapped open, fear clenched in my gut. I sat up slowly, looking at my open window. The thin curtains danced in the wind. When I had fallen asleep my window was closed.

No, maybe you opened it and don't remember.

I tossed my blanket aside and stood up. I glanced around my room, looking for anything out of place. Everything looked exactly as I had left it. I could see no sign of intrusion. Shaking my head, I reminded myself that I had barely slept. I needed tea and breakfast. That would help settle me, surely. I padded over to shut the window and as I stood there I noticed a crowd of people down in the village square. Arms waved and I could hear faint shouting. They were in a very heated argument.

Curiosity overwhelmed me. I slammed the window closed and hurried to my wardrobe. I rushed to pull my clothes off when blood and dirt on my shirt and trousers caught my eye, reminding me of my stumble. There was a little more there than I remembered. It must have been a worse fall than I had realized in the moment. I lifted my palms, the wraps from the night prior were gone. I didn't remember discarding them. The scrapes were healed completely. I silently thanked Hellen for her herbs.

Red eyes flashed in my mind again. I shook my head, not wanting to think about it anymore, and slipped out of my clothes. I picked a pale pink dress from the wardrobe and tugged it over my head, smoothing down the wrinkles. I yanked my brown boots on, leaving only a sliver of skin showing between the tops of them and the trim of my dress. As I looked at my reflection I noted how drained of color the pastel dress made my skin look and how it clashed against my red hair.

I frowned, rubbing my fingers along my dark circles and the splatter of freckles across my nose and cheeks. I brushed through my long hair, ripping at the tangles. The voices outside rang louder, urging me to rush out of my bedroom, all but running down the stairs. I swung the front door open, making my way out to the commotion. The village square was just past my front yard. The voices became clear as I approached.

"It was probably that *hag* that lives in the woods!" Gallus, an older man, said. A musket– that I had no doubt he would use– hung across his shoulder. He was well-known in the village and mostly well-respected. I had never liked him. "I've always said she was a witch!"

"No," argued a young woman, Jaen was her name. "I saw some men come into the tavern a few days ago. Heard them tell Marnie they were just passing through. I say it was them!"

They flew into a flurry of accusations. I gazed around at all of them, trying to decipher what had happened by what they were saying. My frustration grew as I was unable to reach any conclusions.

"What happened?" I asked, pushing my way into the midst of everyone.

They did not answer me. My frustration flared to anger and I glanced around them, aware I was being ignored. I had been an outsider since I arrived in the village. I was nearly a ghost, acknowledged only when it benefited them.

"What happened?" I demanded louder.

Everyone paused and stared at me. Finally, Tyne, an older woman with graying hair, stepped towards me. "It's old man Theo, Kora. He was found dead outside his house this morning."

Everyone continued to stare at me silently. Dread coiled inside me as I recalled those red eyes... And my open window. Nausea mixed with guilt as I wondered if I had almost been a victim as well.

"And... We think he was murdered? Is that what you're all implying?"

I hoped that maybe they had no viable reason to believe that. Perhaps he had died of natural causes. People were easily spooked, eager to burn a witch or hang someone they thought guilty of a crime.

"Go see for yourself," Gallus said.

He pointed in the direction of Theo's home. He didn't have to, though. It was a small village, everyone knew everyone. I walked forward and the crowd of people parted for me. I made my way down the dirt road, feeling their eyes on my back. My grandmother's voice invaded my thoughts again. *'The Gods are evil, child...'* My whole body was vibrating, and each breath I took was strained.

Everything around me was quiet, save the baying of sheep that wandered loose through the village. And the sound of a screeching bird. It echoed through me every time it called out. I craned my head to the sky. A single crow was flying in circles above me.

"One for sorrow…" I mumbled under my breath. My eyes drifted back ahead, the old man's house coming into view.

As I drew near, I could see him. Or what was left of him. His body was contorted, limbs broken. Bones jutted out of his arms and legs. His torso was facing up, while his head was snapped around unnaturally. His chest cavity was ripped open and his insides appeared to be partially eaten. Blood was splattered and bits of organs were strewn around him.

My eyes were wide, my mouth ajar. As I took in the gruesome sight, I became sick. I turned, unable to even take a step, and emptied the contents of my stomach onto the ground. Once my retching subsided I started back to the square. I could not bear to see anymore. My mind was full of fog, I was unable to form any thoughts and my body was violently shaking. My walk back was a blur.

When I returned everyone stared anxiously, waiting to see what I had to say. I closed my eyes, Theo's mangled body was the only thing I could see.

"Could it have been a wolf?" I asked, looking around at them all.

I heard whispered disagreements, and debates. I didn't wait for their responses. I moved through them, unable to hear all of their theories, and walked towards my grandmother's house. She lived just down the road from me. I had moved out when I reached adulthood, needing my own space and a bit of solitude. My grandmother was one of the Hegemon, one of the elders, and had seen more than all of us combined. It was she who kept the stories of monsters and Gods alive. I couldn't imagine why she was not also in the crowd, relaying her knowledge.

As I walked through her front yard I heard an unfamiliar voice coming from inside. It wasn't uncommon. She had visitors all hours of the day. People regularly came from neighboring villages to meet with her. I stepped up to her door, glancing around at her bare yard. Nothing ever grew for her, despite her efforts. I had tried several times to help her raise a garden or even a few flowerbeds. Nothing lived very long. My yard was covered in an array of flowers and vegetables. I supplied more crops to the village than anyone, not that they had ever cared what my contributions were. As if they could thrive like they did without me.

    I twisted the knob and pushed the door open, stepping inside. Her entryway was narrow, several pairs of worn boots lined the wall. The house was painted a sad beige, as it had been my whole life. I walked down the hall towards the den. Her furniture was relatively new, handcrafted by the carpenter who wanted to thank her for delivering his wife's baby the summer prior. I heard her voice, along with the stranger's voice, become more clear. I slowed my steps, walking carefully along the creaky boards so I could hear what they were saying.

    "Fray, you must know it's not safe here any longer. She needs to be moved immediately. Last night's attack was too close," the man I did not know said. Concern laced his voice.

    "We will handle the attack accordingly. Theo was a stubborn old man, he went outside after dark all the time. We have curfews in place for this very reason. We will enforce the curfew, I assure you. Everyone will be very careful moving forward, including *Kora*." My grandmother sounded sure of herself, as she always had.

    She was a proud woman, in everything she did. She had raised me to be the same way, proud and stubborn. The way she mentioned my name caught my attention, but the thought was fleeting.

    Silence followed her comment and I decided that was the best time to show myself. I stepped around the corner, into the kitchen. My grandmother was seated at the small, round table, her white hair pulled into a tight bun. She was wearing the brown dress she usually wore, with a knitted shawl pulled over her shoulders. Her eyes shot to me, a look on her face I was unable to place.

I glanced from her to her guest, who was now also looking at me. He was tall with lean muscles. His hair was as red as mine, brushed back and perfectly in place, unlike my wild curls. He was dressed in fine clothing, everything just as flawless as his hair, making him look out of place in our impoverished village. His hazel eyes locked onto mine and a mischievous grin spread across his face. Something about his expressions and mannerisms was vaguely familiar to me.

"You must be *Kora*. Pleasure."

He stood, holding his hand out in front of me. I took his hand in mine, giving it a firm shake. His brows shot up and he gripped my hand tighter. He raised it to his lips, brushing a kiss on the top. Heat bloomed across my cheeks. Embarrassment nearly consumed me. I should have realized by his clothing and demeanor that he came from a more prominent area than I had been raised. Somewhere women certainly didn't wear boots and shake the hands of men.

"The pleasure is mine, Mr....?"

My words hung in silence as if he wasn't sure he was going to give me his name. At that moment I realized exactly why he was so familiar to me. He reminded me of Hellen.

"Hermes," he said with a nod. He looked back to my Grandmother. "Well, Fray, it was nice to have this time with you. I should be leaving, though. Think about what I said."

At that he turned, brushing past me, and made his way out of the front door. I watched him until he was out of sight and then returned my attention to my grandmother.

"Who was that?" I tried to smother the curiosity, but she had known me my whole life. I could tell by her furrowed brows she knew exactly what I was doing.

"Hermes, as he told you."

Frustration bloomed. I hated that, avoidance and information withheld. She caught that as well. She let out a heavy sigh, picking up her tea cup.

"Sit down, we need to talk." She waved to the now unoccupied seat. I sat down, leaning back in the chair.

"So you heard about what happened to Theo?" I asked, accusation thick in my tone. She looked up from her cup, her face tense.

"Yes, I did, Kora." She offered nothing more than what I asked. We stared at each other, neither one of us wanting to relent. Finally, I caved. She was more stubborn than me, it seemed.

"Do you have an idea of what might have happened?" My voice came out more harshly than I intended.

"There is no way for us to know what happened to him. No one is supposed to go out at night. We have these rules in place to keep everyone safe. You know this." As long as she had known me, I had known her. I could tell she was lying to me, I could taste it. A bitterness washed through me.

"I don't think you're being honest with me, Grandmother. I saw Theo. His body was not only ripped open, it was feasted on… and his bones were broken. There is no way a human or an animal could have done that." I couldn't shake the suspicion that she knew more than she was telling me.

She sat there, eyes burning a hole into me. The silence was loud between us as I stood my ground. I would make her tell me what she knew. She put her head in her hands, shoulders slouched forward.

She sat like that for several minutes as I continued to watch her. Finally, she sat up, looking defeated.

"You're right, Kora. I do not think that was something any human or animal could have done."

My anxiety grew, and my hands started shaking.

Say it, I thought. *I need to hear you say it.*

"I fear the Gods are back, and they're sending us a message."

Her face seemed to age as her admittance rang in my ears. I felt like I had been hollowed out. Shock coursed through me like a raging river, even though she had given me the answer I both expected and feared.

"What sort of message would the Gods be trying to send to us? What could they possibly want?"

Her eyes glassed over and I noticed her hands trembling slightly. She took a deep breath in, closing her eyes. She paused, contemplating her words and I felt like I was going to burst with anticipation. Her next words clanged through me.

"The Gods are vengeful and angry creatures. They do not like to be scorned or slighted. We have cast them aside for many years, leaving them forgotten, taking control of our own lives and our fates. I am afraid our time is up."

THREE

I was almost through the woods, the sun still high in the sky. My bag was slung over my shoulder, full of vegetables from my garden, and I had braided my hair back out of my face. The wind was strong, as if it could sense a storm coming. Gods and monsters were back to hunt and eat us, like in the days of old. Images of red eyes lurking in dark woods, of broken and twisted bodies, filled my head. A shiver went through me. I continued trudging on, determined to get to Hellen's cabin with enough time to have a real conversation and still get home before dark. She was older, possibly, than my grandmother. She had to have some knowledge that could help us.

Hecuba did not greet me in the woods to walk me to the cabin, nor was she outside waiting for me on the porch. As I crossed the treeline I noted Hellen's chimney had no smoke. Her curtains still hung in front of the windows. Somehow, with no signs of activity, the cabin had a menacing aura. It seemed like a trap, waiting to snap the leg of any unsuspecting prey.

Don't be ridiculous, Kora. You have been coming here for months.

I shook my head, moving up to her porch. The creaking of her steps seemed to echo through the trees, causing more anxiety to build inside me. I thought again of Theo's ravaged body. I was not close to anyone in the village, save my grandmother and Hellen. But the death had still shaken me, if nothing else just for the abhorrent nature of it.

I stepped up to her door and knocked. I stood there, straining my ears to hear anything at all that may be stirring around inside. My stomach sank as I heard nothing. I could only imagine her body broken and bloody inside her home. I wondered if she had screamed for help, if Hecuba had also been killed.

I couldn't take another second of my imagination. I grabbed the doorknob, twisting it gently, and swung the door open. I glanced around the room. Everything seemed to be in place. Stepping inside, I quietly laid my bag down by the door. I crept through the house, tiptoeing to the kitchen. There was no blood, no sign of a struggle. Relief mingled with confusion.

Maybe she went to town. I must have just missed her.

As I entered the kitchen my body finally relaxed. I decided I would make a pot of tea and wait for her to get back. Shock hit me like a ton of bricks when I looked at the old wood stove. A young woman stood there with her back to me. Her raven hair was pulled into a loose braid that hung down to the bottom of her back. Her black dress was… familiar. It was the dress I had seen Hellen in the previous night.

I stood there, staring at the woman's back. As I watched in silence, she used a stick of incense to light several candles. Once they were lit she ran her fingers through the smoke, muttering something I could not decipher. The smoke flashed a deep green and the flames flickered angrily. A gasp flew from my lips before I could catch myself.

The woman turned quickly, shock and outrage plastered on her face. As soon as our eyes met, I was stunned. The young, beautiful woman I was looking at... She was Hellen. A vibrant version of her, full of life. What once was. I stood there, mouth agape, unable to speak. '*Hag,*' they had called her. '*A witch*'. I had been blind. What signs had I missed?

She relaxed when she realized who I was, then a wicked grin spread across her face. I understood at that moment that I did not truly know her. Something about her seemed almost feral. Cruel. I swallowed hard, fear slithering through every part of me like a snake. I took a shaky step backward, not taking my eyes off of her.

"Now, Kora... I'm going to need you to take a seat so we can talk."

Her eyes seemed wild, but her hands were raised in surrender. She bowed slightly, motioning me to her table. I glanced from her to her table, then back. I knew I should run, yet I could not stop the curiosity sneaking up to smother my fears away.

I stepped up, pulling out a chair to sit. My eyes stayed glued on her as if she might pounce on me at any moment. She nodded, turning back to the stove to put the tea on. I glanced around her kitchen. The jars and bottles of unidentified liquid and herbs now stood out to me like a sore thumb. The candles crammed anywhere she could make them fit, most half-burned or more. Dried plants strung upside down from her ceilings, bones. and fur scattered about. I had always thought of her as an eccentric old woman. I never imagined she was an actual witch.

She turned to the table, two cups of tea in her hands. She passed one to me and sat down across from me. My words came out more hostile than I meant for them to. "You're not poisoning me are you?"

She let out a harsh laugh, as she leaned back in her chair and sipped her tea. "Now, child, if I wanted you dead then you would already be dead."

She stared at me over her cup, her lids heavy. I held her gaze, eyes narrowed. I brought the cup to my lips, smelling it deeply before taking a sip. She grunted and rolled her eyes.

"Please, if I poisoned your tea do you think you would smell it?"

Frustration and embarrassment flared. I set the tea down abruptly. "Who are you?"

I was not going to play her games any longer. Everyone was feeding me lies and half-truths, and I was sick of it. I felt betrayed. Wrath moved through me. She could turn me into a toad for all I cared.

Her smile spread wider, her red lips parting. She looked at me as though she could read my thoughts. Her eyes seemed to glow a faint purple. She stood, the chair clattering as it slid out from behind her. With her arms outstretched and her chin held high, she spoke. Her voice came out as three separate voices speaking in unison.

"I am The Maiden, child. I am the Keeper of Keys, She Who Wanders at Night. I am The Mother. The Moon Mistress, The Light-Bringer. I am The Crone. The Torch Bearer, The Guide. I am the Trinity Goddess, Hecate."

Her words reverberated through me. She was not only a witch, but a *Goddess*. I had been in the presence of a Goddess and had no idea. She could have killed me many times. I would not have stood a chance. Old man Theo's body flashed in my mind, followed by images of red eyes in the woods, my open window. I felt sick and my head started spinning. She was staring at me like she expected me to say something. But as the images flooded my mind, and the room swirled around me, I found no words.

I grabbed at the table as the feeling of falling washed over me. Then everything was black.

Perhaps she had killed me.

***

I woke with a lurch, a putrid smell filling my nostrils. I sat up, gagging and coughing. My head was throbbing. I reached up to rub my temples and as the fog lifted my memories returned. My eyes flung open. Hellen, or Hecate I supposed, was kneeling beside me, a bottle of smelling salts in her hand. In a panic, I scooted back away from her. I didn't want to end up like Theo. I wondered if he had just been in the wrong place at the wrong time.

Or perhaps he had seen something he shouldn't have.

"You! You killed Theo."

Her eyes met mine, and a look of sympathy flashed across her face. She reached towards me, causing me to jump. She laid her hand on my knee, shaking her head softly.

"No, child. I did not kill Theo. Had I killed him it would have looked like he went to sleep and never woke up."

Maybe it was the time and friendship we had shared, or maybe it was the soft expression she gazed at me with, but I believed her. As the recognition settled, fear boiled over again. My whole body started shaking.

"If you didn't kill him, who did?"

Her eyebrows knitted together, as she spoke. "The veil is thin, Kora. It could be a number of monsters or Gods that brought that unfortunate end upon him."

I shook my head, I could sense the lie in her words. She had to at least have an idea of who, or what, did that. I pushed myself off the floor, crossed my arms, and looked down where she still knelt on the floor.

"I don't believe you. I think you know exactly what happened and you're going to tell me! You have spent months lying to me, you owe me this much."

Anger flickered through her eyes like a hungry flame. Regret coursed through me, but I refused to back down.

"You speak to me, child, like you have any sort of rule over me. You may speak to me as a friend, that much I owe you after months of *real* friendship. I may have withheld information, but never have I lied to you. What you will not do is speak to me as though you have some sort of authority over me. *I* am a Goddess, and *you* are a mortal child."

My arms fell loosely at my sides, my expression softening. She was right. She had been a friend to me. She had been kind to me.

"Please, Hecate. If the village is in danger please tell me. If you know who did this and how I can avoid this happening again…"

Her eyes narrowed. She stood, pulling her chair back to the table and sitting down. "If I give you any information regarding the Gods, you have to promise me you will do nothing but encourage safety on your people. You cannot try to confront the Gods. If you approach another God the way you did me, you will be struck dead where you stand."

I nodded, eagerly. I would comply with whatever she said to get the information I wanted. I sat across from her, holding her stare, waiting. She sat in silence, seeming to weigh her words before she spoke them.

"I believe this was the work of the Harpies, the Hounds of Zeus."

I considered her words. "The Hounds of Z–" she jumped towards me and covered my mouth quickly. My body froze, eyes wide. She was so fast I didn't even have time to react.

She shook her head, keeping her hand on my mouth. "You mustn't utter the names of the Gods, child."

I swallowed hard, feeling sick. She slowly removed her hand from my face and sat back down. I thought about my next words before I spoke them, trying to tread lightly around a subject of which I knew nothing, really.

"I've spoken your name?" I wondered for a moment if she had given me another false name. The thought made me feel small and insignificant.

"Yes, you have. I am here before you, I know you. If you speak the names of the Gods, they hear it. Wherever they are. If you speak his name he will know it and he will come. It has been a very long time since mortals have spoken the names of the Gods. You may refer to Zeus as the God of Lightning, for safety's sake."

"Why can you say his name?" I was trying to understand, but the rules seemed complicated.

She waved her hand dismissively. "Oh, the Gods gossip about one another all the time, we don't even acknowledge it anymore."

"And you said he has hounds? Am I allowed to say their name?" I spoke slowly, dancing around saying anything that may cause me to be struck dead. She smiled, it was a soft smile that time.

"The Harpies, yes. You can say that."

"The Harpies…" I echoed, the word feeling foreign on my tongue. "Why do you think that they killed Theo? What do they look like?" My words came out hurriedly. She looked slightly disappointed by my questions, making me consider what I should have been asking instead.

"The Harpies are a vicious creation. They have the body and face of a woman, the wings of a bird, and talons on their feet. They follow Zeus, ravaging any who slight him. I hope you never have the misfortune of meeting him. He is easily angered and throws tantrums like a child." She became distracted by her disdain for the God of Lightning, contempt dripping from her voice.

I took in the information she gave me, contemplating everything it meant. "What happens if I come face to face with a Harpy?"

Pride showed on her face as I spoke. She nodded, sipping her tea again. That was the right question, then.

"Very good, child. If you come face to face with a Harpy the first thing you must realize is where you see one, several more are hiding out of sight. You must never run in the presence of a Harpy. You stand perfectly still and you call my name as loudly as you can. I will hear you." Her face was serious, causing a wave of uneasiness to wash over me.

"I have another question." I paused, almost scared to ask. "Do the Harpies have red eyes?"

Shock flashed on her face. Her lips pursed, and she leaned forward on the table, placing her hand over her lips. We held each other's gaze, silence hanging in the air between us.

"Why?" Her question came out clipped. Dread coiled in my stomach. I wanted nothing more than to take my question back. I wasn't sure I wanted the answer.

"When I was going home from your house last night I saw a shadow in the treeline, it had red eyes." Her eyes widened and her brows furrowed. She breathed in slowly and then let out a shaky exhale.

"No. The Harpies do not have red eyes. They have beady, black eyes– like a rat. I had a visitor last night. I was hoping he wouldn't see you." I could feel the sweat beading down my back as she spoke. She narrowed her eyes on me. "You did as I said, yes? You did not speak to him?"

I grimaced slightly before I could control myself. "Well…"

"Kora! I told you, in no uncertain terms, to speak *to no one*!" Her voice raised, sounding again as though she had three separate voices speaking as one.

"I only said I was trying to go home," I said defensively.

"That absolute *ass* couldn't even have the decency to tell me he saw you! What in the Hells was he thinking?"

She stood abruptly as she spoke, her chair hitting the floor loudly. Her anger seemed to swirl around her like a beautiful vine of roses with thorns springing out to impale anyone who may venture too close. I decided against telling her about my open window.

"How many Gods are walking around among us without us even knowing?" I asked, more to myself than to her. It pulled her from her rage-filled venting.

She looked at me, her eyes full of curiosity, her temper simmering down. "Why do you ask that, Kora?"

"I never would have guessed you were a God, and I'm assuming who I saw in the woods was also a God? My grandmother had a strange visitor today. He mentioned to her that the attack was too close. I think they were talking about moving me. I don't understand why I would need to leave."

"Mortal lives are fleeting, child. They probably just want to keep everyone safe." She spoke to me softly, as if I didn't know a life could be tamped out like the flame of a candle.

"The man who was visiting her, I had never seen him before. He had red hair…" I leaned back in my chair trying to remember his name. She eyed me closely as I sat quietly.

"Hermes!" I shouted, lurching forward in my seat. Hecate's eyes widened, and her mouth flew open. As we stared at each other I had a sneaking suspicion that I had said something I shouldn't have.

The winds infiltrated her home, swirling around both of us. Dread and fear filled me. My grandmother's voice echoed through me again…

'The Gods are evil, child.'

FOUR

As the air swirled around us, tendrils slipped loose from our braids. Pure power circulated the room, snuffing out candles and scattering dried herbs. Hecate was beside me in an instant, arms around me protectively. I sunk into her touch, fearing I had just gotten myself killed. How stupid I had been, shouting his name after I was given ample warning about my words.

The wind died down and silence fell around us. The sound of Hecate's breathing filled my ears. I glanced around the room, Hecate still held me tightly. As the seconds ticked away I felt a dark and thick dread come over me.

A bright flash of light blinded me, my hands flew up to my face instinctively. I could feel his presence burst into the room with us, but my body refused to move. I couldn't lower my hands. I swallowed hard, trying to calm myself.

"Well, well… If it isn't Kora." His tone was taunting. Slowly I dropped my hands, lifting my eyes to meet his. My heart sank when I saw him. Gone were the fine clothes he wore earlier, replaced with robes and sandals. His hair was no longer pristine, but hung in loose curls around his face, framing his fair skin. His eyes were bright, the hazel seemed almost incandescent. He had an aura about him, one that sent all my senses screaming. My mind fumbled over itself trying to piece together why my grandmother was holding council with a God. Had she even been aware?

"Hermes." As Hecate spoke, my body thrummed.

I had forgotten she still stood with me. Her fingers tightened around my shoulder, her nails digging into my skin. I tore my eyes from Hermes to look back at her. She was staring at him with malice, daring him to move. Her power radiated off her body, reminding me how very fragile I was in comparison.

Movement drew my attention back to Hermes. He swaggered up to the table, picking up the chair that had been knocked over. He sat, leaning back until the chair was balanced on its back legs. My skin was on fire. Every instinct I had told me I was a deer staring down a wolf, waiting to be ripped apart. The Gods were apex predators and I was most definitely their prey.

"Hecate. I always knew you had a soft spot for the mortals, but what on Earth are you doing?" There was mischief sparkling in his eyes and a familiarity in his voice.

"This young woman is mine, Hermes. You will not speak of this to the other Gods." Her voice was cold, but her eyes were pleading. I could not tell who held the power, or which side of the coin my fate would be landing on.

"You should teach your pets to be more careful, Hecate. Don't forget– she's the one who called me here." He leaned forward, propping his head up in his hand, elbow resting on the table. "How did this come about?" I could feel my fear turning into anger as he spoke about me as if I was not in the room.

"Between the Harpies ripping open old men and you gallivanting around the town like you fit in, how could she not become curious? I feel like everything I do lately is just covering up your all's messes!"

He arched a brow at her. Her pleading eyes turned cold again. Her hold on me loosened, her body relaxed. She moved from me and took a seat across from Hermes, leaving me standing there alone. I felt exposed; vulnerable. I moved quickly to sit beside her, folding my arms over my chest.

He turned, taking in every inch of me slowly. "You're going to get yourself into a lot of trouble, kid." He had a twinkle in his eye that made me wonder if he would enjoy my strife. A shudder went through me. He moved his attention back to Hecate. "We should wipe her memories, Witch. She'll be much less trouble that way."

Her eyes flared and she slammed her hand down on the table, causing me to jump. "Absolutely not! I told you– she's mine. You'll not lay a finger on her."

My relief was short-lived as Hermes spoke again. His words sent me spiraling into my own thoughts.

"I don't think she's yours at all, Hecate."

She fell silent, seeming to mull his words over as thoroughly as I was. Her eyes slid to me, narrowing. She leaned into me and sniffed heavily. Her eyes widened and she turned back to Hermes. They stared at each other in silent conversation.

Finally, I spoke, unable to contain my temper any longer. "I'm right here, stop talking about me as though I'm some object to be possessed!"

Their heads snapped to me, surprise clear on Hermes' face at my boldness. Hecate opened her mouth, I could only assume to scold me, but Hermes held a hand up to cut her off.

"You cannot belong to Hecate, because you've been claimed already. Long before you were born. Your mother hid you here hoping to conceal you from your destiny. Even the Gods cannot escape The Fates, though."

I replayed his words over and over as they both watched me. I had thought my mother had abandoned me, that she had never loved me. The idea that she tucked me away somewhere to keep me safe from the Gods ignited a sliver of hope that I would one day see her again.

Memories of my mother I had held on to so tightly, flashed through my mind. Golden hair, green eyes, a blanket of freckles across tan skin. The smell of clove and cinnamon, hugs, and promises of a future together. After so many years I couldn't tell if they were memories or things my mind had crafted to keep me from breaking.

"Who?" The question escaped my mouth before I could even decide if I wanted to know the answer. Hermes and Hecate glanced at each other in yet another silent discussion. "Who claimed me?" I pushed.

The only other God I was familiar with was Zeus. I hoped that it was not him, after what Hecate had told me about him. *'Easily angered'*, she had said. Certainly not the kind of God I would want to be at the mercy of. I had a tendency to get under people's skin. I would certainly be dead within minutes around him.

It was Hecate who spoke first. "You were promised by The Fates to the God of the Dead, child." Her words clanged through me. God of the Dead…

I looked at Hecate, my anger flaring up. "Did you know this whole time?" She flinched at the accusation, then shook her head. "Then how do you know this?"

She leaned into me again and I pulled back slightly. She inhaled deeply through her nose, closing her eyes. When she opened them a shadow rippled across her face. "You smell like her. Not wholly, but there's a hint of spice about you. Clove?"

My eyebrows shot up. I hadn't made her up at all. The memories of my mother were real, and Hecate seemed to know her.

"The question is, Hecate, will you run to the God of the Dead and hand her over? Or will you risk his fury and keep her tucked away?"

Hermes was grinning, that fiendish gleam in his eyes again. He seemed to revel in all of the chaos. I turned back to Hecate, feeling sure she would keep me safe. She had been doing everything she could so far. My confidence in her shattered as I met her stare. She looked torn, unsure.

I stood abruptly, backing up a few steps from them both. I should never have trusted a God. I needed to leave, to hide somewhere.

"Where can you hide from a God?" that voice inside me murmured.

I continued to slowly back away from them.

"I won't let you take me." My voice was quiet, barely more than a whisper. Hecate looked at me with pity in her eyes.

"Even the Gods cannot escape The Fates," she said to me softly.

I turned from them both and ran out of the cabin, my grandmother's words reeling through me. I had made a grave mistake in trusting Hecate after finding out she was a God. I was reckless and gullible.

I swung the door open, barreling down the stairs, heading to the woods. The sun was bright, but was starting to hang lower in the sky. I made it to the treeline and glanced over my shoulder, Hecate stood on the porch watching me. There was sadness in her eyes and she was hugging her arms tightly. My heart pulled at the sight, my body urging me to stop, but my head screamed for me to keep running.

As I ran deeper into the woods, my fear turned to rage. I felt tricked and lied to. I would not belong to the Gods. I would not let myself be used and discarded like trash. I had my whole life ahead of me. I was strong and full of potential. I would find a way out of it. Certainly my grandmother would know some way to avoid such a future.

Another pull hit me, deep in my bones. The hair on my arms stood, and a chill went through me. I slowed to a stop and stilled. The smell of smoke and iron filled the air and brought with it flashes of red eyes. I turned, looking to my right, expecting shadows and darkness. Instead, I saw the most beautiful man I had ever seen.

He was tall, the trees above us casting shadows along his dark skin. His inky black hair was pulled back into a bun and a well-groomed beard covered his jaw. I swallowed hard and my eyes trailed down. He wore a white button-down, the sleeves cuffed up, and a black tie hung loosely around his neck. When my gaze flicked back up he was staring at me intensely and his eyes… They were red.

Realization sunk in; he was the God Hecate had been waiting for. I should have been scared, but I felt no fear looking at him. Just a dangerous curiosity, a tug. He was looking at me with the same interest, both of us standing perfectly still.

I wanted to turn and run, I wanted nothing else to do with these Gods. I told myself to leave, to heed the words Hecate had told me the previous night. Instead, my lips parted and I spoke.

"I'm just going home." The same words I spoke to him last, the words that saved my life. I hoped they would bring me home safely once more.

He tilted his head to the side. I was unsure what to expect of him. Maybe fire and brimstone? He took several steps towards me, not breaking eye contact. His movements were slow, as if he was scared I would startle and run away. But as I stood there, holding his stare, I decided I didn't want to run. I wanted to stay there in those woods, looking at his face forever.

He stepped up next to me and I realized exactly how much taller than me he was. I only reached his chest. My eyes were locked on his, as if he held me in a trance. He reached his hand up to my face, brushing a strand of hair behind my ear. His touch sent another chill through me.

His eyes peeled from mine like it pained him, and he glanced in the direction of Hecate's cabin. I turned away, closing my eyes and breathing his scent in again. It reminded me of a cool autumn night, sitting around a fire. I opened my eyes, and I could feel his stare back on me.

"I'm just going home," I said again. It felt more like a reminder to myself– that I was going home– I was not staying here. They were dangerous Gods, not my friends.

In an instant he was gone, vanished into thin air, leaving only his burning aroma surrounding me. I felt a hole inside me, then. Something missing from me that I had never noticed before. I didn't let myself linger on the thought of it. I breathed in one final time, memorizing everything I could from that moment, and I made my way back to the village. I didn't run, my steps were slow and steady. All the anger I held for Hecate and Hermes had been smothered by him.

As I exited the woods, the village coming into view, I told myself I would see Hecate again. I needed to learn what I could of the Gods, to keep myself safe. She was my best chance at getting the information I needed. The Gods were dangerous and capable.

And if they planned to come for me, to take me…
I would be prepared.

FIVE

I marched through the village, my head still spinning. As I made my way to my grandmother's house I passed several people. They were scurrying inside, beckoning children behind them. They ignored me, as they always did. I wondered, as I walked, if it was some curse from the gods for avoiding The Fates. My mind wandered back to the God I met in the woods, the way his eyes held mine, his smoldering scent.

    I shook the thoughts away as I approached my grandmother's house. I opened the door and entered without knocking. Silence filled the space as I walked through and found her alone in the kitchen. She was sitting at the table, drinking her tea. She looked weary. I hadn't realized before how much she had aged over the years.

    Her eyes flicked up to mine. "Kora. I didn't expect you back today." She stood, making her way over to her small wood stove. Every move she made seemed strained. "Sit, I'll make you some tea."

    I obliged, pulling a chair out and sitting at the table. I couldn't help but wonder, as she made my drink, how much she had hidden from me over the years. I ran my fingers along the worn wood of the table, one of the only pieces of furniture she had left from my childhood.

She hurriedly brought over a cup of hot tea, sat it down in front of me, and took her seat again. I looked at the woman who had cared for me most of my life. She had fed me, had raised me. She was the reason I was the person I was. Right?

I picked up the small glass cup and sipped the tea softly. It was full of honey, and almost disgustingly sweet compared to the tea Hecate always served me. My mouth had adjusted to the bitter drinks, making me blanch at the tea I had just received. I put the cup down, deciding I couldn't finish it.

"We need to talk, grandmother." I noted how hard she swallowed, the concern showing in her wrinkled face. She nodded silently, allowing me a moment to collect my thoughts. "I know about The Fates, and what was foretold of my future." Her eyes widened, and her thin lips parted slightly. She tried to recover quickly, but I continued.

"I have no plans to let myself be taken by the Gods. I need you to tell me what you know so I can stay safe. I need to find a way to keep myself hidden." She wrung her withered hands, her anxiety undeniable.

"How did you get this information?"

Her words came out short, and the way she avoided my question had my anger bubbling up again. I tried to tamp it down, to choke it out. I didn't have time to be angry. I needed to gather information.

"How I obtained it is not important. I need you to tell me what you know. I don't have time for games." She must have been able to see my rage threatening to erupt, because she nodded and took a sip of her tea.

"Very well, Kora. It was a crisp, spring night 21 years ago. I was already settled in for the night when a loud banging on my door pulled me from bed. When I answered it, a young woman stood there with her small child. You couldn't have been more than three or four years old. You were bright-eyed and inquisitive and your mother was scared."

I could see the memories flashing across her face as she spoke. She paused to take another sip of her tea, before continuing. "She told me that she had you in secret, that if the Gods learned of you, your fate would be grim. She begged me to take you, to keep you tucked away here in our quiet village until she came back for you. I thought she would be back within a couple years at most, though she never said as much."

She paused again, a smile spreading across her face. "The time never came, however, and I am thankful for that. I was never able to have my own children. You completed my life, Kora. I made sure to keep the fables of the Gods alive, to ensure you knew how dangerous they were. Just in case one day you crossed their paths. Your mother wanted you safe."

As her story ended I felt more of myself hollow out. The woman before me, the one I had loved for as long as I could remember, was not even my real grandmother. The anger I was trying to tamp down flared again. My entire life had been a lie. I didn't know what to think, or how to feel anything other than burning wrath. I wanted to scream, but I couldn't.

Wrath begged to be released, she wanted to hurt someone the way she had been hurt. I pushed her aside, trying to focus myself on the task at hand. Information. I needed information.

I sat in silence, holding her stare. She let me process her words while she sipped her tea. "Do you know who my mother was? Her name? Where she went? Did she say how this curse was laid on me?"

My questions came out as quickly as I thought of them. I kept my eyes locked on her, watching her mull them over before she answered them. My skin was on fire.

"I did not know your mother. She did not offer her name, only yours. She did not tell me where she was going, she said it was safer if I didn't know. The only thing she said to me about this curse was that you were destined to end up in darkness, surrounded by death. She said you were full of life and you deserved to be in the sun, among the living. I had heard stories of how evil the Gods were, she did not have to say anything more than that for me to know I had to do everything I could to keep you safe."

The answers she gave left me disappointed. I had hoped she held some key information that would save me, but she was just as blind to everything as I was. With my hope shattered, I covered my face with my hands. I would have to go back to Hecate. She would know something. I wasn't sure I could trust her, but did I really have a choice?

"You're a force of nature, Kora." Her words drew me out of my thoughts, like a moth to a flame. I lifted my face, my eyes meeting hers again. "We may not know where to go from here, child, but I believe in you. I know you will figure this out. You are a strong, capable young woman. If anyone can defy fate and the Gods, it is you."

Her words filled those holes inside me. She was right. I had always found a way to get what I wanted, she had raised me to be unstoppable.

I stood slowly, pushing my chair back. "Thank you, grandmother. For everything."

She smiled at me, and there was sadness there. I brushed a kiss against her temple, and as I turned and left her house, I couldn't help but feel like it was somehow goodbye. I wasn't sure what I would be doing next; if I would leave or stay, but it felt like the end of something for me.

When I opened the front door and looked around at the quaint village, it was empty. Everyone had retired for the day, hiding away in their homes so they didn't end up like old man Theo. The sun was setting, a muted pink spreading across the sky. I made my way over to my own house, passing by the rose bushes in my front yard. They were still blooming, even this late in the year. It didn't seem to matter what time of year it was, my flowers and crops always did well.

I reached over and plucked a bloom from its stem. I turned it over, inspecting the perfect red petals. I brought it to my nose and smelled deeply. It smelled sweet. My thoughts drifted to the tea Hecate always served me and I was angry again. Angry at The Fates, at the Gods, at my mother. I crushed the bloom in my fist and tossed it to the ground.

I walked into my house, closing the door behind me and latching the bolt. Red eyes and blood flashed into my mind. I tried to piece together what the Harpies must look like, and how they must have ripped open and broken Theo. If the Gods and the Harpies existed, what else was lurking around out there, waiting to devour us? A shiver went through me.

I wandered into the kitchen, suddenly very aware of how empty my stomach was. I rummaged through my cabinets, pulling out some stale bread and dried figs. I sat down at the table and ate, lost to my thoughts of monsters and what I might face if I left the village.

When I finished, I left the remnants of food on the table and made my way upstairs. I considered what I might do to keep myself safe. I didn't own any guns or swords, I was no fighter either way. I had no way to keep myself safe. I would have to use my wits to stay alive, and to do that I would have to arm myself with as much knowledge as I could. Hecate was the only one I could think of who might be able to help me, but I still wasn't sure that she would. Hermes seemed like he wanted me to fail, and I did not think I could trust him.

Hermes… I had forgotten to ask my grandmother how she knew him. I shrugged the thought away, deciding I could ask her the next day.

I opened the door to my bedroom and a chill washed over me. Immediately my eyes flew to my window, which was open again. The curtains were blowing softly in the breeze. My eyes darted around the room, looking for anything amiss, or any intruder. My bedroom was on the second floor, I had no idea how anyone could even get to that window from the outside.

'The Harpies are a vicious creation. They have the body and face of a woman, the wings of a bird, and talons on their feet.'

My stomach dropped. Surely if the Harpies were the ones opening my windows they would have killed me. My eyes fell to my bed. A single flower lay there. I walked over, glancing around the room again. I picked the white bloom up, looking it over. I brought it to my nose, breathing its scent deeply. Its smell was a tangle of sweet and bitter. Paperwhite Narcissus. I had not seen them growing anywhere in the village before. I could not imagine where it had come from, or who had put it there. Perhaps a peace offering from Hecate.

Again my thoughts drifted to those red eyes. I considered leaving right then to go to Hecate's cabin. I glanced out of my open window, darkness now sprawling across the sky, and fear settled in my chest. I would wait until daylight to trek across those woods again. I wondered if he would be there when I walked through. I felt a flush come over my cheeks as I pictured him and remembered his hand touching my face.

"Get yourself together, Kora." I laid the flower on my bedside chest, and rubbed my hands across my forehead, feeling frustrated with myself. I would not let my curiosity drag me into oblivion.

"Sleep, and tomorrow you will find what you need to survive this."

I pulled my dress off, putting on loose trousers and a big shirt to sleep in. I left my dress and boots in a heap on the floor, crawling into bed. With my hair still in a loose braid, and my window still open, I settled in to try and sleep.

My eyes drifted to the narcissus and my mind to the mysterious God in the woods.

I dreamed of his red eyes, of Hecate's booming voice, of the catlike grin spread across Hermes' face, and of mangled monsters not quite human but not quite birds. I dreamed of a God, wreathed in lightning, cursing mortals below his feet. I tossed and turned all night, waking several times covered in sweat, the smell of fire and metal surrounding me.

The last time I woke, the sunrise was peeking in through my window. I heaved a sigh, throwing the covers away, and decided I might as well get an early start. I glanced at the flower I had left on the chest– its white petals were black and dried, like the very life had been sucked out of them. My stomach dropped and my chest burned at the sight.

"The Gods are evil, child."

SIX

I threw on a muted green dress and my brown boots. Giving one last glance to the withered narcissus on my chest, I headed downstairs. I stopped by the kitchen to grab a dried fig and then made my way outside. As I stepped out, the village was already alive and people were bustling about. Several hens scratched around the dirt road, and a rooster called out loudly somewhere in the distance.

    I started walking through town, heading towards the woods to Hecate's cabin. I looked at my grandmother's house as I passed it. The inside was dark, she was probably still sleeping. As I made it to the tree line I saw Hecuba sitting, waiting for me. When she saw me her tail started wagging. Once I was next to her she started whining anxiously. She jumped up and started running to Hecate's cabin.

    That voice inside me urged me to hurry, something felt wrong. I started running after Hecuba, trying not to trip on rocks and roots. She was far ahead of me, but still within sight. If I fell too far behind she would stop and stare at me, giving me time to catch up. Fear kept my legs moving, even though my muscles were burning. Maybe the other Gods had punished her for the information she had given me. I disregarded my anger with her from the day before, she had been my closest friend for so long and I cared for her deeply.

Please be ok.

As I rounded the familiar corner of the woods, her cabin came into view. I stopped dead in my tracks as I took in the mess. Her garden had been ripped from the ground. The pots on her porch had been busted, and remnants of her herbs and toxic plants were thrown about. Large gouges were cut along her cabin and windows had been busted out. I stood there looking at the destruction and I wondered if the villagers had done it.

'Witch', *'hag'*, they had said. They were looking for somewhere to place the blame for Theo. But if it was the work of the townsfolk then Hecate would certainly be ok. There was no way a group of mortals could take down a God. I had seen her speed and glimpsed her magic. I could only imagine what else she had flowing through her veins.

I took slow steps up to her porch, Hecuba sat at the door waiting for me. The door was hanging on its hinges, like it had been ripped loose. My face fell with dismay as I reached for the knob to open what was left of it. I had to yank hard to get it open, it was wedged in place.

I pulled it free and stepped inside. The inside was in worse condition than the outside. Her jars and bottles had been busted on the floor and against the walls. The mystery liquids had stained everything it touched, the same gouges that were outside the cabin lined the walls inside as well. Curtains were torn to shreds, furniture was broken, and pieces of dried plants and herbs littered the space.

Surveying the destruction I could tell it had not been done by humans. I thought of the Harpies and my stomach knotted. I glanced across the cabin to the kitchen just in time to see a large pan fly across the room. I jumped as it slammed into the wall. Hecate appeared in the doorway, staring at where the pan had hit. Once I saw her, well and in one piece, relief washed over me. She threw her arms out, her eyes glowing a deep purple, and screamed. It was an ear-shattering, symphony of voices as she cried out. I bent over, covering my ears. It chilled me to the bone as the haunting sound vibrated through me.

She fell to her hands and knees, bowing her head. Her dark hair, streaked with gray, was down, waves spilling around her. *The Maiden, The Mother, and The Crone.* I stood slowly, stepping around the rubble towards her. Her head snapped up. The deep purple glow ebbed away, leaving her brown eyes staring directly at me. I stopped, holding my hands up. If she had wreaked this havoc on her own cabin, what would she do to me? When she realized who I was, her face crumpled. A small sob escaped her lips.

When I heard the defeat in her voice and saw the desperation in her eyes my body moved on its own. I was by her in seconds, wrapping my arms around her. She leaned into me, grabbing fistfuls of my dress, and cried. The sound of it shattered my heart. I pulled back to look at her, tears stained her cheeks and her lip trembled.

"What happened here?" I asked. She shook her head slightly and wiped the tears from her face.

"You need to leave, Kora. It's not safe here anymore." Her voice was gravelly, telling me she had been crying, or screaming, for a long while. I brushed her thick hair back and wiped her eyes with my sleeve.

"Absolutely not. Tell me what happened." My words came out demanding and harsh as my anger started boiling inside me. If someone had hurt her…

"Kora you need to listen to me. I didn't tell you everything yesterday. You are the daughter of Demeter, the Goddess of Harvest."

Her words sank into me like a knife, slicing and carving away. My body numbed, and then that burning ignited inside me. She didn't give me time to respond before she continued. "Your father was a mortal, but you are the Goddess of Spring. You were promised by The Fates to the God of the Dead, King of the Underworld. Your mother hid you away to keep you from being enveloped by his darkness. She wanted to keep you pure. He knows you're here now, and he's going to come for you. You have to leave; run far away and hide."

    I stared at her, silently. I bit my lip until I tasted blood, my nails digging into my palms. I tried to take in her claim, but it felt outlandish. I would know if I was a God.

    "Would you?" That Wrath-filled voice questioned. Rage bubbled up, igniting my blood. All my anger, that vicious voice that whispered to me... I was a God.

    "Hecate." My voice was shaking, or was that my body? "Tell. Me. What. Happened."

    As I spoke the earth beneath us shuddered. Her eyes never broke from mine as she raised herself to her feet and took several steps back. Was that fear on her face? I stood after her, my skin felt like it was cracking apart. All I could feel was that scorching Wrath, yanking her chain as it strained against her. I wasn't sure I could hold onto her much longer.

    "He came here," her words came out quickly and panic brimmed her eyes. "He came here and questioned me. Said he saw you in the woods and wanted to know who you were. I... I had to tell him." She had backed herself up against the counter, her hands gripped the edge.

    The rage dissipated instantly. My skin cooled, and Wrath stopped pulling at me. The earth beneath us calmed as I took a deep breath.

"He's the God of the Dead." The words came out softly. My heart felt like it was being ripped in two. That feeling of longing when I looked at him, it was The Fates, it was not me. "He did this? To your cabin?"

I felt her tension within me again, that Wrath I had inside. I hated the Gods, I hated The Fates, and I hated her.

"I am you," she purred in my ear. *"Hate me all you like, but you cannot escape me."*

"Yes, he did this. He was angry that I didn't call him as soon as I realized who you were." Her words drew me from myself

"You all just destroy each other's property? Wreak havoc on each other?" The behavior disgusted me, and it was evident in my voice. A hollow laugh escaped her lips. She shook her head, her body finally relaxing a little.

"You don't understand, Kora. There are hierarchies within the ranks of Gods. I sit far below that of Hades." As she said his name a hum went through me. "I answer to him above all else. He is the head of the Chthonian Gods."

"Chthonian Gods?" I frowned, my eyebrows knitting together.

"Yes, the Gods of the Underworld. There are quite a few of us, but not as many as reside in Olympus. Hades rules the Underworld and all the other Chthonian Gods by proxy. When he calls, we answer. When he makes demands, we fulfill them." I understood politics, but the barbaric nature of the ransack still left a sour taste in my mouth. It was cruel.

"Where do I go?"

I felt defeated before she even responded. How could I hide from the Gods? Even if I managed for a while, knowing now that I might not have a mortal life span complicated things further. I could spend years hiding and moving, and might still be caught.

She shook her head, bringing her hands up to rub her eyes. "I honestly don't know, Kora. I…" Her voice trailed off as her eyes met mine once more. We stared at each other, both of us at a loss for words. Unsure where to go or what to do.

As we stood there, lost in thought, a breeze blew between us. It picked up dirt and debris from the wreckage, sending it circulating around us. I shielded my eyes with my hands, leaning back against the wall. I knew who it was before the bright light flashed. When my vision returned I saw Hermes standing in the middle of the room, a grin on his face. He was wearing his robes and sandals again, his hair windblown and messy.

"Ladies." His smile faded as he looked around the room, taking in the wreckage. He whistled softly, putting his hands on his hips. He turned to Hecate, whose face was now contorted with outrage. "Hecate, have you considered hiring a maid? This place is a mess."

Dark tendrils oozed from around her. I watched, stunned by the tangible magic she drew out. They lashed out at Hermes like whips and I crouched down, drawing my knees to my chest. He vanished, reappearing on the other side of the room. The black tentacles slammed into the floor with a crash. He smiled widely, brushing hair out of his face.

"You should calm yourself, Hecate. You're scaring poor little Kora." He wagged a finger at her and let out a small laugh.

She roared, throwing her magic at him once again. He was gone an instant before they made contact with him, and they blasted into the wall. When he appeared again he was beside me. He grabbed my arm, yanking me upright, and twisted me in front of him.

"You spineless pile of shit!" She screamed, her eyes glowing that same dark purple they had been before. "You had to open your big mouth. You caused all of this!"

"He would have found out eventually. Isn't that right, Kora? Tell the Witch she needs to relax."

He pulled me into him, one hand on my arm and the other wrapped around to grab my chin. I could tell he was being gentle with me, but I could still feel he was much stronger than I was. I swallowed, slightly nodding my head. I tried to beg Hecate to calm down with my eyes. I did not want to be caught in the crossfire of their fight.

She lowered her hands, her eyes returning to normal, and her magic retreating. She snarled and pointed her finger at him.

"You're a prick!" She spat. "Let the girl go before she rips you apart." Shock and confusion fell over my face at her words. I could rip no one apart, let alone a God.

"You are a God," that voice assured me. *"You are powerful. Show him. Show him your power."*

I closed my eyes tightly, pleading with her to be quiet. Her voice faded away, but her feelings stirred around inside of me still. I wiggled against Hermes and he released me. I turned on my heel and slapped him. My palm made contact with his face and his mouth flew open. He turned to me and I expected him to kill me on the spot, but instead, he smiled widely.

"Feisty. He's going to have a blast with you." With a wicked gleam in his eyes, and his words hanging in the air, he vanished.

I turned to Hecate, her eyebrows were furrowed and she was frowning deeply. I felt even more helpless to my fate than I did before. I could see no way to escape any of it. I brought my hands to my face and rubbed my eyebrows, my frustration coming to a head.

"Is he always so insufferable?" I asked.

She cracked a smile, the tension leaving her face. "Oh yes, unfortunately, he is. I've had to put up with him far longer than I care to think about."

I returned her smile, feeling entirely normal for a moment. The feeling melted away as silence hung between us and the reality of my situation set in. I was doomed.

"Hecate I–" My words fell as I caught his smoldering scent. It burned my nose and threatened to entrance me.

I glanced around the room and then back to Hecate, her face mirroring my growing anxiety. Her eyes were wide and her lips pulled into a tight line. I looked at the door, weighing how quickly I thought I could make it outside and back to my home. I knew it wouldn't matter how fast I was. I could run forever, and I knew deep in my bones he would still find me.

Magic billowed across the floor, pooling around us like black smoke. The Wrath inside me sang with anticipation, like it was calling to her. The magic weaved up, snaking around itself, forming a dark archway between me and my only exit. My heart skipped a beat.

The God of the Dead stepped out, red eyes darting around the space. He wore a black shirt and matching trousers, his shoes shined as the light from the broken windows hit them. His hair was pulled back into a low bun, like the last time I saw him. He was even more beautiful than I remembered. His eyes met Hecate's and she bowed her head. He stood there, staring at her silently. I was holding my breath, scared to move at all. His eyes slid from her and landed on me.

Fear tried to settle inside me, urging me to bow as Hecate had, but that wrathful voice sliced it away.

"You bow to no God," she said. *"Lift your chin and stand tall."*

And I did just that. Head held high, back straight, I stared at the King of The Underworld. I felt so small, standing there in front of him. His eyes trailed down my body and back up to my face, I fought the urge to squirm under his gaze. He looked back to Hecate, who was still bowing, and he spoke.

"Hecate." His voice was deep and husky, sending a shiver through me.

Contempt burned in her eyes as they flicked up to him, but she kept her head low, waves of hair spilling around her. I could feel anger radiating off of her.

"You're dismissed." He waved a hand at her as he spoke.

Her eyes shot to me, surprise and guilt clear on her face. She lingered, keeping her eyes locked onto mine. She didn't want to leave me with him.

Her red lips parted, and her voice came out timid and pleading. "Hades…"

"Hecate." It was a command. Annoyance was thick in his tone, as he repeated her name harshly.

Still, she held my stare, her body not moving an inch. Worry filled me at the sight of her blatant defiance. He had destroyed her home the last time she had done so. I wouldn't let him cause her more suffering.

I nodded my head, trying to reassure her. "You may leave, Hecate."

My words came out more confident than I felt, as I tried to imitate the inner voice that whispered to me often. She bobbed her head, black and purple magic swirling around her. It engulfed her completely, and then she was gone. Unease washed over me when I looked from where Hecate had been standing, to *Hades*. He was already glaring at me, outrage plastered on his face. His nostrils flared as he breathed in deeply. I kept my eyes fixed on him, feigning composure.

I waited for him to erupt with rage, to lash out and hurt me. He took several steps towards the broken table, reaching down to pick up a chair that was still intact. He sat it upright, then grabbed another and set it across from the first. He took a seat in the second chair, crossing his legs. He closed his eyes and pinched the bridge of his nose. I waited, silently, still expecting him to explode.

He opened his eyes, motioning to the chair in front of him. "Sit, Kora."

His voice was composed and even. He crossed his arms, waiting. He was obviously used to being obeyed. My eyes slid to the chair and then back to him. I considered refusing, yelling at him, running… But my body betrayed me. I slowly walked over to the chair and lowered myself into it, not breaking eye contact with him. I tried to read what he was thinking, but his face was now straight and void of emotion. I tore my eyes from him, I saw a muscle in his arm flex. *Still angry, then,* I thought.

"You do not order my Gods again, do you understand?" His words were rigid. My eyebrow arched, and I bit the inside of my cheek. I wanted to argue, but I wasn't sure how much I could get away with. "Do you understand?" He repeated when I did not respond.

Wrath yanked her chain hard and sudden, and I spoke before I could stop myself. "Maybe if you didn't treat them so poorly they would listen to you."

He huffed a laugh, shaking his head. "Do not pretend to understand our laws, *Goddess*. You have been hidden away in the lands of mortals for a long time. You know nothing." His condescension set me ablaze.

"You say this, but it is *I* whom Hecate answered to." I was nearly shouting, my whole body vibrating.

My skin was tight, and my insides were on fire. Wrath thrashed against her restraints and screamed to be released. She was impossible to ignore. The earth shuddered beneath us. His eyes shot to the floor, like he could see the ground through it. We sat in silence, the quaking under us settling as my anger subsided slightly.

He looked back at me, curiosity on his face. "Interesting," he murmured under his breath.

My eyebrows furrowed and I crossed my arms. "What?" I snapped.

A smile crept across his face. I decided then that I definitely did not like him. I wanted to rip him apart, watch him suffer. I imagined what it might feel like to tear him open, as the Harpies had done Theo. I was pulled from my fantasies as he spoke again.

"Let us start over," he said. "I'm–"

I held a hand up, interrupting him. He raised his brows and smirked at me, but allowed me to speak.

"Yes, yes. Hades," I sneered. "God of the Dead. King of the Underworld." My voice dripped with disdain and I rolled my eyes. His very existence grated on my nerves.

"Aidoneus." He said softly. I looked at him, confused. "You may call me Aidoneus."

I felt a lump in my throat. All my annoyance and anger evaporated. Something about the way he said it made it feel significant. Like he was offering a very intimate piece of himself to me.

I blinked at him, faltering, then cleared my throat.

"Aidoneus." I echoed weakly.

The corner of his mouth turned up slightly. I felt that pull to him again, like our intertwined fates were palpable. It didn't take long for him to spoil the moment.

"I'm bringing you back to The Underworld with me." His words fell into silence as panic took hold of me.

I rose from my seat, ready to argue. I was too slow, though. He stood, lifting his palms to the ceiling. His black smoke of magic rose from the ground like fog. It was entwined with bright red flames. I could feel the heat from the hellfire as it swallowed both of us entirely. I tried to scream, but no sound escaped my lips. My throat burned, I could not tell if it was the fire and smoke or my silent screaming.

I reached out, trying to grab anything I could to ground me, but there was nothing to hold on to. Terror was the only thing I could feel as my body tumbled through the void.

Then everything went black.

SEVEN

Soft light broke through the darkness. My feet hit the ground unexpectedly and my ankle twisted under me with a crunch. My body slammed into the hard floor. The marble was cool against my skin, which had warmed considerably by the heat of his scorching magic. I lay there, glancing around at my surroundings.

I was in a large, open room. I sat up slowly, continuing to look around. It was a dining hall. A long table stretched across the floor, covered in more food than I imagined I could ever eat. A large chair was seated at the head of the table. I stood up, spinning around, the most breathtaking sculptures and art adorned the room. I had never seen such extravagant decor and furniture in my tiny village in the mountains.

I was startled when Hades cleared his throat behind me. I turned to face him, the shock of my sudden change in scenery apparent in my expression. He had his hands in his pockets and a look of pride on his face. I blinked away my astonishment, trying to compose myself. I didn't want him to see my dismay.

He stepped towards me and I tensed, but he brushed past me, continuing to the table. He reached out and plucked a red grape from the bowl of fruit and turned to me, raising it to his mouth. My eyes dropped to his lips as they parted slowly. I felt heat in my cheeks and I turned away from him.

"You should eat, Kora. You must be hungry." His voice was taunting, like he had seen the pink blooming on my face. I glared at him, my skin growing redder against my will.

I opened my mouth to speak but felt a thrum of power pulse through the room. I whipped around to see a man standing there with us. His eyes moved from Hades to me. He looked gaunt and his skin was so sickly pale one could have argued it was gray. He had dark circles under his almond-shaped, brown eyes. Long black hair spilled down his back. He wore gray robes, which hung loosely on his body, and his feet were bare. I slammed my mouth shut, realizing I was gaping at him. He looked at me as if he was just as dumbfounded by me as I was by him.

He opened and closed his mouth several times, searching for words. He looked back to Hades. "Who have you brought here?"

His voice was quiet, but he spoke with a familiarity that told me they were on much friendlier terms than Hades was with Hecate. Hades shrugged, as if his stealing me away was not a monumental, life-changing ordeal. Like turning my life upside down was nothing to him. I wanted to be angry, I wanted to shout or break something. But I couldn't.

You're in shock, I thought.

"You're home," that voice inside me hummed.

I pushed back against her. I would not lay down and accept any of it. I would fight tooth and nail against it, against him.

The God I did not know walked by me, stealing another glance as he passed. His feet padded along the marble floor. He made his way up to the far side of the table pulling out a chair and slumping into it. He stretched one of his arms out along the table's surface and rested his head on it. A heavy sigh escaped his lips, I could hear the exhaustion in it.

"I guess it's your style to bring in strays." A corner of his mouth lifted as he smiled lazily. He was blinking slowly, his lids heavy. Was he falling asleep?

Hades took a seat at the large, ornate chair at the head of the table, filling a plate with whatever was in his reach. "She's not a stray, Hypnos."

He said it with an indifference that had me fighting to keep my anger in check. Was every God I came into contact with going to insist on speaking about me like I was not in the room with them?

My stomach growled loudly. Both Hades and Hypnos glanced at me, amusement on their faces. Feeling embarrassed, I stomped over to the table and yanked a chair out. I plopped down in it, deciding if I was going to be there I might as well eat.

I reached out and grabbed a plate, piling various foods on it. There were exotic fruits and cheeses I had never seen before and meats I could not identify. I tried not to think about what they might be as I added them to my plate. The smells wafting from the table had my mouth watering. I looked up as I took a bite of bread, Hypnos was watching me intensely. I felt a twinge of embarrassment.

"What?" I demanded, my mouth full of bread.

His eyebrows shot up. Surprise, and what I could only guess was disgust, on his face. He wrinkled his nose, sitting up and then leaning back in his chair.

"Oh, dear," he mumbled, looking at Hades with a concerned expression. "Where did you find this one?" Hades gave him a disapproving look, then went back to his food. Hypnos' face became more serious when Hades did not answer him. "Hades... Where did you find her?"

Hades put his food down and looked at me. Our eyes locked. I swallowed hard, the food turning to lead in my throat. "She was with Hecate."

He turned his attention back to Hypnos, who narrowed his eyes, mulling over what that might have meant. Finally, Hypnos sighed again, bowing his head in defeat.

"Please, Hades. I am so tired, I do not have enough energy for this today." He rubbed his cheek, eyes pleading.

I couldn't take the back and forth any longer, I could feel Wrath stirring under my skin. She itched for freedom, for release.

"He *stole* me!" I exclaimed, slamming my hand down on the table.

Paintings shifted and decor shook as the walls around us rumbled. Hypnos sat up abruptly, his eyes wide. Hades gave me a bored look and shook his head.

"Easy, Goddess. I have spent more money furnishing my castle than you could imagine. I don't need you destroying my priceless art with your childish tantrums." His words ignited the fire inside me.

I was pulled from my thoughts before I could become too enraged, by Hypnos speaking again. "Hades, please tell me she isn't Demeter's daughter." Hades responded with another shrug and Hypnos groaned loudly. "You'll start a war," he whined, leaning back in the chair. He looked utterly defeated. I felt a twinge of satisfaction knowing I was not the only one the God of the Dead had that effect on.

"I didn't steal her," Hades snapped. "She's mine, by decree of The Fates."

As he proclaimed his ownership over me, I felt myself tipping over a ledge. It felt like I was being shredded from the inside out, a thousand thorns trying to tear their way through flesh and bone. I would not be another God to add to his belt of minions.

"Will you all stop talking about me like I'm not sitting right here?!" My voice was shrill, and another rumble echoed through the castle.

I realized then, that quaking within the earth…it was me. As it sunk in, I could feel Wrath crying out with glee. She loved it, reveled in it. She wanted more. I could feel it, that magic coursing through me. It felt as though the string of a harp had been plucked deep in my core and a wave of power followed. I grasped for it, trying to replicate it.

Another strong tremor shook the castle, the glasses on the table rocked, and priceless art threatened to topple over.

"Yes!" she begged. *"More!"*

I reached for that string of magic again, but it slipped through my fingers, just out of reach.

"Enough!" Hades roared.

He stood, towering over me. It was gone then, I could no longer even sense it within me. Wrath quieted herself into the shadows. I stared at Hades, and the anger on his face made me sink into my seat. Quietly I sat there, willing my body to be still.

"I'm trying to be patient with you, Goddess, but if you cannot keep yourself under control I promise I will make your life here miserable." The edge in his voice told me I did not want to know exactly what that entailed.

I melted deeper into my chair, wishing I could just disappear. I dared to glance at Hypnos, who looked like he was fighting to keep his eyes open. He was no help at all. Hades relaxed, my obedience satisfied him. He sat back down, turning his attention to his food. Hypnos was now laying his top half across the table, eyes barely cracked open. He was completely unfazed by the waves of my power and Hades' shouting. I wished Hecate was with me. I thought of her wrecked cabin, and how she must be piecing it back together slowly. Maybe her magic would help mend her home quickly.

"Would you like to see the courtyard?"

I blinked, looking up to Hypnos. He was sitting up again, waiting for my answer. His face was calm, or was he just that tired? When was the last time he had even slept? Instinctively my eyes darted to Hades. He glanced up from his plate as if he already knew I was looking at him. Our eyes locked briefly, and then he nodded his approval.

I jumped up, eager to put some distance between myself and the God of the Dead. "Yes, please," I said quickly.

If the inside of this castle was that beautiful, that full of riches I had never seen, I couldn't wait to see the outside. I imagined there must be exotic plants and flowers I had never even dreamed of. I tried to contain myself, but I could not dampen my excitement. Thoughts of escape trickled in, rotting my enthusiasm. It would be the best course of action; to survey the area and plot my freedom.

Hypnos stood slowly, passing across the room. "Come, then," he said, giving me a sidelong glance.

I hurried to follow him, trying not to appear too eager. We approached two large doors at the end of the dining hall. I trailed my eyes up the doors, taking in all of the intricate carvings covering them. A large tree was etched into the center of both, each one had a single pomegranate hanging low in their branches. There were figures, Gods I supposed, scrawled along the edges. Images of war, worship, and monsters, told some forgotten story.

I reached my hand out, trailing my fingers across the wood. It sung in response to my touch. I could feel life still somewhere inside, slumbering… waiting.

Hypnos reached out to the doors, pushing them open wide. Disappointment surged through me as they swung from my hand and I walked through the archway. I glanced back over my shoulder to appreciate one last time the sacrifice the tree had made to create something new.

I saw Hades out of the corner of my eye, still seated in his chair at the end of the table. His arms were crossed over his chest, and though I dared not look at him fully, I could tell his eyes were on me. I couldn't tell if it was the dim lighting, drab colors of the manor, or just the idea that he had his eyes on me so intensely, but unease washed over me. I turned my attention back to Hypnos. He was walking slowly, eyes straight ahead, as if he was walking alone.

I took the moment of silence to inspect the room as we moved through it. Somehow it was even larger than the dining hall. It was wide and open, a few sculptures and tables lined the dark walls, but the middle of the room was empty. Except the massive chair that sat towards the back of it, near the entrance to the dining area we had been in before.

My mouth sagged as I took in the large throne, and that's exactly what it was. It was intricately carved, the same style as the double doors. I couldn't quite make out what was depicted. I caught myself yearning to touch it, to run my hands along the wood and ask to hear all of the stories it held within itself. I imagined what he might look like, peering down at whoever might be kneeling on the floor in front of him.

My mind scrambled as I walked directly into Hypnos' back. He had stopped directly in front of me to open the door leading outside. I stumbled backward, trying not to fall.

"Sorry!" I exclaimed, expecting him to tear into me. He glanced back, the same exhausted indifference on his face.

"It's fine." He yawned as he spoke, and the drastic contrast between him and the other Gods I had met shocked me. He was so calm, though I wondered if he would still be so level-headed after a long nap.

He reached out to the iron door in front of him. It had no window, no stories to tell, just a slab of pure iron with a handle. It was cold, uninviting. *Fitting*, I thought blandly. Of course the King of the Underworld would want to make his entrance as unapproachable as he was. I couldn't imagine he had very many friends.

The door swung open and my heart dropped into my stomach. My eyes drifted around, taking in my surroundings. Disappointment and dread coiled deeply within me. I had hoped for bright colors, flowers, and foliage, for trees towering above everything. How naive I had been.

Hypnos stepped out, his feet crunched along the dried and cracked earth. It was inky black, like it had been scorched clear of any growth that might have been there long ago. I lifted my eyes from the ground and saw there was nothing. It was rolling hills of blackened earth as far as I could see. No sign of life anywhere. It was desolate.

I craned my head back to take in the sky; if you could call it that. It was a soft gray, like a cloudy day, but there were no clouds in sight. No sun or moon, just a blanket of gloom. I couldn't see where the source of light was coming from, it was as if the sky itself was illuminating everything. Something told me it was like that no matter what time it was, just a constant state of depression.

I looked to Hypnos, who was staring at me, judging my reaction. I could feel the dissatisfaction on my face.

"Well?"

"It's... different." I could find nothing pleasant to remark on. I watched as his face crumpled slightly.

"I know it's not as bright as the upper world, but it grows on you."

I nodded absentmindedly, still trying to take it all in. Even if there was some secret passage out, I would get lost without any landmarks.

"Let me show you around. You'll learn to love it here." He said it with such conviction it made my heart hurt.

"Lead the way," I said, forcing a smile.

EIGHT

We walked for what seemed like hours along the charred dirt. I had been right, I would have been lost without a guide. Large iron formations were jutting up from the ground as if they had erupted from the core of the earth. They all looked nearly identical.

Hypnos offered quiet commentary as we passed by things he felt were significant. I tried to memorize all of the information he fed me, but there were so many names and terms I had never heard that I gave up quickly.

"What did you mean," I asked as we walked. "When you said he takes in strays?"

Hypnos shot me an apologetic look. "I meant no offense. It's just he tends to," he paused briefly, "allow refuge to those who wouldn't be accepted elsewhere, for one reason or another."

"How very hospitable."

The sarcasm in my voice did not slip past him. He gave me a tight smile. "He has a rough exterior, but he means well."

"Did he mean well when he destroyed Hecate's cabin?"

Hypnos stopped and stared at me. "Hecate and Hades have a… Strained relationship. I won't make excuses for his behavior, but if that had been another God that Hecate lied to as she did, it would have gone much worse than it did."

I turned and continued, not caring to proceed with the conversation. It still felt like an excuse. After that, we walked for a while in silence. Neither one of us seemed to know what to say.

I heard it before I saw it, the sound of flowing water. My heart leapt at the thought of it. Finally something worth seeing in the absolute hellhole that was the Underworld. I stepped faster, the sound of crunching echoed around us.

As we crested the small hill, a wide river– stretched as far as I could see– came into view. There was a small waterfall, cascading down from a cave formed in one of the many iron formations. I lifted my hand to my chest, in absolute awe of it. I turned to Hypnos, who was staring at the river longingly.

I had been below mere hours. It was a lifeless, colorless place. I ached for the upper world and anything that bore any semblance to it. Before I even registered what I was doing, I was sprinting down the other side of the hill. I wanted to jump into the river, to submerge myself in the water. I needed to feel the chill and the currents against my skin.

I vaguely heard Hypnos shouting behind me, but I didn't care to listen. My mind was set on bathing in the river. As I ran, there was no wind on my face, no breeze to blow my hair. I hated it, I hated everything about the Underworld.

I was feet from the river when a crevice in the ground caught my boot, sending me slamming down face first. Pain erupted through my face as it collided with the earth. I grunted, lifting myself up on my hands and knees. My hands were covered in black granules. I realized at that moment it was not even dirt beneath us. It was iron. I wiped my hands along my dress, leaving smears that looked like soot across the green fabric. I reached up, rubbing the particles from my face. My eyes lifted to the water. It was crystal clear.

Hypnos touched my shoulder, interrupting my thoughts. I glanced up at him, his face was full of worry. "You cannot touch the water, Goddess."

"Kora," I corrected.

He nodded, lifting his eyes from me to the river. "Kora. You mustn't touch the water, lest you accidentally ingest some of it. Drinking too much would pluck every memory from your mind."

Shock contorted my face. I tried to form questions, but I could string no words together. He must have seen them there, my unspoken thoughts flitting across my face. As I sat there, staring at him, he continued.

"The River Lethe. Its sole purpose is to help them forget. The shades. They come here distressed, sometimes."

"Shades?" The word brought images of shadowed figures into my mind.

"The souls of the dead," he clarified, patiently. "Sometimes death can be traumatizing. They need help in order to rest peacefully."

It seemed strange to me, that only sometimes death would be hard to process. I would have imagined all death would be. To go from the upper world to the Underworld, I was not even dead and I was struggling with it. But the thought of forgetting everything… It haunted me. I thought of my grandmother. She would die one day. Would she have to drink from the River Lethe?

Hypnos stood, offering his hand to me. I placed mine in his; his touch was soft as he pulled me to my feet. He walked past me and motioned for me to follow him. I stole another look at the river and a chill went through me as I considered how close I had been to losing myself completely. I turned, walking quickly to catch up with him. He was heading straight to the cave near the waterfall.

"Where are we going?" I asked, coming up beside him.

"To my home."

As we approached the base of the iron formation, I craned my head up to take it all in. It was the size of a small mountain. It was steep. I wasn't sure how anyone even got up to the cave.

"May I?" he asked, reaching out to me. I looked at him and then up to the mouth of the cave again.

"Yes?" My voice was laced with uncertainty.

He wrapped his arm around my waist carefully, pulling me closer to him. He raised his other hand in the air. I felt that same thrum of magic pulse from him and ripple around us, like a drop of water in a puddle. The air twisted, dust from the iron earth swirling with it. A tornado of iron encased us, and then everything went black. My stomach turned and I tried desperately to orient myself. I couldn't tell what was up or down. I felt his arm tighten around me.

Light broke the darkness, just as it did when I arrived in the underworld. My feet landed on the ground. I nearly toppled over again, but Hypnos held on to me firmly, keeping me in place. I braced myself against him, fighting off a wave of nausea.

"You'll get used to it." He let out a soft chuckle.

As I regained my balance, he released me. I looked around, we were standing in the mouth of the cave, way closer to the edge than I was comfortable with. I breathed in deeply, turning away from the cliff and taking several steps deeper into the cave. It was nearly empty. There was a flat form of iron carved out of the wall, a small fur cover, and a pillow sitting on top of it.

That cannot be comfortable.

I continued glancing around, and my eye caught on a pile of dried flowers. I strode over to them, crouching down to get a closer look. I picked one of the blooms up, it was brittle. *Poppies*. I turned to Hypnos, he was rubbing his hands together. He seemed…embarrassed.

"They're my favorite," he mumbled under his breath.

I felt sad, as I thought of how he must have watched the poppies wither and die. With no soil or sun to nurture them, they wouldn't have stood a chance. How often did he visit the upper world?

"Why do you live in a cave, Hypnos? Surely Hades has plenty of room in his manor?" It seemed cruel when I thought about it, that the God of the Dead would seclude himself away in his castle while another God lived in a cave.

Hypnos smiled as he walked over to his bed, sitting down on the edge. He slumped over and sighed. "He offered," he said softly. "He's offered it many times. His home makes me feel confined. There are no windows, no open doors. Here I can sit at the edge and look out at the vast underworld. I can hear the flow of Lethe. I don't sleep, but it brings me peace when I lay here and listen to it. It reminds me of the upper world."

He looked out of the opening of the cave as he spoke. I saw that longing in his eyes again. I was shattered for him.

"Couldn't you live in the upper world? Must you stay here like this?"

He turned his attention back to me and smiled as though I was ignorant. And I supposed I was. I didn't understand anything. Everything seemed so complicated and there were so many rules. It made me realize how simple my life had been before Gods and monsters turned it upside down.

"I leave, sometimes. I gather poppies while I'm there and bring them back here. They never last long, though."

"Hecate lives in the upper world. I'm sure you could find some agreement with Hades to–"

He laughed abruptly, cutting me off and startling me. I stared at him, as he wiped tears from his eyes.

"Ahh yes. Hecate lives part of her time in the upper world. She and Hades argue often. As I said, they don't get along well. She's abrasive and stubborn and he is much the same." There was a sparkle in his eyes as he spoke. As if their turmoil was his favorite form of entertainment. "The other half of her time is spent here," he continued. "She has a small hut, as far as she could manage from his castle, without encroaching on the territory of The Erinyes."

"Erinyes?" I was beginning to think I would never learn everything I needed to.

"They're also known as The Furies. They were granted refuge here after they were banished by the other Gods. Hades gave them a job to earn their keep. Everyone else felt they were too vicious and sadistic to have around. Zeus tried to release them in the upper world but they ravaged mortals until it became a problem."

I felt fear and unease as he explained the Erinyes. I hated the thought that I was even in the same realm as them. At my hesitance, Wrath stirred within me.

"Do you, though?" She prodded. Her words made me feel confused. I should want to stay far away from them, so why did I feel so conflicted? *"Birds of a feather…"* she whispered in my ear. *"They could be yours. Take them, leash them… Unleash them."*

I pushed back against her, disgusted that those thoughts even entered my mind. Trying to distract myself, I forced myself to speak.

"These Furies… What is their job here?"

He considered his words before he spoke. Like he was weighing how much to tell me, leaving me frustrated as I waited for him to answer.

"They punish the sinful," he said simply.

I felt Wrath's excitement deep in my bones. She wanted them.

"I am you," she reminded me hastily.

I had always felt her, wriggling around inside me like a parasite. Whispering cruel things in my ear. She was louder since I had arrived at the Underworld, though. Her urges more demanding.

I opened my mouth to change the subject, but she yanked her leash and my mouth betrayed me. "Where do they reside?"

Hypnos looked at me, his eyebrows furrowed, concern in his eyes. I could feel my body aching with anticipation as I waited, anticipation that I was not sure was my own. We sat there, eyes locked, as the seconds passed. He stood, shaking his head.

"We should get back," he murmured as he walked towards the ledge of the cave.

I felt Wrath writhe around in anger at his blatant disregard to my question. I tried to soothe her as I stood, following him.

"Of course." I looked down at the River Lethe, the fear I felt from being up so high earlier was now gone. The flow of the river had quickened, its current crashing against the banks. It looked as angry as she... as *I* felt.

He wrapped an arm around me and iron swirled then darkness engulfed us. I thought of Hecate. I needed to find her.

"You need to find The Erinyes."

If she was somewhere in the Underworld then she could help me escape.

"They can help you rule."

I had to get back to the upper world.

"A crown could sit on your head."

Back to my old life.

"You could be queen."

I belonged there.

"You belong here..."

We were back at the castle in an instant, my feet planted on the ground firmly. I did not stumble, no nausea or disorientation hit me. Wrath's voice echoed over my own, drowning out my thoughts of escape and my childhood home. We were back in the throne room. I lifted my eyes and they locked with Hades, who was standing near the door to the dining hall.

A woman stood next to him, her beauty caught me off guard. She had long, blond hair, her figure slim. Her lips were painted a bright red, which looked harsh against her soft features. Pointed ears peeked through her wavy hair. She was wearing a low-cut dress, its color matched her lips, and it had a slit clean up to her hip. She stared at me with brown doe eyes, but rage burned there.

My eyes shifted from her back to Hades and I felt Wrath struggling against her restraints. She screamed and flailed. Her hatred burned through me at the sight of the woman standing so close to him. It snuffed out all of my thoughts and feelings.

And then I felt the chains snap…

NINE

I couldn't stop it. Power coursed through me as if it had a mind of its own. It ripped at my flesh, trying to tear my skin apart. My body burned like it was on fire. The earth beneath us rumbled and shook, sending paintings falling from the walls and clattering onto the ground. The marble floors cracked and busted under our feet.

    I couldn't even make sense of the anger– it wasn't mine– it was *hers*. I could hear Hypnos shouting, his voice muffled like I was underwater. Shock was plastered on Hades' face, and the woman I did not know reeked of fear. Everything moved in slow motion.

    My hand lifted on its own as magic forced its way down my arm. I wasn't sure what I was doing, I was not the one in control. I could only watch in distress as thick, thorny vines erupted from my palm. They shot directly at the woman in red. Her mouth opened and I expected her to scream, but the only sound I could hear was a high-pitched ringing in my ears. The ringing invaded my head, deafening me.

    Hades opened his arms, shadows billowed around him like smoke. The shadows lurched forward, becoming solid, and shredded my vines into nothing. Pain shot through my entire body like the vines had been connected to every nerve inside me. Wrath screamed– no… It was me. I doubled over, grabbing my arm. It was bleeding where vines had torn through violently. I looked up at Hades, my anger blending with Wrath's, becoming so entwined I wasn't sure how deep my own feelings even ran. Tears ran down my cheeks. I reached up with my uninjured hand and wiped them away, but it was not tears, it was black ichor leaking from my eyes.

Hades held his hands up, and his mouth moved like he was trying to reason with me. But that damn *ringing…*

"Kill her!" Wrath screamed. It echoed in my head, causing the ringing to intensify.

I gripped my hair, feeling as though I was going mad. I looked past Hades, at the woman who was now running through the dining hall. Wrath took hold of me again and I roared in anger, in pain, and threw my other hand out. Another blast of vines sprung out towards the woman. Hades was ready, his shadows ripped at my magic again, but I was prepared that time.

With sharp pain throbbing through my body, I launched myself to the floor. I slammed my bloody palm against it as hard as I could. I willed my power through the floor, into the black iron beneath the castle. It struggled and flickered against the metal, but I pushed harder. The shadows continued tearing my vines apart as if they were made of paper. Hades was distracted.

Wrath let out a savage warcry that sent a sharp, stabbing pain through my head. A blast of large green whips exploded from the floor in the dining hall, marble went flying. Those vines were thicker, several wrapped around each other. I watched as Hades wheeled around, surprise on his face. The woman fell to the ground and screamed, the most beautiful fear I had ever seen in her eyes.

Right as they were about to crash down on her, shredding her, Hades vanished and reappeared between her and my magic. He threw his hands out and a black shield of shadows covered them. My vines slammed into the shield over and over. Wrath was molten inside me. I felt like I was burning from the inside out.

I begged her to stop, to calm herself, but she would not. She was in complete control and I was helpless to her fury.

Finally, it busted through, crashing into the floor. Sculptures toppled over, shattering as they fell. Hades and the woman were both gone. I let out another rage-filled scream, and the whole manor shook.

I turned, looking for where they had gone. Dark magic caught my eye across the room, Hades appeared there seconds later, alone. With the woman gone, the ringing subsided, and I could hear again. Wrath was quiet. Content. Hypnos' voice filled my ears.

"Hades, calm down!"

I noticed it, then. Hades was snarling at me– a savage, inhuman gleam in his eyes. Black smoke circulated around him and my eyes widened in fear. With Wrath gone, I felt foolish for doing everything I had done. I wanted to hit my knees, to plead with him. He had no idea that I had not been in control, and his anger at me was misplaced.

"You insolent little brat!" He shouted as his power shot towards me.

Panic settled in my stomach as I watched. I didn't know what to do. I crouched down quickly, covering my head with my hands. I heard a loud impact and looked up in time to see a wall of vines in front of me. I could see his magic tearing my shield apart. I took a shaky breath and then ran.

Shit time for you to disappear on me!
But Wrath stayed silent.

I fumbled around inside myself searching for her. More of Hades' shadows darted toward me, and everything they touched crumbled into dust. He was going to kill me! I screamed as they nearly reached me and a tree erupted from the ground in front of me. His magic collided with the trunk, sending splinters hurling through the air.

"I am you," I whispered to myself.

I reached deep, looking for that string of power. I found it, and with a gentle pluck, it sent a power that burned like lightning through my body again. Flesh tore down my arms and legs as those thorny whips flew toward Hades. Blood ran down my body, dripping onto the floor, but I paid no mind to it. My magic slammed into his. I could see him struggling to overcome them.

"Please," Hypnos begged from the sidelines. "Please, both of you just stop!"

My eyes darted to Hypnos and I immediately realized my mistake. I could feel my magic sputter, as my eyes met his. My hesitation was exactly what Hades needed to gain control. In an instant his shadows overthrew my vines, blasting into me. I went flying back.

The air left my lungs as I made contact with the wall. Pain shot from my back into my limbs. I hit the floor with a thud, gasping wildly, unable to get enough oxygen. White specks filled my vision, and my chest burned. I was going to die. My life in the small village flashed before my eyes. I saw my grandmother's face, then my mother's. I saw Hecate and Hecuba. My garden and then the sun.

Finally, I inhaled deeply and then started coughing. My head throbbed. I looked up, and Hades stood above me, glaring down at me. My body begged for rest; using all of that untapped power left me feeling drained like I had never experienced before. My breath came in hard gulps.

"Finally had enough?" He sneered.

His words sent a flare of madness through me, and I felt Wrath threatening to take over me again. I tried to push against her. I was done. I was no match for the King of the Underworld. He was stronger than me; more experienced. He would overpower me again. I couldn't stand against him.

I opened my mouth to plead my case, to beg for forgiveness, but Wrath answered instead. "No!" she screamed from my mouth.

Sharp thorns sprang from my nails, and I dove on him. He fell, landing on his back and I straddled him. He tried to grapple me, but my nails ripped at his skin and tore his shirt. Blood sprayed from his arms and chest while he struggled under me. I clawed at his face, leaving deep gashes across his cheek.

"Fuck!" He drew back and I expected magic to come for me, I could take it.

But he punched me in the face.

I fell back on my ass, crying out in pain and surprise. My vision went white. He jumped on me, pinning my arms to the ground. "Hypnos!"

I could tell he was using all his strength to hold me down. Power pulsed through my veins as I fought against him.

"No, no, no, no, no!"

Wrath tried to rip her way through me but she couldn't, she was too overspent. I could feel the black ichor sliding down my cheeks again, the ringing in my ears returning. My skin burned as I felt thorns trying to erupt, my back ached and cramped.

"Let me go!" I shouted, my voice feral.

Hypnos ran up to us, kneeling by my head. "Hades I don't think–"

"Do it!" He growled.

Hypnos looked down at me, sadness and remorse in his eyes. "I'm so sorry, Kora."

His voice was soft, soothing the Wrath inside me. He placed his hands gently on my temples, and a warmth rushed through me like water. *Like a river,* I thought. Dust swirled around us, and I coughed and gagged as I inhaled it. My mind drifted against my will to the River Lethe, to the sound of the current, to poppies. I tried to fight it off, to hold on to my anger, but the river sounded so nice…

And with peace finally filling me to my core, I drifted off to sleep.

TEN

My eyes fluttered open, and I blinked heavily, trying to get my bearings. I sat up slowly, the details of the fight falling into place. I glanced around. I was in Hypnos' cave again. The iron beneath me was hard and cool to the touch. I could hear Lethe rushing down below. I looked at my arms and my palms, the skin clean and clear of any wounds my vines had inflicted. Had someone healed me?

"You're weak."

I jolted and turned to see myself sitting on the iron bed. No. It was Wrath. Her red hair was a mess of curls, a mirror of my freckles splattered along her face. Where my bright green eyes were, hers were solid black. The ichor that had seeped from my eyes before also streamed from hers. She sat there, snarling at me, hatred radiating off of her.

"What do you want?" My voice cracked as I spoke. I was scared of her.

She laughed, it was a harsh and crude sound. She smiled at me wickedly, the sight unnerved me. I tried to steady my shallow breathing.

"I want power, control. Vengeance." As she spoke, a shiver went through me.

"Why?" I could see the irritation in her expression as I prodded her.

I pushed myself off the floor. It was uncanny staring at myself. The side I had spoken to frequently, but had never seen. She scoffed.

"Because I deserve it. I have done my time, quietly in the shadows"

My brows furrowed and I shook my head. *Just because you deserve something doesn't mean you can use whatever force you have to take it.*

"Doesn't it, though?" My eyes widened as she responded to my unspoken statement. *"I am you,"* she sneered at me.

"Right." I swallowed hard, trying to avoid letting my mind wander to any specific thoughts.

I hated that she had attached herself to me, like a parasite, feeding off of me. I wanted to be rid of her, and all of the chaos she brought into my life. I backed against the wall of the cave and leaned against it, not wanting to take the only seat available. Which was right next to her on the bed.

"Have you known this whole time?" I asked. "That I'm a God."

She tilted her head to the side, seeming to contemplate my question much harder than I thought she would have to. Red curls spilled over her shoulder, nearly reaching the bed.

"No."

I hummed, leaning my head back. I studied the texture of the ceiling in the cave. Not the answer I expected. I had so many more things I wanted to ask her, but I wasn't sure she would know the answer. Did her knowledge end where mine did?

"No." Her eyebrow raised, and she crossed her arms. Annoyance was thick in her voice. She didn't appreciate me thinking, instead of just speaking to her.

"Why did you attack that woman earlier?"

A smile spread across her face. *"She's in the way."*

"In the way of what?"

"Of us ruling the Underworld." She scowled as she spoke.

"Why are you so hellbent on ruling the underworld?" I couldn't stop the frustration in my tone. I didn't understand it at all, her insatiable need for it. I missed the blue skies, the sun on my skin, the smell of flowers. I missed the upper world.

"It's our right. If The Fates promised us to the God of the Dead, why shouldn't we rule?"

My eyebrows knitted together and I shook my head. "Do you not see how many Gods he has as underlings? He just wants another notch in his belt, he doesn't want someone on a throne by his side."

She let out a soft chuckle and crossed her legs, making herself comfortable. Her head tilted to the side again, and she stared at me in silence before speaking.

"Have you asked him?"

It was my turn to laugh. "Oh yes, I'm sure I can waltz right in; 'Hello Hades, King of the Underworld. I know I just tore into your face and destroyed your home, but could I be Queen?' I'm sure he would love that!"

Her eyes narrowed at me. I tried to push past how uncomfortable the sight of it made me.

"If he will not give it willingly, we will take it!"

I shook my head again, rubbing my eyes. She was exasperating. "I don't want this. I don't want to rule anything. I just want a quiet, uneventful life." There was pleading in my voice.

"*You do want it, I know because–*"

"Yes, yes." I rolled my eyes. "You know because I am you. I'm sick of this!" I stomped my foot against the iron floor of the cave and everything shuddered. I looked around us, worried if I got too angry I might bring the cave in on itself.

"*Careful,* Goddess,*"* she said mockingly. My face flushed at her words.

We were getting dangerously off course. I wasn't sure how much time with her I had, and I needed to get as much information from her as I could. She had to know something that could help me. Something to get me out of the wretched place I was stuck in. I just needed to keep her talking, to distract her enough to get her to let something slip.

"So you want to find The Furies, rule the Underworld, and then what? What's your big plan?"

"*We rebuild the Underworld entirely,*" she said as if it was obvious. "*Think about it, Kora. We could bring life here. Have this whole place bursting with color. We will have The Furies continue their duties of punishing the sinners, and we will build a paradise for those who lived righteous lives.*"

Her words hit me forcefully. I did not expect her to want change. I expected her to want destruction and pain. Shock was apparent on my face. She flashed me a soft smile that was out of place against her rage-filled eyes.

"*We can make this place beautiful. We can give Hypnos his poppies. The Shades will have something pleasant to look at for eternity, instead of this ugly black iron everywhere. We can do it. Only us.*"

She was convincing. She was right.

"Hades will never let us…"

"Then we crush him and take what we want. He has ruled this place for all this time and this is how he does it?" She laughed coldly. *"It's pathetic, really."*

I fidgeted with the sleeve of my dress. I did want that. I wanted to change the entire place. I wanted to make it everything I knew it could be. I couldn't imagine myself overthrowing Hades, though. He was so much stronger than me. And he had so many Gods at his disposal. I had no one.

"We have Hecate," she said proudly.

"One God on our side will not win us a war, which is exactly what we would be in for if we do this."

"You're missing the point, Kora. We enticed Hecate to defect; to side with us. If we can do that once, we can do it again. We will just have to get as many on our side as we can. Surely there are others who feel the same as she does."

"It feels too simple, too easy." I shook my head again. It would never work.

"It will work because we will make it work."

A sharp pain throbbed through the side of my head and I winced. It felt like someone had their hand in my brain, it was disorienting. What was I doing? I didn't want to take the Underworld. I wanted to be above, in the mortal realm.

My vision rippled and blurred. I looked around, confused. Wrath whipped her head around as well, then her black eyes slid onto mine.

"We don't have much time, Kora. You need to listen to me. Go to The Furies. Find them and convince them of our right to rule. They will listen to you, I know it. Once you find them, go after the other Gods."

My vision rippled again, everything around me growing fuzzy. "What's happening?"

She stood, striding over to me. She placed a hand on my cheek. I couldn't feel it. I took several rapid breaths, my heart began to race and panic took hold of me.

"You're waking, Kora. Remember all we talked about. Convince them, take the throne." There was fire burning in her black eyes.

That's right, I was supposed to take the throne. I needed to change the Underworld. Wrath was right.

"But how? How do I do that?" I grabbed her arm, I couldn't do any of it without her. She smiled and brushed her hand down my cheek again.

"Kora, how many times must I say it?" She leaned into me. *"I am you,"* she whispered into my ear.

I felt tears spilling from my eyes. I reached up and wiped, black ichor streaked across the back of my hand. A chill went through my body.

"You're a force of nature, Kora. Never forget that."

My lip quivered as she spoke my grandmother's words. Determination consumed me, driving away my fear and confusion, and I straightened my back. I would sit on the throne… One way or another.

White light enveloped her and flooded the cave, blinding me. Then everything was black.

I lurched upright, gasping loudly. I blinked and rubbed my eyes, expecting to still be in the cave. Expecting to see Wrath with me. She was not. I was sitting in a large, soft bed, covers and furs layered over me. I tried to sort out my thoughts and remember everything Wrath and I had discussed during my sleep. There was a hole in my memory, some missing piece of a puzzle. Like as I was waking I lost something important. I couldn't tell if it had all been a dream, or if she had really been there with me.

I looked down at my hands, they were covered in bloody wraps. Fresh cuts and abrasions peppered my arms. My head throbbed, and every muscle in my body was screaming. His voice cut through the silence like a knife.

"Welcome back, Goddess."

I turned and saw Hades, sprawled out in a cushioned chair near the bed. He was drinking something that smelled strongly of alcohol. He had changed out of his bloodied clothes and into a loose-fitting shirt and trousers. His hair was down but brushed out of his face. His red eyes were gleaming in the candlelight. His face was completely healed.

I took in a shaky breath, trying to steel myself.

"You are a force of nature."

"Hello, Hades."

ELEVEN

I noted the tension in his face when I said his name, the furrow of his brows. He had asked me to call him Aidoneus. It felt far too intimate, too personal. After he snatched me and brought me below I had decided that I would only call him Hades.

"It would help our cause if you play nice."

Play nice? You nearly brought his entire castle down!

"I don't like that woman."

I ran my fingers across the fur cover, my eyes still on the God of the Dead.

"We need to talk, Goddess." His voice was stern, but I couldn't blame him.

I nodded but kept my mouth shut.

"What happened out there?"

Hells. I tried to spin a quick lie, but I could think of nothing. "I just… Was angry. You brought me here without even asking me."

"The anger," he said carefully, "I understand. What I cannot seem to piece together is how you managed to wield your power with such expertise, when you did not even know you had it just hours before."

Embarrassment washed through me. How could I admit that Wrath was not only in my head but also managed to control my body and my power the way that she had? I would be chained and confined if he found out.

Wrath writhed around in the shadows of my mind. Hatred seeped its way into my heart, her hatred. She did not want to be restricted even further than she already was.

"I'm not sure," I lied. "I was just so angry."

He sighed heavily, shaking his head. "Well if you're going to be a risk to my manor–"

I cut him off. "No! No, I promise it will not happen again."

He stayed silent for a moment, considering. "I have rules for you, moving forward."

"Of course."

Anxiety pushed against my lungs, constricting my breathing. He stood and crossed the room, taking a seat next to me on the large bed. I fought against the urge to scoot away from him, my body still sore from our fight. The smell of smoke and iron burned my nose.

"If you feel like you're going to lose control again I need to know. I cannot have you destroying everything I own."

"Okay," I said hurriedly. "I will."

"And," he continued, "I want you to have a guide with you, for a while at least."

"Until you trust me?" It was meant to be a genuine question, but there was a bite to my tone.

His face was serious. His hand twitched, like he thought of reaching out to touch me, but decided against it.

"I have no desire to be your enemy, Goddess."

I averted my eyes. Somehow his words ignited guilt deep in my belly. There was a moment of silence between us. I could feel his stare, even though I kept my gaze lowered. I became distinctly aware of the heat radiating off of his body. He was far too close.

"I have one more thing."

My eyes flicked up to his.

"You cannot kill Minthe."

I saw a gleam in his eyes that told me he knew my earlier attacks were not aimed at him. He was aware, even if he did not know why, that my rage had been for her.

"Minthe is that woman?"

Minthe. Her name on my tongue might as well have been poison. It nauseated me just to say it. Wrath let out an angry hiss from the back of my mind.

"Yes. She's a River Nymph from the mortal realm."

"Why is she here?"

He looked away, settling his attention on a painting on the wall. I followed his eyes and my gaze was momentarily consumed by it. It was a forest scene, the sunlight cast in bright rays between the leaves, onto the meadow floor of the earth. It was breathtaking.

"She was cast out," he said. "I gave her refuge here."

My mind drifted to the conversation I had with Hypnos.

"I understand," I said quietly. I was in his domain, I didn't have a choice but to follow his rules.

"So I will reiterate; you cannot go around destroying my home, and you cannot attack Minthe. I will not tolerate that behavior here."

I shifted my eyes back to him. It stung to have him scold me, regardless of how much I deserved it.

"I understand."

He sighed, his face still lined with concern. I was sure he did not believe me. But I could not risk getting myself locked away, so I would abide.

"If I may?" he said, leaning into me.

I looked at him with confusion on my face, and I did not speak.

"I would like to heal your wounds."

Heat crept up my neck into my cheeks. "Oh. Yes, thank you."

He placed his hands gently over my cuts and torn flesh, and black flames sparked under his touch. It did not burn, but the warmth kissed my skin and trailed along my injuries. It spread, leaving my skin clear and unmarred in its wake.

"How did you do that?" I asked, inspecting myself. There was not a scratch left on me.

"Perks of being a God." When I looked up at him, the corner of his mouth was turned up, I looked away quickly.

He stood and then started heading towards the door. "There are clothes in the closet for you, and a hot bath in the washroom. Feel free to explore the manor, if you would like. Don't get into any trouble."

With that, he left me alone. I sat so long my body was stiff before I got up and decided to look around the room. I found the closet full of clothes, as he promised. It was mostly extravagant dresses, expensive shirts, trousers, and boots that appeared brand new.

It didn't take long for me to slip out of my torn, bloody dress and slip into the steaming wash basin in the adjacent room. Once I was clean I made my way back into the bedchamber to try on some of the clothes that he had left for me. Everything fit perfectly.

***

I wandered through the halls of the castle. Candles hung from thick gold chains, lining my path. It was still dim, thanks to the lack of windows. The candlelight danced eerily against the dark stone walls, casting shadows along my way. Hypnos was right, there was a panic deep in my bones that made me feel like a caged animal.

My footsteps echoed down corridors, enticing me to look over my shoulder to ensure I was not being followed. I had gotten lost several times over the last few days and had to call for Hypnos to guide me. He was far more patient with me than I would have been.

I had not seen Hades since our conversation in my bedchamber. Hypnos told me he stayed busy often and was rarely seen throughout the manor. I was thankful for the time to adjust without his scrutinizing eyes. I had been too scared to pull at my powers again, concerned if I plucked that string I might lose myself to madness, rather than learn to control it.

Wrath had been quiet since I dreamed of her. I could faintly feel her stirring, but she did not speak to me. The words she had spoken to me in that vision haunted me often, her ambitions of power and control teased me. I had contemplated sneaking out to look for The Furies many times, but fear of being lost in the vast Underworld kept me confined within the walls of the manor. I spent my days wandering around, trying to memorize every room.

I turned a corner, fear lurched through me. A scream threatened to burst from my lips. My entire body went rigid, eyes wide. I sighed deeply when I realized it was not some flesh-eating monster, but the woman in red I had seen on my first day in the underworld. She had also made herself sparse since the incident.

"You spook easily, half-breed." She was leaning against the wall, glaring down her nose at me. She was donning another red dress, it was tight and hugged all of her curves. The silk shone in the light of the flames around us. Her long blonde hair fell in perfect waves down her back. I inhaled deeply, trying to remind myself of all the rules Hades had given me.

'Do not kill Minthe'.

Minthe. Even her name grated on my nerves. I caught myself imagining my hands wrapped around her throat, imagining them ripping her body open.

"They told you, didn't they? Your mother is a God, but your father was some poor mortal man. I heard he died." She pretended to examine her fingernails.

I ground my teeth, trying to focus on my breathing. *Do not kill Minthe*, I reminded myself. I tried to think of some witty comeback but everything seemed juvenile. I rolled my eyes and brushed past her, deciding the smartest thing I could do was ignore her. I made it several more steps down the hall when she stopped me.

"Wait!"

I turned back towards her, her face crumpled and tears lined her eyes. I tilted my head, trying to understand why she had so quickly gone from taunting me to appearing upset.

"I'm sorry," she started, hugging herself. "I… I think we got off on the wrong foot. I haven't had a friend since I've been here. It's lonely. Maybe we could start over?" Her voice cracked, she sounded sincere.

Perhaps I had judged her too quickly. I sighed, shaking my head. Wrath broke her silence.

"She lies," she whispered. *"Don't trust that two-faced harlot."*

I felt the malice in Wrath's voice, felt a tingle of power ripple through me. Minthe's eyebrows furrowed. She must have felt it, as well. I closed Wrath off, drowning her out entirely.

"I would love that," I said with a forced smile.

She returned my smile, her eyes softening. Maybe having her as a friend would be nice if I was going to be stuck below forever. She took a few steps towards me, glancing around.

"I have to tell you, Kora. I'm sure you're still learning your way around. I think you're going the wrong way."

I blinked, then looked around. I had been sure I was going the right way, but suddenly I didn't feel so confident in myself. I glanced down the hall, then the opposite way. Everything looked exactly the same.

"I'm trying to get to the dining hall. I'm supposed to meet Hypnos."

She smiled at me again, nodding her head. "Of course. It's just the other way, there." She pointed to the other side of the hall.

She must have lived in the manor a long time, I wasn't sure I would ever know how to navigate it. I was relieved then, that I had bumped into her. Thankful I had not ended up lost somewhere, having to call for Hypnos again.

"Thank you, Minthe. Maybe we can meet for lunch soon?"

She smiled brightly, "I would love that! Have a nice day with Hypnos."

With that, she sauntered off in the direction I had come from. I watched her walk away, wondering how she had changed her tune so quickly. I had been the one to attack her, though. Certainly that had caused ill feelings. I shrugged, deciding that was a matter to worry about later. The less conflict I had while stuck in the Underworld, the better.

I turned on my heel and headed down the path she had pointed, feeling excited to get to the dining hall. Hypnos had agreed to take me to Hecate's hut and I was eager to see her again. We had so much to catch up on. I wanted to know everything that had happened since I left.

I walked for several minutes down the hall when I started to feel uncomfortable. Something was off. The hall cut sharply to the left, leaving me no choice but to make the turn. As I moved, the next path was pitch black. There were no candles to light the way at all. My stomach dropped. *I should turn around*, I thought.

But something pulled me onward. I swallowed thickly and stepped into the darkness.

My hand rubbed across the wall as I stumbled forward, unable to see a thing. My other arm was stretched out to make sure I didn't walk into anything. The stone was rough against my palm. It was definitely not the right way to the dining hall. Minthe had most certainly led me astray. But for some reason, I couldn't bring myself to stop. I couldn't even bring myself to be angry with her. The curiosity overpowered any outrage I should have felt.

My outreached hand met stone and I fumbled around until I found another pathway. The darkness was unending, as were all of the twists and turns I was making. It seemed like I had been walking forever. I wondered if Hypnos had tired of waiting, or if he had gone looking for me. Silence was heavy as I walked, causing my footsteps to echo around me.

Light broke in the distance. It was faint, like it struggled to cut through the black that hung around me. I quickened my steps, eager to see where I was being led. As I drew nearer to the light, the room started coming into view. It was a large, round room. It was empty. There were windows, the only ones I had seen since I had arrived.

Thick iron barred them off from the outside world. There was an enormous, open doorway on the other side of the room. The adjacent room was just as pitch black as the hall I had come from.

I stepped into the open space, looking around slowly. It smelled old and stagnant. My heart rate quickened and I felt Wrath awakening inside me. I walked up to the window, placing my hands around the bars, and tip-toed to peek outside.

There was a river in the near distance. I hadn't seen that river on my outing with Hypnos. It must have been in the opposite direction that we had traveled. I heard movement behind me and my stomach tightened. I swallowed, slowly dropping my hands from the barred window. I felt a thick, hot breath hit me in the back. It blew my hair slightly. Dread hit me all at once.

"Turn," Wrath whispered.

As slowly as I could manage, I turned around to face what was behind me. My eyes widened, and I clenched my teeth so I didn't scream. I feared any sudden movement or sound might spring it to attack. A massive three-headed dog stood before me. Its body was black with traces of brown up its legs. It had long noses and erect ears. The same brown on its legs crept up its noses and sat atop its eyes, like eyebrows. All three heads were a foot from me, its eyes piercing into my soul. It did not growl or bare its teeth, but its presence was no less frightening. It was as big as a bear. I stood there, unable to breathe. Unsure what to do. Hades had not prohibited me from wandering the castle, but I was sure I had entered an area that was off-limits.

I tried to sidestep around the beast, and its eyes tracked me. A low growl rumbled from its throats and I stopped again.

Fuck. I shouldn't have come down here.

I could feel Wrath's satisfaction. *"Touch it,"* she said. *"Show the beast he is yours."*

"You're crazy," I whispered to Wrath under my breath. I was about to be killed by the monster. "Who keeps something like this in their home?"

The dog tilted its large heads in unison.

"Touch it!" she demanded again.

My hand slowly lifted, as if Wrath herself was controlling it. Shaking uncontrollably, I reached out towards the middle head. The beast stood frozen. It kept all of its eyes locked onto mine as my hand inched closer to it. My hand gently brushed down the side of its cheek and, to my surprise, it leaned into the touch. I stroked its fur again and its ears laid back against its head. I saw its nub tail wagging. My fear melted away slightly.

"Good," she hummed.

I scratched under its chin, and it closed its eyes. The other heads slammed into it abruptly, lips peeling back and monstrous growls coming from their throats. I snatched my hand away, gasping. The heads stopped their bickering and swiveled back to me. Concern sat heavy in their big brown eyes.

"No need for that," I said, voice shaking still.

It stepped closer, lowering its heads. I hesitantly reached both hands back out, petting the beast as equally as I could manage, hoping to avoid another fight between them. Their whole body began to wiggle as they aggressively wagged their tail. A smile broke across my face, the sight of the giant animal being sweet was too much to bear.

"*What* are you doing here?"

Hades' voice cut the silence like a blade. I whirled around to face him, the King of the Underworld. He was standing at the entrance of the room, arms crossed.

"I–"

I wanted to throw Minthe under the bus, to tell him how she had lured me in the wrong direction. How she had pretended to be my friend and then lied to me… But I refused to look like a fool in front of him.

"You didn't say there were areas off limits."

He tilted his head. Intrigue on his face, not anger. His eyes slid from me to the dog. The beast sighed heavily and then sat down with a thump. Their ears were standing tall again, the tail no longer wagging.

"Lay down," Hades said to the dog sternly.

The beast laid down instantly. He had him well-trained. "His name is Cerberus," he said, turning his attention back to me. "He's my guard dog. A very shit one, albeit." He shot Cerberus a sidelong glare. The dog laid its ears back and whined.

"I don't think he needs to guard anything from the people living here."

Hades raised an eyebrow at my retort. My face flushed as I remembered the destruction I had caused just days prior. "Fair enough," I mumbled.

"Come."

Cerberus hesitated. I looked from the dog to Hades and I saw his jaw twitch. When my eyes flicked back to Cerberus, he was staring at me. I looked up, and Hades was also staring at me. Wrath was overjoyed at the sight of the dog looking at me when Hades had given him a command.

Hades walked over, crouching down near Cerberus, who flopped over onto his back. Hades reached down and scratched the large beast's belly. A back leg kicked in reflex. I watched as Cerberus rolled around on the floor in front of Hades like a giant puppy. He stared down at the dog with what I could only gather was love. A smile crept across his face.

"How long have you had him?" I dared to ask.

His eyes flicked up to me, a softness there I was not expecting. "Since he was a small puppy. I've lost count of the years."

I nodded, tearing my eyes away from his. I tried to distract myself with images of what Cerberus must have looked like being so young.

"Is he your only dog?"

The corner of his mouth lifted in a half smile. "Yes, he is. I've never cared much to add to my already overflowing plate of responsibilities, but Hecate brought him to me and said he was too unruly for her to manage. He's always been well-behaved for me. I think she just lacks patience."

"That does sound exactly like her." I grinned, then my eyebrows furrowed. "How did you know I was here?"

He looked up from Cerberus, his face serious. "This is my realm, Kora. I know everything that happens here."

His tone was not threatening, but his words sunk deep into me. I would never be able to find The Furies without him knowing, if he could truly see everything that happened within the Underworld. I would be lucky if he did not already know of my plan. I tried to speak, to distance myself from the guilt that tried to slip in my mind.

I could find no words.

He stood, brushing off his trousers. Cerberus jumped to his feet, striding over to me, and leaned against my legs. I looked down at the dog, his large round eyes locked onto me. I could feel his loyalty. When I looked back at Hades, his face still held that same kind expression. He looked... pleased.

"We should go. I think Hypnos is probably still waiting for you in the dining hall."

I swallowed, unease still settled deep into my bones. I tried to keep thoughts of The Furies buried, fearful he might even be able to read my mind.

I plastered a fake smile across my face. "Of course."

I was in trouble.

TWELVE

Reality warped around us as we appeared in the dining hall. I managed to land on my feet and keep my balance, with the help of his arm wrapped tightly around me. I squeezed my eyes shut, trying not to allow the nausea to take me. When I opened them I saw Hypnos leaning across the table, staring at us. I watched as a smirk spread across his face. I became increasingly aware of the grip Hades had on my waist. I pulled out of his grasp, taking several steps away, making sure not to look at him. My face was hot as I strode to the table.

"Sorry, Hypnos."

He shrugged, pulling himself up from the table. "No matter," he mumbled. "Would you still like to visit Hecate?"

I nodded, eagerly. "Yes. Please."

"Of course." He brushed his hair out of his face, his eyes still lined with dark circles. He made his way into the throne room, which had been repaired completely, by magic I assumed. I walked after him, feeling Hades' heavy stare on my back. I felt a wave of guilt as I followed him into the room. I was thankful to not have any physical reminders of my actions. I hated that I had caused such a mess, but I did not regret attacking Minthe. She had tricked me. I hated the thought that she had gotten one over on me. I wondered at first if that was Wrath's feelings or my own, but quickly realized it was mine.

We stepped out of the castle and I instinctively looked up to the sky, hoping for sunlight. There was none. Just the same sad sky, no sun to warm my skin. I sighed heavily, my heart ached for the upper world. It was easy to pretend I was still above while I was stuck in the manor, but stepping out and seeing all of the gray above me and all of the black iron under my feet… It was disheartening.

"So what happened? Why were you late?" Hypnos' eyes locked onto me. I considered lying, telling him I had just been lost. But I was sure he would see through me.

"I bumped into Minthe. She gave me false directions to the dining hall." I rolled my eyes as I spoke, trying not to sound too bitter.

"Ah. That sounds about right." He kept walking but glanced over at me. "And you called…Hades?" He raised his eyebrow.

I felt my face warm. "No! I ran into Cerberus–"

He cut me off. "You ran into Cerberus? Are you ok?" His eyes were wide with concern.

I shot him a puzzled look. "I'm fine. He's a surprisingly sweet dog."

Hypnos was frowning, his brows furrowed. "Sweet? Are you sure you met Cerberus? He's a temperamental beast."

I smiled over at him as I thought of Cerberus wagging his tail and rolling around on the floor. He was intimidating to look at, but he still just seemed like… a dog.

"It was a little difficult to keep each head from getting jealous, but once I figured out what order to pet them in–" He interrupted me again, startling me.

"Wait, wait. You *pet* him? Like… with your hands?" His eyes were wide and his mouth slack. I wondered, at that point, if I had been extremely lucky by having such a pleasant interaction with Cerberus.

"Yes, I pet him! I like him." I smiled, feeling extremely pleased with myself. "Oh! While I was in the room with him I found a window. I could see another river. How many are here?"

"There are five. You saw the River Styx."

"What does that river do?" After learning of Lethe I was apprehensive about bodies of water in the Underworld.

"Styx is how the dead are brought here. They are ferried across by Charon."

"No horrid repercussions from ingesting that river?"

He gave me a very tired look. I couldn't tell if it was true exhaustion or if he was just weary from all of my questions. After spending a few days with Hypnos I had learned he was the God of Sleep. As such, he never actually slept himself. It sounded like a miserable existence to me but aside from the bags under his eyes and constant yawning, he didn't seem to mind it.

"Styx is not only dangerous to ingest, it's dangerous to even touch. Anything that touches the water, aside from the wood that Charon's boat and oar are made of, immediately disintegrates."

He spoke with an indifferent tone, but I was horrified at the knowledge of a river having that sort of power. Everything about the Underworld was scary and dangerous. I missed the peace I had in my life before.

"And who is Charon?"

Hypnos smiled, shaking his head. "I'm going to have to write all of this down for you."

"That would be nice, actually."

He bumped his shoulder into mine and a laugh escaped my lips. He had become my favorite thing in the Underworld. Our friendship blossomed quickly, he was kind and easy to talk to. I was thankful to have his company.

"Charon's only job is to escort the dead across the river. No one knows how long he has been the ferryman. He doesn't speak."

I wondered how anyone could be silent for so long. How he must have been below before any other Gods or creatures. I thought he must have been very lonely for a long time. Would I end up lonely? Would I be stuck below for so long that the new Gods told stories of me the way we spoke about Charon?

"Will Hades eventually let me spend some of my time in the upper world?" My voice broke as I looked at Hypnos.

"Eventually I believe he will let you leave. I know it's hard being here when you long for the life above. I'm truly sorry, Kora."

He held my stare, his eyes full of sympathy and understanding. I believed that he was sorry. Remembering his cave above Lethe and the pile of poppies, I thought maybe he felt the same as I did. Perhaps he also yearned to be amongst the living.

"I just wish there was a way to make this place more like the upper world. I miss flowers, I miss the sun."

I looked down at the iron earth beneath us. I tried to imagine the smell of my garden, the warmth on my face, my fingers in the dirt.

"I wish I could change this place."

When my eyes lifted, I saw something in Hypnos' eyes. My heart ached at the sight of it. It was sorrow and pain. It was affection. It was faith and confidence.

"Then change it, Kora. Hades may be king, but you are a Goddess. You are strong and capable."

He spoke to me like he believed I could. Like he knew I could make it everything I wanted it to be... Everything, I thought, he wanted it to be too. We spent the rest of our walk discussing things we loved the most about the upper world. Things we missed. Places we thought would be the best for trees and gardens. We talked about our favorite flowers, and which might look best together. It was comforting, even though I was unsure if I could actually get anything to grow. I decided I would try. Both for myself and for Hypnos.

Hecate's hut came into view in the distance. It was smaller than her cabin in the woods and stuck out like a sore thumb amidst all of the iron and rigidity of the Underworld. The wooden foundation looked old and weathered. Smoke rose from the chimney. My mind drifted to the night my life changed.

Wrath stirred around inside me as we approached, making me realize how quiet she had been since we left the castle.

"The Witch will teach us," she whispered to me. *"She can show us how to control our power, how to grow it."*

My body hummed with excitement that I was not sure was my own. My steps quickened, the need to be reunited with Hecate urging me forward.

"Kora."

I turned back to Hypnos, who had stopped several steps behind me. My eyebrows furrowed. I had expected him to stay with me through my visit, but I felt his hesitation.

"Yes?"

"I'm going to let you go on ahead, I have something I need to do. Hecate can take you back to the manor when you're ready."

I could sense the deceit in his words. Not wholly a lie, but he wasn't telling me everything. I forced a tight smile. It hurt that he would hide something from me.

"Of course. I'll be fine."

He nodded and with a swirl of dust around him, he vanished. I stood there, staring at where he had been. My chest ached. I pushed it away and turned back to the hut. I didn't have time to let it affect me, I had to see Hecate.

I stepped closer to the door, a genuine smile replacing the fake one. The door burst open, and the young and vibrant face of Hecate appeared. Her eyes were wide, a wild smile on her face. Her long black hair was split into two braids hanging over her chest. She wore a long black dress, the collar hung slightly off her shoulders. A large skeleton key dangled on a chain around her neck, and a golden crescent moon was painted on her forehead.

"Kora!"

She ran to me, grabbing me and pulling me into a tight hug. She had my arms pinned to my sides and her face was buried in my neck. I huffed a laugh, trying to get my arms around her. Her shoulders trembled then, and I realized she was crying.

"Hecate, I missed you."

She pulled away to look at me, her cheeks lined with tears. I felt my lip quiver and my own tears threatened to fall. She wiped her eyes and laughed.

"Please, come in! We have so much to discuss, Kora. I'll put some tea on."

I let her pull me into the hut, eager to finally sit after such a long walk. My mouth watered at the thought of her bitter drink. When I stepped inside I was surrounded by dogs. There were a dozen coming over to smell me. Most of them were rather large, thin dogs with long noses and legs. They were unlike anything I had ever seen. Then Hecuba rounded a corner and our eyes locked. She bounded over to me, jumping up, paws on my shoulders, and licked my face. Her tail wagged and she whined excitedly. I brushed my fingers through her shaggy hair, holding her tightly.

"Oh! I have missed you, you mangy hound!"

The dogs all hastily followed Hecate into the kitchen. I trailed behind them. When I made it to the kitchen the dogs dispersed, finding a place to lay. Hecate was already standing at the wood stove boiling water for tea. My eyes fell to the table and widened.

"Hecate… is that a weasel?"

She turned, glancing at the creature lying on a blanket across the table.

"Her name is Galinthias." She smiled at me devilishly and turned back to the tea.

I walked to the table slowly, peering down at the little animal. It stretched out, yawning widely. Its small black eyes met mine, then it rolled over and went back to sleep. I wondered how Hecate got anything done with so many animals wandering through her home. The kitchen was so small, and the dogs so large, we had to step over them to move around.

She hurried over with two cups, placing one on either side of the table. She took a seat and I followed suit. I brought the tea to my lips, inhaling deeply. I could smell the familiar pungent aroma she had served me so many times before. A smile spread across my face.

"So! Tell me everything. What have I missed?" The excitement in her voice was comical.

"Well, Hypnos has been showing me around. I must admit, everything is very… gloomy here." She nodded as I spoke, taking in every word.

"And Hades? How is he treating you?"

My mind flashed to my first day, the destruction I brought upon his manor. The way I had clawed at him.

"He stays to himself mostly. We had a rocky first day, but I haven't seen much of him since. I met Cerberus!" I tried to veer the conversation away from the God of the Dead.

"Yes, awful beast," she muttered. "But when you say 'rocky first day'? What happened?"

Her eyes drilled into me as she waited for me to speak. I shifted in my seat, trying to find a way to tell her without giving too many details.

"Well... It was going ok. Then I met Minthe."

"Oh Gods! Does he still have that pathetic Nymph living there? Please tell me you killed her."

"No! ...I tried." My face flushed and I rubbed my hands together. I expected Hecate to lecture me about the politics of the Gods, or life being precious. Instead, she laughed loudly.

"How dreadful. There's always next time."

I stared at her, confusion clear on my face. She continued sipping her tea, waiting for me to finish my tale.

"I sort of destroyed the throne room in the process. And I clawed his face, I think." She barked another laugh, and I grinned. "It's really not funny, Hecate."

"Right, right. Sorry."

"Hypnos told me about the rivers here and The Erinyes."

She shivered at the mention of The Furies. "Those three unnerve me."

"He said you might be able to teach me how to control my power."

Her eyes lifted to mine. "Of course, we can't have you tearing this whole place down." She winked at me. "What did your power manifest as?"

"Flora, it seems. At first, it was vines erupting from my palms, but I managed to grow a tree and make the vines come from the ground too. Oh! At one point thorns grew from my fingernails."

She listened intently as I spoke, taking everything in. Her brows were furrowed together, and she nodded her head. Once I finished describing the chaos I had caused she sipped her tea again.

"Sounds like you made quite the scene, Kora."

I sighed heavily, leaning back in my chair. Hecate picked up Galinthias, the animal dangled from her hand as she moved it to her lap. She stroked its brown fur as she thought.

"I think I know exactly how to help you."

THIRTEEN

Sweat beaded down my forehead and my hair clung to my damp face. My arms trembled and every muscle in my body cramped. My eyes were locked on the potted hemlock in front of me. I ground my teeth as my vision blurred. I had lost track of how long I had been kneeling on the floor, arms outstretched to the plant. *'Make it grow,'* she had said. Dizziness washed over me as I frantically searched for that hungry power within.

"Breathe!"

Her sudden shouting startled me and I gasped, the air finally filling my lungs. I hadn't even realized I had been holding my breath. I hunched over, my palms flat on the floor. I took several more ragged breaths as my eyes managed to see clearly again.

"If you refuse to breathe during these exercises you will end up passing out."

"I…am…trying!" I managed between huffs.

"We have been here for hours and made no progress, Kora. We need to consider a new angle. What were you feeling when you managed to tap into your power before?"

"Rage," Wrath snarled. *"Jealousy."*

"I don't know. I can't remember."

"Try harder. You must remember something."

"*Say it!*" Wrath demanded. *"Tell her how angry you were when you saw that Nymph standing there with him."*

I whirled around to Hecate, anger boiled deep inside me. I felt like I was going insane, Wrath prodding me from one direction and Hecate from the other. Silence. I needed silence. For just one fucking–

"Kora."

"I don't know!" My scream echoed around us, power coursing through me. It both burned and intoxicated me as it jolted through my veins like lightning. The hut shook. The animals all jumped to their feet, fear in their eyes. Wrath thrummed through me with excitement. The power filled me to my core, my body begged for more.

"That's it, Kora. Do you feel that? Grab it and take it!"

As Hecate urged me on, I pushed into it. I let my anger take hold of the reins. Another quake rumbled through the earth beneath us. I felt incredible. I felt invincible. I frantically grasped for more and felt that tearing sensation across my skin again.

"The hemlock, child."

My eyes ripped from Hecate to the plant I knelt in front of. My head cocked to the side as my eyes focused on it. I soaked in all the tiny details it had to offer me. I could see every vein running through its soft petals, and feel the pulse through its leaves down to its roots. I could sense the very life within it.

I reached my hand out, feeling it hum as I drew near. My fingers brushed across the petals and my power surged into it. The hemlock drank it in, and before my very eyes, it grew. Its stem shot up, blooms bursting open, and new leaves unfurling. My eyes widened. I stared as it continued to sap my magic; it continued to grow larger and larger. It hung over the edge of the pot, unable to support the weight of the abundance of leaves and flowers. The plant began to feel like an extension of myself, I couldn't tell where my fingers ended and the hemlock began.

Suddenly I could see nothing, I could hear nothing. I was the hemlock and the hemlock was me. My mind was quiet. Everything was peaceful, everything was life. Nothing else mattered.

The beautiful, serene connection shattered as my body was shoved backward, my fingers separated from the bloom. Sound and thought filled my head instantly, bringing me to a point of panic and dismay. It was too much. Every noise screeched painfully through my head. The very feeling of my body became overstimulating. I needed that peace again. I launched myself back to the plant, clawing at the air, desperate for that blissful silence. My body and my mind needed it more than I needed air. I craved it.

My scalp screamed as Hecate yanked me away by my hair. I fell onto my back, the ceiling of the hut filling my vision. I lay there taking raspy breaths, my chest burning as it rose and fell. She stood over me, looking down at me as she smiled. I settled back into my own mind, my panic subsiding, my body feeling like itself again.

"Interesting."

I stayed frozen as my mind tried to collect itself. She knelt beside me and ran her hand across my cheek and then lifted it to her face. Black ichor coated her fingers. She glanced down at me, pride in her eyes.

"You are remarkable, child."

I pushed myself up, drawing my knees to my chest.

"That was euphoric." My words came out soft and breathy.

I looked at the hemlock, it was massive now. I hadn't even realized how much I had given it. All I could think about was how much more I had to offer, how magnificent I could help it become. I could feel it radiating my own power.

"That was beautiful," Wrath whispered. Her own pride mirrored Hecate's and sent a shiver down my spine.

My eyes stayed glued to the plant and I realized I wanted to be lost in that feeling forever. I wanted to lay down and be swallowed by the earth. For grass and flowers to drain me completely. I could give every ounce of myself to nourish them. It felt like my only purpose; to bring life to everything. *'The Goddess of Spring'*, Hecate had called me.

But I was more than that. I could feel it humming just below the surface, right within my grasp. I was not just the Goddess of spring. I was birth, I was growth. I was life in its entirety.

Determination burned in my eyes as they lifted to Hecate. "I can do better."

There was no question in my mind, then. I knew I could tap into it again, I could grow anything. The feeling of it all was so fresh I feared if I stopped too long it might slip out of reach.

I didn't wait for a response. I stood tall and raced for her door. I wanted to try it on a larger scale, from scrap. I rushed outside, my boots crunching across the iron ground. I looked around, the vastness of the Underworld no longer felt like a blight. It felt like… a clean slate. A smile spread across my face.

I turned to see Hecate standing in the doorway. She was watching me intensely, waiting to see what I was going to do. I swiveled away from her and knelt down to the blackened earth.

My fingers raked against the cold, hard ground. It felt so different from laying my hands on the hemlock. I could feel no pulse of life from within it. *A clean slate*, I reminded myself. I reached for that power, still feeling it just below the surface stirring and dancing within me.

"You are life," I whispered.

My mind melted into that force. I could feel it growing and spreading. I urged it into the iron earth, willing it to produce anything at all. I shut my eyes tightly as I felt my magic pour out of my fingertips. Feeding... I wasn't sure what. I didn't care. It could be whatever it wanted to be.

"Kora."

Her voice was muffled as if she was far away. I felt my mind slipping again. I didn't care about that either. My mind didn't matter, neither did my body. The only thing that held any importance to me was whatever I was growing. It begged for more and I obliged. I would give it anything. I would give it everything.

It sapped my power until my bones ached. Until it hurt to breathe. I could feel Hecate's hands on my shoulders, her fingernails digging into my skin. I knew she was speaking to me, but I could no longer hear her. I was somehow distinctly aware of everything around me, but nothing at all. It didn't feel like the blissful silence and peace I had with the potted hemlock. It felt like chaos. Like agony. It felt like death.

My body was hit with a blast of pain beyond my imagination. I was thrown through the air, my back slammed into the ground. A scream shattered the silence. It was my own scream. I clawed at my chest, my skin felt like it was on fire. My eyes flew open, the gray sky above me like a blanket. I was still screaming and clawing at myself. My nails ripped at my clothes and my skin.

Hecate rushed over to me, grabbing my wrists. I fought against her, trying to pry myself free. Panic and pain were the only thing my mind could register. I was a feral animal.

"Breathe, child. You're ok."

She spoke to me softly, like she was consoling a babe. My body started to shake violently. My screaming turned to sobs as tears mixed with black ichor poured down my face. She sat there, holding me tightly and stroking my hair until I was quiet.

I reached up and wiped my eyes, pushing myself away from her. She looked at me with so much pity I had to turn away. When my eyes settled on the land I had tried to grow life from, my heart sank.

I hadn't grown anything. The ground was cracked worse than it had been, leaving craters and crevices skittering across the surface. It looked like I had sucked everything right out of the iron. Even the color had been drained. There was a massive circle of gray where I had been sitting in front of her hut.

As I stared at the destruction I had wrought upon the land I did not feel like a Goddess of life, I felt like a Goddess of death.

"There can be no life without death." Wrath's words left me hollow.

Everything after was a blur. My mind and my body both felt empty. Hecate had gathered me up, helping me walk inside. I watched her lips move, but I couldn't hear what she said to me. She sat me down at the table, wrapping a small blanket around my shoulders. My gaze fell to the pack of dogs who stood as far away from me as they could, pinning me with their watchful eyes. Hecate brought me tea, but my arms were so heavy I could not lift the cup to my mouth.

I sat with my hands wrapped around the warm cup and lost myself in silence. I wasn't sure how long I sat there staring. Hecate didn't speak, didn't push me. She allowed me the time I needed to come down from the devastation I felt after what I had done.

After what could have been minutes or hours my mind finally started stringing thoughts together. I wanted to hate the Underworld. I wanted to hate my power. Instead, I found myself desperate to try again. There was no avoiding my abilities forever. Eventually, someone would expect me to do something with it.

My eyes lifted from the now cold tea to Hecate. She was already staring at me. She must have seen it in my eyes, that hardened perseverance. That inability to back down. As our eyes locked, she nodded.

"Again, then." She stood as she spoke, brushing past me.

I rose to my feet, the blanket falling into a heap on the floor. I turned to follow her, not bothering to utter a reply. My eyes stayed in front of me as I walked through her home. The dogs parted for me and bowed as I passed them. Hecate was waiting for me outside the opened door. My eyes fell to the ruined ground and I felt a flicker of doubt.

"None of that. You are a queen."

I turned from the shame and the guilt of what was inside me. Wrath was right, there was no place for that. I stepped past Hecate, trying to ignore the weight of her stare. Every step I took was exhausting. Too much of my power had been used already, but I could not stop until I understood how it worked. I had to be able to control it, at least to some degree.

I knelt on the ground, not bothering to move past where I had tried last. I placed my palms down and closed my eyes. I inhaled deeply, and on the exhale I released myself again. I tried to focus on it this time. I couldn't allow my power to do as it pleased, I was its master.

Visions of what I wanted to grow filled my head. I knew before I stepped outside what I needed to create. Power flowed down my arms, through my fingertips, and into the ground again. My mind tried to slip and I fought to hold it in place.

"Focus."

Hypnos' face flashed in my mind. I thought of his cave above Lethe, the pile of poppies he kept beside his bed. I thought of his sleepy smile and his kindness. I could feel the ichor trailing down my cheeks. My body ached and burned all over. Peace filled me. I could hear Hecate gasp, could hear the earth parting for me. I could feel it, that time, the life springing out from the ground. I knew before I ever opened my eyes that I had been successful.

"Look, Kora."

"Open your eyes."

So I did. A single poppy had grown from a small crack in the iron. Its stem was thin and frail, the lone bud unopened. It was small. I wanted to be embarrassed by how poorly it was, but I couldn't. I had done it. I had brought forth life where before there was none.

I lifted my shaking hand out and caressed the bud. It unfolded slowly, exposing the bright red petals completely. A smile spread across my face. Hecate knelt beside me. I lifted my eyes to hers, a corner of her lip turned up in a half smile.

"The Goddess of Spring."

I shook my head, turning my attention back to the bloom.

"No," I said weakly. I touched the flower again, grasping at the tiny flicker of power I had left still inside me. The bloom wilted and withered before me until it dried and crumbled into dust.

"I am so much more than that."

FOURTEEN

We appeared outside the front door of Hades' castle. Hecate had her arm tightly around me, my body was far too weak to stand on its own. I had drained myself completely, growing and destroying several more flowers after the first poppy, until she had made me stop. I had been too exhausted to argue with her and had agreed to let her bring me back.

"Make sure you get plenty of rest. Sleep as much as you can."

She stepped up, still supporting the weight of my body, and pushed the door open. When we entered the manor my eyes fell on Hades. He was seated on his throne, glaring at us. Fire burned in his red eyes and anxiety washed over me.

I peeled my gaze from his to the God standing in the middle of the room. He brushed his copper hair back, flashing us a devilish grin.

Fuck. He had the worst timing. I felt Hecate's grip on me tighten and her body still.

"Care to tell me, Witch, why I had to find out from Hermes that you helped my Goddess expend every drop of power she had in her?"

His voice was quiet but his tone was cold and filled with rage. The hair on my arms stood up and a chill went through me. I was too tired to speak so I silently begged Hecate not to be combative. There was not enough energy left in me to deal with a fight. She either did not see my inaudible plea or did not care. I couldn't tell which.

"Someone has to teach her how to control herself, Hades, or she will destroy everything in her path!"

I cringed as she spoke. I knew deep down her words were not meant to hurt me, but they sliced at me like a knife. My face fell and shame threatened to consume me. She was right. If I didn't perfect my power I could wreak havoc on everything.

Hades stood, his eyes locking on to mine. He strode over to us, not bothering to look at Hermes as he walked past him. He stopped before us and I lifted my head to look at him. There was so much anger on his face and a deadly aura radiated off of him. I had thought he would be happy to see I had gained some control over my abilities. He did not break his eyes from mine as he spoke.

"Leave us. Both of you."

Hermes vanished instantly, but I felt Hecate hesitate. I kept my stare locked on Hades and slipped my arm away from Hecate. My legs trembled and my body swayed as I stood on my own. Pure stubbornness kept me upright.

"You can go, Hecate." I felt her eyes on me, but I refused to look away from the God of the Dead.

"Very well."

In a plume of smoke and darkness, she left us. I felt my heart sink as soon as we were alone. I waited for his fury, for shouting and sharp words. They did not come. His face softened and relaxed. He slipped an arm under mine, as Hecate had been doing before. My lip trembled and I leaned into his body for support. I could not rationalize the relief that washed over me. It was the debilitating exhaustion, I told myself.

"Come, Goddess. You need to eat and rest."

The gentle understanding in his voice cracked something inside me and tears rolled down my cheeks. I let him guide me into the dining hall, and let him sit me in his large chair at the head of the table. I watched in silence as he filled my plate with food and my cup with water. He sat to my right and his eyes met mine. There was something there… Something I wasn't sure I had ever seen in anyone before. I brushed the thought off before I could place it.

"You need to eat. It helps."

I looked down to my plate and with shaking hands I started to eat.

Food had never tasted so good. The flavors and textures were extraordinary. It was all food I had eaten at that very table before, but something about being so drained made it so much better. My trembling subsided as my stomach filled. My mind was clearer. He had been right, the food did help. I gulped the water down like I had been days without it. I set the empty cup down and he refilled it immediately.

Once I had eaten until my stomach hurt and drank several cups of water, I leaned back in the chair. My eyes slid to his.

"Feel better?"

"I do."

He opened his mouth but then closed it as if he decided against whatever he was going to say. I was too drunk off the meal I had eaten to wonder too much about it.

"I made progress today."

"You overexerted yourself today."

My eyes dropped to the nearly empty plate in front of me. I couldn't figure out why I wanted his approval so badly. I wasn't sure which was more frustrating; the fact he was not excited about what I had accomplished, or that I craved his validation.

I looked around the room, scanning the area for the God of Sleep. He would be proud of me. He would celebrate my success with me.

"Where's Hypnos?"

Hades' eyes narrowed and his brows furrowed. He drummed his fingers on the table as he contemplated his words.

"He will be unavailable for a few days," he said flatly.

He pushed his chair back and stood up, walking around the table to the stairs.

"You should get some sleep."

And with that, he left me sitting at the table alone. I sat there, taken aback by the sudden change in his demeanor. I must have said something wrong. Or perhaps he was just incapable of having a decent conversation. I huffed loudly and folded my arms. I wanted to go upstairs and retire to my own bechamber, to sleep for as long as my body would let me. But my full stomach and cramping muscles begged me for a moment of rest before ascending the long staircase.

A breeze stirred around the room, rustling my hair. I rolled my eyes and moaned loudly. I already knew exactly who was about to be in the room with me. With a flash of bright light, Hermes was back. He sauntered over to the table and sat where Hades had been sitting, looking ridiculously proud of himself. I hated his smug face.

"I thought you were gone? What do you want?"

He whistled, looking me up and down. "Wow, Kora. Looks like you have slithered your way right in. Sitting in Hades' big, fancy chair?"

I shot him an annoyed look. "You have some nerve, Hermes. Do you enjoy causing problems for people?"

"Actually, yes."

His smile widened. He grabbed a grape from my plate and leaned back in his chair, popping the fruit into his mouth. He was a thorn in my side.

"Kill him, then."

Wrath's sudden interjection shocked me. My mouth dropped and I scrambled to hide my expression. I was not fast enough though. Hermes raised an eyebrow, scrutinizing me.

"Can't be that surprising, Kora."

I reached out and grabbed a strawberry, examining it intensely. I had been so careful to keep Wrath's existence a secret, I was not about to let Hermes of all people learn about her.

Hells, Wrath. Shut. Up.

"You must lead an awfully boring life if this is your idea of fun."

He shrugged, eating another grape. "It passes the time. After so many years you have to find things to keep yourself entertained."

"Sounds miserable. You should end his suffering."

Can't you keep your opinions to yourself, for once?

"And where would the fun be in that?"

"You never answered my question, Hermes. What do you want?"

He smiled a wicked, toothy smile. It made my skin crawl. There could be no good reason. Dread coiled inside me as I waited for his response.

"I just came to check in on you."

There was a gleam in his eyes as he spoke, and my stomach soured as I tasted his lie in the air. There was a storm coming. One I was not prepared for. I shot him a soft smile, made it as sweet as I possibly could.

"I'm fine."

"Indeed you are, Kora."

Without another word the air around us picked up, swirling across the room, and with a flash of light, he was gone.

I sat there alone, the silence hanging heavily, like a bell yet to be rung. The weight of impending doom crushed down on me. I couldn't shake the feeling that things were about to get very complicated.

FIFTEEN

The smell of smoke and iron coaxed me awake. I blinked slowly, the fog of my sleep slipping away. I sat up and my eyes darted to the chair across the room. Hades was stretched out, his head leaned back, hands clasped in his lap. I stared as his chest slowly rose and fell. He was asleep. I gently pushed my cover away, sliding my legs over the edge of the bed. His eyes snapped open and he pushed himself up. He looked at me, a disoriented expression falling over his face.

"You're awake."

His voice was still gravelly and laced with sleep, his lids heavy. I fought against the blush threatening to creep across my cheeks. His long, dark hair was down, his shirt partially unbuttoned. I forced my eyes back up to his.

"You say it like you're surprised."

The corner of his mouth lifted in a half smile. "You slept for three days. So yes, I am surprised. I wasn't sure you would wake at all."

My eyebrows shot up. I didn't feel like I had slept that long. I had never slept more than a night before. My body was still weak, my muscles ached.

"How long have you been here with me?"

He shrugged, standing up and stretching. He started walking to the door and I got up from the bed. My whole body buzzed as my feet hit the floor. It was power thrumming through me. I looked down at my hands and then up to Hades, who had stopped at the door and turned back to me.

"It will do that, once you start using it. It will build up and need to be released again. Get dressed. I want to see what you can do today."

I scrambled to the large closet crammed full of clothes that I learned had been filled specifically for me. He opened the door and spoke to me over his shoulder.

"I'll meet you in the throne room." With that he left me to get ready.

I pulled my clothes from three days ago off and left them in a heap on the floor. I dug through the countless dresses, all of them looked too nice for what I was going to be doing, and grabbed a plain black shirt and dark green trousers. The shirt was loose enough to move freely but not so much it would hinder my movements. I shoved on the brown boots I had been wearing since I was brought below.

I glanced at the looking glass above the small vanity, my curls were wild and tangled. Sighing, I stepped over and brushed them out as best I could, then tied my hair back out of my face. My eyes fell to my reflection. Somehow my face looked hardened since I had arrived. Gone were the soft expressions and gentle eyes. I barely recognized myself.

I shook the thoughts away and left the room and my past self behind. I hurried down the stairs and through the manor to the throne room. I was eager to push myself, to show Hades what I could do. My power rippled through me, begging to be used.

When I walked through the large, wooden doors, he was standing there waiting for me. His hair was pulled back, his sleeves cuffed up. His red eyes met mine and a smile spread across his face. Before I even realized what I was doing, I was grinning back at him. My chest felt light. I wondered when it had happened. When I had stopped thinking constantly of the upper world. When I had stopped plotting how I would get back to my village and my grandmother. When excitement for my days shifted from the idea of getting back into the sun to learning my power and spending my time with Gods.

I brushed past him, the grin still wide on my face. I made my way to the door leading outside and pushed it open. As I stepped out I was met with the gray sky and blackened iron under my feet. I didn't feel the wave of sadness and loss that I felt the last time I had stepped outside. I could make the Underworld beautiful.

And I would.

He glided to my side, and I could feel his eyes on me. They burned into me in a way that both scared and enthralled me. I looked up at him, his expression was kind. He held his hand out to me.

"We're going out a little ways, just in case." He had a gleam in his eyes as he spoke.

"Was that supposed to be a joke?"

His cheeks flushed and his brows furrowed. "You say that like I'm humorless."

I laughed loudly, it felt foreign. His face softened and he shook his head. I reached out, taking his hand in mine. The touch sent lightning through my whole body. My power pulsed and I felt a ripple of his own power in response. Our eyes locked and time stopped for me momentarily.

Darkness swirled around us. It enveloped us, everything around us disappeared. I could see nothing but pitch black. His hand tightened around mine, grounding me. I couldn't comprehend what had happened to me over these days in the Underworld. The only thing I knew was that I was finally excited about what I could accomplish.

The darkness dissipated, the cool light breaking through. My feet hit the ground confidently, no sickness washed over me. Another wave of power coursed through me. I could feel it nearly burst free. My eyes shot to Hades, who was already looking at me. I knew he could feel it trying to escape my body just as well as I could.

"We're out far enough. You need to let some of it out."

He stepped back a few steps and watched me. I looked from him to the ground, unsure what to do and where to start.

"It doesn't matter where you start."

Wrath's voice echoed in my head. It oddly comforted me to know she was still there inside me. My constant, in this fast-changing life that was now mine. I nodded and knelt to the ground, placing my palm flat on the cold iron earth. I inhaled deeply, and my power reared back ready to strike. I felt the air around me stir, lifting my hair. With a long exhale, a shudder rumbled through the ground. I could feel it leave my palms. I could feel it slither beneath us. The surface of the earth cracked and from the crevices grew dozens of paperwhite narcissus. They sprung forth, leaves unfurling and blooms opening perfectly. They surrounded me entirely. I looked to Hades, a smile beaming on my face.

He was smiling back at me, hands crossed over his chest. Finally, the approval I had been looking for. I stood, looking at them again. They were such an uncommon flower that I had rarely had the pleasure of seeing them. The last had been… the flower left on my bed. I had never asked Hecate if she had been the one to leave it.

I looked back at him as he walked over, leaning down to inspect my work more closely.

"Paperwhite narcissus." His eyes flicked to mine. "Did you know these are my favorite?"

My stomach fluttered as I stared at him.

"You."

He stood, taking several steps back again. His face was unreadable. How had I not guessed that before? He had been the one to leave me that gift. I thought of my open window. Anger flickered inside me like a flame. I had been living in his home for over a week and he hadn't told me.

"Hermes said you can do more than this. Show me."

My anger swelled. Of course he wouldn't care about something as trivial as my ability over flora. He wanted the destruction. He wanted death. I had woken from my three-day sleep naive. I should have known better. All of the enthusiasm I had felt just moments before melted away completely. My smile turned to a snarl.

"Of course. What use would this be to you, right? You want to see the *good stuff*." My voice was cold and harsh. It didn't sound like me. It sounded like Wrath.

I stepped back, crushing several blooms as I moved. I didn't care. I was about to destroy them anyway. He wanted desolation? He wanted a blight? I would give it to him. I would show him exactly what I could do.

I let the magic crash through me, I slammed my hands down onto the iron earth. It rushed through my arms and quaked under our feet. The ground was leached of color, of life. The flowers wilted and turned black, crumbling into dust as my power billowed through the air. It spread across the ground, destroying everything as it moved. I stopped it right before it reached him. I lifted my arm, wiping black ichor from my cheek onto the back of my hand.

I stood, glaring at him. Waiting for the praise. Waiting for the same look to come across his face. My anger still bubbled inside me. I could feel Wrath whispering for more. I ignored her, my eyes locked onto Hades. He glanced down at the ruin I had caused, his face flat.

"Interesting."

His bland indifference caused my anger to grow into rage. But as his eyes lifted to mine, his expression softened, causing me to falter. I stood there, feeling conflicted and confused.

"Do you think you could maintain things here that you've grown? Would they wither over time?"

I blinked at him. My mind was reeling. I had no idea what he wanted from me. I considered it, whether or not something I made in the Underworld could thrive and survive.

"I'm not sure."

"Would you try?"

I glanced around, trying to grapple with the whiplash I had received from all of the emotions that had flooded through me so quickly. Did he want a garden? I looked back up at him. He was still looking at me, expectantly.

"I…"

"Say yes," Wrath urged.

"Yes."

He smiled at me softly. "Good."

He walked up to me and I lifted my head to hold his gaze as he approached. He reached out, wiping more black ichor from my cheek.

"I just wanted to see what you could do, Goddess. I have no intention of using your power for some hidden agenda. Though," he smiled. "A garden in the courtyard would be nice."

My cheeks flushed and I looked down at my feet, embarrassed at the way I had behaved. I had assumed when I shouldn't have.

"I'm sorry, Hades."

He lifted my chin gently, and our eyes met.

"Aidoneus, please."

He spoke softly, and his eyes… My heart skipped and my face grew hotter.

"I'm sorry, Aidoneus."

He smiled and held his hand out to me. I placed mine in his, the touch electric again. The smell of smoke filled me completely.

"I think that's enough for today. I don't need you sleeping for another three days." I huffed a laugh and rolled my eyes. He pulled me closer to him and as his darkness swallowed us he whispered softly.

"Let's go home."

SIXTEEN

We arrived in the throne room. The manor was empty and quiet, as it usually was. His words were replaying in my head as my feet planted on the floor, his fingers still intertwined with mine. I told myself he thought of me just as he did Hypnos or whatever other Gods might live in his realm. I told myself the way his hand felt in mine was all in my head. That the heat in my face and the butterflies in my stomach were pointless. I tried to remember the cold glares and Hecate's ruined home back in the upper world.

He was no different than any other God I had been warned about. He was dangerous.

"If you're not too tired, I thought maybe we could walk around the courtyard outside to plan for the garden?"

He looked at me with those eyes again. Those eyes that made me forget my life above completely. That made me want to start over with him. No matter how much I liked the idea of him walking through a lush garden, it was a game I did not need to start playing.

He's dangerous, I reminded myself again.

"He is dangerous," Wrath echoed in a tone that made it sound more like a promise than a threat.

"I'm not too tired."

My mind urged me to break my eyes away from him, to go outside and build my plans for what I would grow. But my body was frozen in place. I couldn't force my legs to move, I couldn't avert my eyes. He stared at me like he felt exactly what I did. Like we could stand there lost in each other forever.

We were both jolted out of our trance by a voice I was not familiar with. It was sharp and harsh. As Hades peeled his eyes from mine, resentment coiled inside me.

"Hades. We need to speak."

I turned to the man standing several feet away. My stomach churned at the sight of him. I did not feel the air stir, did not feel any pulse of power around us. He had entirely snuck up on me. I hated the thought of anyone being able to surprise me like that.

My concern melted into confusion as I looked at him. He was tall, as was every God I had met so far. His body was lean but muscled. His dark hair pulled back into a tight braid. His skin was sickly pale. His brown almond-shaped eyes were locked onto me. They were familiar. He had no bags or dark circles from lack of sleep, but even so, they were the same eyes Hypnos had. They looked like twins, though the God before me looked much healthier than Hypnos did.

"Well? Go on." I could hear the annoyance in Hades' voice. I looked from one God to the other.

"Alone."

Hades shook his head. "Anything you have to say can be said in front of Kora."

The God raked his eyes from Hades to me. I felt uneasy under his gaze. I wanted to melt into the floor.

"I mean no disrespect, but I believe you'll want this to be said in private, Hades."

The God of the Dead turned to me, his eyes apologetic.

"I'm sorry, Goddess. Can you step outside for a moment? I'll meet you out there when I'm finished here with Thanatos."

I wanted nothing more than to argue, to beg to stay. Curiosity filled me to the brim. That had always been one of my greatest weaknesses. *'Nosy'* my grandmother had often called me. I nodded, fighting against myself. I left them standing there in silence. Every step I took was forced as Wrath pressured me to stay. I pushed the door open and stepped outside. I leaned my back against the door and closed my eyes.

"You're going to let them kick you out like that?"

My eyes flew open. Hermes stood in front of me grinning widely. He always showed up dramatically, yet somehow he had also snuck up on me. I must have been more overspent than I had realized.

"What do you want, Hermes?"

"I just thought you should know that they're talking about you."

I scowled at him, crossing my arms. He had no way of knowing that. He had certainly just come to taunt me.

"Make him tell you what he knows."

"Why do you say that?"

He strode over to me, placing his hands against the door on either side of me. He leaned in until his cheek was nearly touching my own. My heart pounded in my chest and heat rose up my neck. He whispered into my ear, causing the hair on my arms to stand.

"I know lots of things, Kora. I hear everything."

He pulled away just enough to look me in the eyes. He was so close to me that our breath mingled. I put my palm flat on his chest and his lips curved up. I pushed him away gently and he took a step back.

"Thanatos was pretty insistent on them being alone. What was I supposed to do, throw a fit?"

He smiled, holding out his hand.

"I can take you inside and they'll never know."

I stared at him, utterly torn between respecting Hades' wishes and letting my curiosity get the best of me. If they were talking about me I wanted to know what was being said. But Hades had shown me kindness, and I owed him privacy.

"Better hurry *Goddess*, before they finish their conversation."

My hand shot out before I had time to fully consider what I was doing, and I grabbed his. His smile turned wicked and in a blink we were standing on the other side of the throne room. His hand was firmly covering my mouth, keeping me silent, the other held me tightly against his chest. My heart was beating wildly. We were standing in the open, he had not even tried to hide us. Hades and Thanatos were standing where I had left them. Fear churned inside me as I stood frozen, hoping they would not glance our way.

"She's getting angrier, Hades. She's making threats now, making demands. You have to send the Goddess of Spring back to the upper world. You cannot keep going like this. It will cause a war."

"She has no leg to stand on. Kora was promised to me years ago. Zeus will not side with her over me."

"You keep saying that. But eventually, Zeus will grow tired of Demeter raging at him and he will side with her. You know how she gets."

There was a beat of silence as they stared at each other. I wondered who the woman they were referring to was. I couldn't imagine anyone starting a war over me. The only person who had ever loved me was my grandmother, and for all she knew I was off somewhere hiding from the Gods. She had no way of knowing I was in the belly of the whale.

"Demeter can throw her tantrums all she likes, but I will not roll over."

Demeter... I had heard that name, but I had been given so many names and so much information I couldn't quite place where I had heard it.

"You're making a mistake, Hades."

"I appreciate your counsel, Thanatos, but I am not conceding on this."

Thanatos shook his head and then vanished in a plume of smoke. We stood there, watching Hades after Thanatos left. He rubbed his face and then his shoulder drooped. He craned his head back, his arms slack at his side. He looked defeated. My heart ached, wondering what he must be dealing with behind closed doors. With a swift motion, he threw his arm out in front of him. Dark power erupted out of his palm. It shot out like black fire and crashed into the wall in front of him. Stone blasted apart and went flying across the room. My whole body jumped at the sound, I threw myself against Hermes roughly.

Silence hung heavy in the air as Hades stood there, staring at what he had done. He was breathing heavily, shaking his head like he was disappointed with himself. I found myself wanting to go to his side and comfort him. To tell him whatever it was he was going through would be ok.

Movement caught my eyes from the other side of the room. Minthe was sauntering over, her long straw-colored hair billowing behind her as she walked. Anger flared inside me at the sight of her. Wrath thrashed around, as Minthe stroked her hand up his arm. I pushed against Hermes, trying to free myself from his grasp. My power rippled, threatening to expose us.

And then we were gone.

I was still trying to pry myself loose when we appeared back outside. Hermes let me go so suddenly that I nearly fell over. I turned to him, my face contorted with anger.

"Why didn't you let me go?"

"He did not need to know we had been there the whole time, Kora. You're going to get us in trouble!" His voice was a whispered shout.

"I don't care!" I whispered back to him angrily.

"You should care!" His eyes flicked past me, to the door. "Keep your mouth shut."

And with that, he was gone. Leaving me standing there alone in my rage. I didn't get the chance to inquire about 'Demeter', or to find out why it was important to him that I heard that conversation.

"I told you– you should have just killed him."

The door opened behind me abruptly and I turned. I tried to make my face uninterested, to smother all the emotions both Minthe and Hermes had caused within me.

"Everything ok?" My voice came out more chipper than I intended.

Hades raised an eyebrow and narrowed his eyes at me. I smiled in return and he sighed.

"It's fine. Thanatos is just..." His words trailed off as he looked at me. "It doesn't matter, everything is fine. Let's go look at the courtyard, please."

I nodded and he brushed past me. I glanced back at the door, wondering what I had missed after Hermes brought me back outside. What Minthe had said or done to console him. I would have to ask

Hermes to teach me how to move about unnoticed like that. I shook my head and followed Hades around the side of the castle.

He stopped in an area I had not been in yet. There were stone benches and tables scattered about. I wondered what the area had been used for in the past. I couldn't imagine him holding parties and gatherings, but it would have been the perfect place to sit and have tea if it wasn't so… bland and cold, just as the rest of the Underworld was. I glanced around it, trying to envision small trees, flowers, and bushes. It could have been beautiful in the upper world.

"It could be beautiful here."

I still have no idea if anything I grow here will survive.

"It's worth trying."

"What do you think?"

I looked up at him. He was standing there by a bench, his face hopeful. My heart skipped a beat, picturing what I could make of the space. I looked around again and pointed to a spot behind the benches and tables.

"A tree would be nice there." I turned and gestured to the ground near the wall of the castle. "And a rose bush there."

His eyes followed where I pointed like he was picturing what I was saying. He nodded along as I began rambling my suggestions to him. I was lost in the vision. I could see it all so clearly that I could almost smell it. Thick bushes in full bloom, trees hanging full of brightly colored fruit and flowers, vines snaking their way along the walls of the manor.

"It sounds perfect."

"Do you mind if I try?" I wanted to get started immediately. I needed to get my mind off of everything I had heard and seen. I needed something pleasant.

"I don't want you to overdo yourself again." Concern laced his eyes.

"Just one thing?" I pushed. He considered it for a moment and then nodded.

I walked over to the bench and knelt on the ground. I put my palms down, willing my power softly. I pictured them in my head, how magnificent they would look there. The earth beneath us shook slightly, and cracks lined the surface of the iron. A handful of flowers crept their way out of the ground, unfurling and blooming flawlessly. I smiled down at them and begged them silently to live. I needed them to. We all needed them to.

I looked up from the paperwhite narcissus to Hades, who was staring at them as if they were the most beautiful thing he had ever seen. No...

He was staring at me.

SEVENTEEN

We made our way back into the dining hall after Hades insisted I needed to eat. I didn't feel drained like I had the last time I used my power, I could tell I had barely scratched the surface. My stomach growled as I saw and smelled the food already laid out on the table. There were never any maids or cooks bustling about, but somehow the table was always full of fresh food. Usually meats, cheese, and fruit. My eyes were bright as I saw that was not what was waiting for us. Cakes and chocolates were adorning the table. Sweets. More sweets than I had ever seen.

    I hurried over, not bothering to sit or make a plate. I grabbed a small chocolate tart covered in fruit and ate the entire thing in one bite. My mouth watered at the rich flavors. My eyes darted across the food as I tried to decide what to eat next. I settled on a plate of flakey bread.

    "I thought you might like something new today."

    I turned to Hades. He was standing there smiling at me, my mouth full of the buttery pastry. I hummed my approval as I reached for a tiny square of cake with my free hand.

    "We didn't have things like this in my village."

He walked over and took a seat in his chair at the head of the table. He grabbed a goblet of wine and took a sip, his eyes still on me. I ignored the blush creeping up my face and turned my attention back to the food.

There was a wave of power behind me and we both turned to see who had arrived. Hypnos stood there. His face was relaxed, his eyes bright. There were no dark circles under his eyes. He looked well-rested for the first time since I had met him. He walked over to the table, examining all of the food.

"Oh, what a nice day this is, indeed!" He dove straight into the sweets, filling a large plate. I folded my arms as I watched him.

"Where have you been?"

He looked over at me and smiled. "Just taking some time to myself."

More secrets. Would I ever get the full truth from anyone? I tried not to be hurt by it, it was just the way the Gods worked apparently. But I longed for true friendship and honesty. It made me realize that was something I had never truly had before.

"Well, you've missed a lot. I have so much to show you!" I wanted to go to his cave immediately. I had been planning a gift for him ever since that first day I gained a sliver of control over what I could do. Hades interjected sternly.

"No. You've done enough for today." The way he gazed at me softly was gone, as were my butterflies. We were back to hardened stares and silent arguments that I knew I couldn't win.

"You still have plenty of power left."

"I'm ok."

"I said no."

We continued to stare at each other, the air thick with words unspoken. I couldn't understand why he insisted on dictating when and where I could use my magic. Hypnos cleared his throat, and I turned to him. He gave me a sympathetic smile.

"Tomorrow, Kora. You can show me tomorrow. If Hades thinks you've done enough for today, he's probably right."

"I *am* right." His voice was harsh.

I glared at him and scoffed. He was going to drive me absolutely crazy with his back and forth, temperamental remarks. I enjoyed his company when it was just the two of us, but he continued to be insufferable when anyone else was around. I turned to Hypnos, ignoring the look Hades was continuing to give me.

"We should go for a walk."

He glanced at Hades, who said nothing, then back to me. He nodded, grabbing another piece of chocolate. I wanted to get out of the castle and I didn't care to heed any advice from the King of the Underworld. I was going to go to the cave and use my power again.

"Very well. I should probably walk some of these sweets off anyway."

I turned on my heel and started walking towards the throne room, leaving Hades to sulk. Hypnos hurried to catch up to me, still much more lively than his usual self. I had so many questions and so many things I wanted to catch up on. I had no interest in doing either around Hades for him to interject with his snide comments the whole time.

Once we were outside I took a deep breath, trying to release all of the frustration I had built up. I just wanted to enjoy the time I had with Hypnos, I did not want to be plagued by a sour mood.

"Where are we walking to?" His eyes trailed me warily as he waited for my response.

"To your cave," I said assuredly.

He stopped suddenly, and I turned back towards him. He was staring at me like I had told him something incredulous. I shrugged my shoulders at him.

"Kora, I feel like that is exactly what Hades was trying to keep you from doing."

"I'm sure it was, but I don't particularly care."

We stood there, at a standstill. Neither one of us wanted to relent. I could see his thoughts flashing over his face as he tried to decide what he wanted to do. Unlike Hypnos, I was sure of my decision. I had no intention of letting anyone control me.

Finally, he nodded, giving in. "Very well."

He walked up to me and held out his hand. I looked at him, his bright eyes locked onto mine, and I took his hand. Dust swirled around us and within seconds we were at the foot of the cliff where his cave was nestled. We stood there, staring at each other. He was looking at me the way Hades had earlier. I felt my face warm and I pulled my hand free, turning away. I glanced around the space, trying to decide where I would bring forth the meadow of flowers.

I glanced over my shoulder at him and grinned. He returned my smile, that gleam still there in his eyes. I knelt to the ground, drawing on the power still coursing through my body. I had plenty left to do what I wanted to do. I pushed it through my palms, keeping them hovering above the surface of the earth. I could see the air blur beneath my hands and the power radiate into the iron. There was a slight rumble underneath us and then cracks snaked around us. From the crevices grew dozens of bright red poppies.

I pushed again, more broke free. I leaned back, inspecting my work. Every single one was perfect. The smell of them wafted around us. I closed my eyes. For a moment I could feel the sun on my skin, I could smell dirt. For a moment I was above again and life was easy.

But I wasn't.

I opened my eyes and turned to Hypnos. He was looking around at all of the poppies, tears sliding down his cheeks, mouth slightly open. He turned to me and smiled.

"Do you like it?"

"More than you could ever know, Kora. Thank you."

I felt completely happy for the first time in a while. Hypnos walked over and knelt down next to me. Still taking in the poppies. He was looking at each and every bloom.

"Do you know why poppies are my favorite?" He glanced over at me.

I shook my head. He turned his attention back to the flowers.

"I've told you before that I am unable to sleep. Con of being the God of Sleep, unfortunately. I spent the last several days sleeping, though. Occasionally when I go above I bring back a poppy. I use them to allow myself the ability to rest. I can't do it often, because I have duties that I must hold to. But sometimes… Sometimes I can't fight the urge any longer. I spend every waking moment thinking of when I will be able to do it again. I crave it so much it distracts me sometimes."

He looked back at me, giving me a sad smile. That was his big secret. What he had been hiding from me. He reached out and brushed his knuckle along my cheek, wiping away tears I hadn't realized I had let fall. My heart hurt for him. How he handled himself so well I would never understand. I would grow the poppies every day for the rest of my life to help him find his peace.

"Don't cry for me, Kora. You have no idea how much this gift you've given to me means. Thank you. Thank you." His voice cracked.

Tears continued to roll down my cheeks. He reached over and tucked some hair behind my ear and I leaned in, wrapping my arms around his neck. He slowly put his arms around me, holding me just as tightly as I was him. I felt his shoulders tremble and I closed my eyes. I wondered how long it had been since anyone had held him while he cried. How long it had been since anyone had held him at all.

We sat there embraced for a long while. Neither of us said anything. I allowed him to cry as long as he needed. When he had no tears left he pulled away from me, his eyes red and puffy. He cupped my face in both of his hands and pulled me closer. I closed my eyes, my heart pounding against my chest. He brushed his lips against my forehead softly. I opened my eyes and he was staring at me.

"Thank you, Kora."

I nodded slowly, unable to form any words. He stood up and offered me his hand. I took it and he pulled me up. His eyes fell to the poppies and he smiled slightly.

"I can't promise they'll survive long."

"That's ok."

"If they die, please tell me. I'll bring them back as often as I need to."

He laughed quietly, looking lighter than he had before. He was the kindest person, God or not, that I had ever met. I decided then and there I would bring the whole world down for him. I wanted him to always be happy.

We took our time walking back to the castle. I wasn't eager to hurry back. I spent the time telling him what he had missed while he was sleeping. I told him my plans for the courtyard outside the manor. I told him I wanted to throw tea parties, though I had no idea who I would invite. He promised to come to any festivity I threw and drink more tea than anyone there.

By the time we returned, I was already hungry again and exhausted from walking. I was ready to retire to my bed and rest. Hypnos said his farewells and went on his way, leaving me at the door alone. I was smiling ear to ear as I opened the door to go inside, pleased with how my day had ended. My good spirit was dashed quickly as I stepped inside and my eyes fell to Minthe. She was sitting on Hades' throne, looking at me like a cat hunting a mouse. The God of the Dead was nowhere to be seen.

    My stomach dropped.

    "Hello, half-breed."

EIGHTEEN

I narrowed my eyes on her and shut the door behind me. I had no idea what she had planned, but dread filled me nonetheless. She was a snake. I didn't trust her in the slightest. She sat, long legs crossed, drumming her fingers on the arms of the throne. The silence hanging between us was deadly.

"The King is absent. You should kill her while you have the chance."

"What do you want, Minthe?"

Her laugh filled my ears like a screech. She leaned to the side and threw her leg over the arm, the slit in her red dress opening enough to expose her. The material was thin and sheer, anyway. It did nothing to conceal her body.

"You had a good time with Hypnos, I take it? You came in smiling and rosy-cheeked. I'm sure Hades will love to hear all about it when he returns."

I felt the heat rising up my neck to my face. It was anger, not embarrassment, I told myself. I had done nothing wrong. And what I did with anyone was not Hades' business either way. But still, guilt washed over me.

"I'll ask again; what do you want Minthe?"

She flashed me a crazed smile, her face the portrait of malevolence. The dread I felt only intensified at the sight of it. Wrath's suggestion was becoming more enticing the longer I stood there waiting for her to answer me.

"I want you to leave. You're a pathetic excuse for a God, and Hades deserves better than to have you tarnishing his reputation."

I could not stop the rage from growing inside me. I felt my power flicker, too weak to course through me the way it could have. I had used too much to grow the poppies. She must have taken my silence for frailty because she continued chastising me.

"You're vermin, half-breed. Crawl back to your mortals and spend your days growing your puny flowers. You don't belong below. You don't belong in his presence at all. He's better off without you."

Her words and her sneering face tilted me over the edge. I pictured my hands, covered in warm sticky blood as I ripped her throat out. I could see her choking and gurgling as she died by my doing. Just the idea of it all sent a thrill through me. I had never wanted to kill anyone before, but my whole life had changed.

"Rip those pointed ears right off her face," Wrath growled.

I walked up to the throne slowly. My body was vibrating from my fury. Minthe continued to smirk at me as I approached. I ascended the steps right up to her. She lifted her chin to look at me, her eyes burning with hatred. My rage had turned lethally quiet. Wrath lingered, eagerly waiting for me to make my move. I wanted to kill her.

I leaned in closely. She held her ground, refusing to move a muscle. She smelled like salt water and lilies. I pressed my cheek gently against hers and whispered in her ear.

"You want to fuck him so badly it's embarrassing, Minthe. Sit on this throne while you can, because one day it will be mine. And I will sit on it, covered in your blood."

When I pulled away her eyes were wide, mouth ajar. I could smell her fear, and it was intoxicating. I breathed it in deeply, reveling in it. She stood, leaning her body away from me, and slipped around me. Her bare feet padded down the stairs and she ran out of the throne room without another word. I turned to watch her leave, half regretting not taking her life.

"You should have. She deserved it."

I know. Time and place.

"This was the time and place."

Not yet...

I ran my fingers across the arm of the ornate chair, then I sat down. I leaned against the back, sitting tall, and looked down at the room. Being feared, having power... It could easily go to someone's head. It could tear them apart, change who they are entirely. It could shred every sliver of humanity someone had. But it wouldn't do that to me. I was raised to be humble and merciful. I could rule with kindness.

And when I killed Minthe...

"She deserved it."

She deserved it.

NINETEEN

I sat alone in the drawing room. Silence stretched for hours. I still had not seen Hades. I replayed the incident with Minthe over and over. Maybe I had gone too far. It would have been better for me to keep my mouth shut.

What if she tells Hades that I desire his throne?

"She will not. There was fear in her eyes after you finished with her."

Sometimes fear makes people do stupid things.

"Funny. I thought that was love."

I huffed a large sigh and flopped back in the cushions of the settee and got lost in thoughts of crowns and thrones. Thoughts of shredding Minthe to pieces and never having to see her again. Thoughts that pleased Wrath.

***

I was curled up on the large cushioned settee when Hades finally returned to the manor. Cerberus had wandered out of his chambers and lay stretched out in my lap. I thoughtlessly rubbed his stomach as all three heads slept soundly. I hadn't seen the beast roam about since arriving, but I was thankful to have his company. I had changed out of the comfortable clothes that I had been wearing before into a black nightdress.

    Hades walked into the room and smiled when his eyes fell on me and the large dog snuggled up together. As he approached us Cerberus raised his heads briefly and then flopped back down to my lap. I pulled my attention from the furry beast up to Hades. Tendrils hung loosely around his face. He wore the same dark shirt and black breeches he usually did. His red eyes were locked onto me. The silence hanging between us was comfortable, all of the friction from earlier in the day was absent from his face.

    "Did you have a nice day?" His voice was quiet, he sounded exhausted.

    "It was lovely, actually."

    I smiled up at him softly and he knelt in front of me, his eyes falling to Cerberus. He scratched the dog's stomach gently then looked up to me, his eyes smoldering. I wished at that moment that he always looked at me like that. I wished that his attitude didn't turn cold as soon as we weren't alone. My eyes dropped to his lips and my core turned molten. My hands begged to reach out and tangle themselves into his hair. I both loved and hated how my body reacted to being so close to him.

    His hand drifted from Cerberus to my knee. His touch jolted through my silk nightdress and set my skin on fire. My chest rose and fell more rapidly. Though it had been years since anyone had touched me, my body knew exactly what it wanted. He stayed knelt there with his hand on my knee, eyes burning into mine. I realized he was waiting for me to give him some sign of permission to make another move.

With a shaky hand, I pushed Cerberus off my lap. The beast took the hint and strolled off with a huff, disappearing into another room. Hades didn't break his eyes away from mine as his hand slid further up my thigh. My fingers brushed across the top of his hand and up his arm. He reached up with his other hand and tucked my red curls behind my ear. My face felt hot as he ran his thumb across my cheek to my bottom lip.

"You're exquisite."

His voice came out barely more than a whisper. It sent me spiraling down a road I told myself I wouldn't go. I knew, as his hand continued to trail up my thigh, I couldn't stop what was about to happen. I couldn't stop it because I didn't want to. I wanted his hands and his mouth on my body. A small gasp escaped my lips as he grabbed my hips, fingers digging into my skin. His gaze darkened as he pulled me to the edge of the settee. He slid my dress up my legs, exposing my skin to the air. Chills skittered across my body. I sat there frozen, my heart hammering in my chest, my mind reeling. I could only watch as he lowered his head, peppering my thighs with soft kisses.

"Kora," he mumbled into my skin.

A whimper slipped from my lips in response. His eyes flicked up to mine. I bit my lip until it hurt, my hands clenched the cushion tightly. His own hands glided back up my bare thighs to my hips. He hooked his fingers around the rim of my undergarment and he slipped them off, tossing them on the floor. Gently he spread my legs and his eyes dropped.

I could not focus. My body was humming with power and need, the throbbing between my legs nearly too much to bear. He lifted my legs up, resting them on his shoulders. Softly he kissed the inside of my thigh and then gently sunk his teeth into the sensitive skin. My power pulsed within me and his thrummed in response. I tossed my head back and moaned quietly.

His fingers were digging into my hips again when his tongue found me. My hand flew to his head and I gripped his hair. I felt the waves building as his mouth did things I never thought possible. He continued feasting on me, one hand firmly grabbing my ass while the other roamed up my chest to palm my breast. My moans grew louder and I drew near my climax.

"Aidoneus…" I managed between ragged breaths.

Saying his name urged him on. His fingers slid deep inside me, his mouth focused on my bundle of nerves. He pinched my nipple with his free hand and it was too much. Ecstasy exploded inside me. I screamed out in pleasure, my legs shaking. When I opened my eyes he was staring up at me, his lids heavy. I took several gasping breaths as I came down from that high.

He reached up and cupped my face, bringing it down to his and kissing me thoroughly. I could taste myself on his tongue. I was drunk on him. My hand ran up his chest, back to his hair and I kissed him deeper.

"Kora!"

My eyes flew open and I sat up, gasping. I looked around the room frantically, trying to gain my bearings. I had fallen asleep on the settee. My eyes found Hades standing in the doorway of the room. He was grinning at me knowingly, an eyebrow arched. My face flushed as I scrambled to pull my dress down, which had slid up to my thighs while I slept. I brushed my wild hair out of my face.

"What?" My voice was weak and shaky as I spoke. I could still feel the waves of my climax pulsing through my walls and I clenched my thighs together.

"Having sweet dreams?"

My face burned hotter and embarrassment consumed me.

"He is rather nice to look at."

"Do you always startle people awake?" I snapped, trying– and failing– to ignore Wrath.

He shrugged then walked over and sat next to me, his arm on the back of the settee. I scooted away from him and shot him an angry look. His red eyes sparkled with mischief as he looked me up and down hungrily.

"You sounded like you were having a grand time, I didn't want to miss all the fun."

I scoffed loudly, pressing my back into the arm of the seat to be as far from him as I could. I was scared to allow myself to get too close. Scared to let my skin touch his. My body still begged for more. I found myself wondering if he could please me so completely outside of my dream. I couldn't let myself find out.

"You are absolutely astonishing, do you know that?" My voice was nearly shrill as I barked at him.

His grin widened. "Oh, I heard exactly how astonishing I am while you moaned my name."

I jumped up and backed away from him. My whole body was on fire. He looked at me like he knew exactly what I had dreamed. Like he could taste the wetness pooling in my undergarments.

I hated him.

"Do you, though?"

I whirled around and stormed out of the room. I stomped through the dining hall and up the stairs to my bedchambers. My heart was beating wildly, every breath I took burned in my chest, and my legs were still shaking. I slammed the door behind me and leaned against it. Finally free from his infuriatingly perfect face, I groaned loudly and hit the back of my head against the wooden door.

I had no idea what was wrong with me, or how I had ended up in such a situation. I shook my head. He *was* rather nice to look at…

When I opened my eyes they fell to my bed. I bit my lip. My body was still reeling from that dream. It had been so long since I had felt that way. I looked over my shoulder at the door. My room was far enough away from everything.

I walked over to the bed and crawled into it. Slowly I lay on my back, staring at the ceiling. I shouldn't. If I allowed myself to, I would end up on a slippery slope. It was a dangerous game I was playing. My fingers lifted to my lips, tracing over where I could still feel him. It was just a dream, but it felt so real. It felt so good.

Against my better judgment, I allowed my fingers to trail down my neck to my chest. They glided across my silk nightdress and brushed against my hardened nipple. I sucked a breath in through my teeth at the touch.

My hand continued to slide down my body. I pulled the hem of my dress up and pulled my undergarments off, throwing them aside haphazardly. I raked my fingernails up my thigh where he had kissed and nipped my skin. Every touch was invigorating. They finally reached between my legs where I was still dripping wet. A soft whimper slipped from my lips as I sunk my fingers inside myself. I felt my walls tighten and I pulled them out before plunging them back in, deeper. My free hand cupped my breast and squeezed. My legs shook.

There were no longer cautionary thoughts drifting through my mind as I stifled moans and cries, my fingers diving in and out. I pictured Hades as I bucked my hips into my own hand until I came undone all over again. The waves of pleasure crashed over me again and again until I lay there, breathing heavily as I stared up at the ceiling.

That would be the only time I let myself cum to the thought of his face. It couldn't happen again.

TWENTY

My eyes fluttered open, exhaustion and embarrassment from the night before crashing into me. I groaned loudly, rubbing my eyes. I forced myself up from the bed, glancing around the room. Slowly sliding out of bed, I moved to the washroom. I hoped if I took my time getting ready Hades would be gone by the time I left my room.

The large basin was steaming. It was always filled with hot, clean water, despite never having seen anyone change or heat it. I pulled my night dress over my head and tossed it onto the floor. I stepped into the wash basin, the water burned pleasantly against my cool skin.

It was the day I would go looking for The Furies, I decided. I thought of what I might be met with when I found them as I soaked.

"No point in fretting over it."

I'm nervous.

"There's no time to be nervous. Wash yourself so we can leave."

I dunked my head under the water, hoping to wash away all of my anxiety. I stayed under until my chest hurt and my lungs burned and I was forced to come up for air. It didn't help.

After I was finished with my bath I padded to the closet, rummaging through to find something fitting to wear. I chose a long, gray dress. It was simple and comfortable. I didn't want to go clad in overly dramatic attire, since I had no real idea what I would be walking into. I wondered if they would try to kill me before I even got a chance to speak. With a little reluctance nestled inside of me, I pulled on my favorite boots and slipped out of my room quietly.

My steps echoed off the walls as I wandered through the empty manor. I made my way to the front door, my nerves mingled with Wrath's excitement. I was still not convinced that I was making a wise decision, but Wrath coaxed me onward.

"We need them on our side."

I don't think we should be doing this. This realm is not ours.

"It will be ours. Now go to The Furies."

I still don't understand why we must do this. They keep to their territory, how will they be any help to us at all?

"The more we have poised at our backs, the better. Everyone fears them to some degree. Why else would they be confined to their own dwelling?"

If they're that bad, maybe we shouldn't go...

"Nonsense. This is the right move if you want the throne."

I couldn't explain why it had happened, but I did want the throne. I wanted to rule over the Underworld, to change it into something beautiful. Or perhaps that was just Wrath's desire twisting my mind.

I stepped into the throne room, glancing around. Neither Hypnos nor Hades were still anywhere to be seen. I hoped Hypnos was making good use of my gift and that Hades was somewhere far away. I didn't need him to know where I was going or what my intentions were. His empty flirtations and mood swings aside, I feared he would kill me if he knew what I was planning.

I cracked the front door and slipped outside. My eyes darted around, making sure I was still alone. My boots crunched against the iron earth. It had become a comforting sound somehow. I craned my head up toward the gray sky, I was starting to enjoy that too.

As I rounded the corner of the castle I was met with a pleasant surprise. My narcissus has survived. They still looked as strong and healthy as they did when I first grew them. A smile spread across my face.

"*I told you.*"

I rolled my eyes at Wrath's remark and continued moving. I didn't have an exact location of The Furies' territory, but I knew it was beyond Hecate's hut. It would be quite a distance to walk and I wasn't sure I could make it past Hecate without her sensing I was there. But my decision was already made.

***

After walking for some time through the vast nothingness I became thankful that there was no scorching sun beating down on me. It would have made my task much more grueling to be hot and sweating the whole walk. My eyes raked the horizon for the top of Hecate's home, knowing it should be coming into view soon. I spotted a stream of smoke in the distance, probably from her chimney. I glanced around, trying to decide the best direction to continue.

"Left."

I veered left slightly, hoping to stay far enough away that she wouldn't spot me out of a window. I walked until the smoke was behind me. My legs began cramping and I was getting thirsty. I thought of all the comments about The Furies I had heard and imagined fresh food and water were probably things I would not be offered once I found them. I cursed myself for not thinking ahead and bringing something to fill my stomach and hydrate me.

Foolish indeed, since I had no idea how long I would be walking still.

I felt her before I saw her. A cool breeze kissed my skin and the crisp smell of an autumn night filled my nose. Nostalgia hit me forcefully as memories of nights around a fire, music, and laughter consumed me. Power pulsed through the air, and my own thrummed through my veins in response. My eyes scanned the area, hoping I had met my goal.

When my eyes fell on her, I knew I had not. There was no way the woman before me was one of the dreaded Erinyes. Her face was too serene, her eyes too kind. She was absolutely bewitching, and I had no idea who she was. I had heard no stories of any God residing in the Underworld that matched her presence.

She stood before me, almost unnervingly still. Her long black hair hung down her back in small braids, and her skin was a deep, rich color. She had high cheekbones and full lips, and her eyes were so dark they looked black. Her dress shimmered as she took a step towards me. Was it black or silver? Large, onyx feathered wings stretched from her back. She smiled at me softly as she approached. When she spoke her voice was alluring. Her accent was thick, one I had never heard before. She was breathtaking.

"Hello, daughter of Demeter."

My eyebrows lifted in surprise. That was where I heard the name Thanatos had said. That was my mother. She was the one raging above to get me out of the Underworld, the one Hades would risk going to war with. How did this God know who I was?

"You look so much like her."

My eyebrows furrowed and anxiety crushed in on me. I considered then, that perhaps I shouldn't have gone out on my own. Maybe Hecate or Hypnos would have helped me in my quest. Maybe this God was dangerous, her beauty a weapon to lure unsuspecting prey to their deaths.

"Can you read my mind?"

A small laugh escaped her lips. It was melodic and calming.

"No, child. I have no need for such things. It was written on your face, the question."

"Who are you?"

She paused for a moment.

"I am The Night."

That meant nothing to me. I tried to remember every story and name Hypnos had told me, but I felt confident I had never heard of her. Why would no one have mentioned her to me before? My palms were clammy, I stood no chance against her if she decided to kill me.

"I'm sorry, I didn't mean to encroach on your land."

"I have no land. I roam where I please, my home is everywhere."

I felt like she was speaking to me in riddles. I didn't know how to respond. I was scared to say the wrong thing, so I stared at her silently, ready to bolt at any moment if things turned sour.

"In any case, you may encroach on any land here you please."

My head tilted reflexively. She looked at me like I should have known what she meant, but I didn't. I was a guest. I had no rights to the lands.

"You seem confused, My Lady."

Her eyes stayed glued to me. I still felt like she could see through my very soul. Her words were formal, a far cry from the way anyone had ever spoken to me before.

"I am," I confessed quietly.

"You are unaware? Forgive me. Perhaps I should not have spoken."

"Some candor would be nice, actually."

She stepped up to me, keeping her dark eyes on mine. She was about a head taller than me, but her presence made her feel larger than life. The shock was like a knife to my gut as she knelt and lifted her face to look at me.

"You are Kora. Daughter of Demeter. Goddess of Spring. Autarch of Life. Promised Queen of the Underworld. All who reside within this domain bow to you."

My lips parted as my world flipped upside down.

TWENTY-ONE

Muffled voices and a high-pitched ringing were all I could hear. My vision blurred. I felt like I was outside of my body, somewhere far away. Fingers bit into my shoulders as someone shook me. Promised queen of the Underworld… Did others know? Surely I was sitting alone in the dark while everyone tiptoed around me, keeping me blind to my own destiny.

I could feel Wrath moving through me, slipping into my skin, taking over my body as I retreated within myself.

Good, I thought. *Let her deal with it.*

Darkness engulfed me, and I let it. Memories flashed faintly in my mind. I curled deeper into the abyss, trying to recoil and hide from them. I didn't want to see them. I didn't want to feel them. My whole life had been perfectly fine without them. Quiet. Peaceful, albeit a bit boring. I had never minded.

"*You did, though. You did mind. You knew from the time you were a child that you were meant for more.*"

No. No. No. I don't need any of this. I was content with my life. I was happy.

"*Lies!*"

Her shrill shrieking blasted through my head, disorienting me. I slipped further into the void, begging her to let me be. The memories grew stronger and more clear. I didn't want them.

My mother, Demeter, brushed my copper curls behind my ear. She cupped my face in her hands as her green eyes gazed at me with pure love. Her lips moved, but I couldn't hear her voice. She glanced over her shoulder and her mouth parted in a silent laugh. Childlike joy filled my small body. That was happiness. True, unrelenting happiness. When was the last time I had felt like that?

The memory swirled and melded into a new one. My heart sang with joy. I sat in a field of wildflowers. I could feel the warmth of the sun on my skin. My little legs were crossed and I ran my chubby fingers through the grass. As I looked up I saw several women sitting in front of me. Their hair was shades of pastel pink, blue, and purple. They all had pointed ears, their skin sunkissed, and their eyes matched their hair. One of them leaned forward and sat a crown of flowers atop my head.

Again the memory changed. Fear flooded me. I sat behind a tree, covering my ears tightly. I hated the screaming. I couldn't hear it, but I could remember the feeling. It always scared me. I twisted myself around to peek, keeping my hands firmly over my ears. My mother stood in front of a tall man. He had long dark hair and a deep complexion. Their arms waved wildly, their faces contorted with anger. Lightning danced across his skin. I shut my eyes tightly, wishing to be anywhere but there. *"Stay strong,"* a familiar voice consoled me.

When I opened my eyes, I was reaching for a rose bush. I looked over my shoulders to make sure I was alone. I didn't want anyone to see. I looked back to the roses and brushed my fingers across their blush blooms. They turned black and rotted under my touch. A thrill went through me. I knew I shouldn't do it. My mother had dared me after the first time, but I couldn't help myself. I watched as the entire bush quickly died and crumbled. I loved it. *"Again,"* that voice whispered. I glanced around looking for my next victim.

When I blinked I was walking hand in hand with my mother. It was dark outside, and quiet. The world around us was sleeping. I looked up at her, my child's mind full of confusion at her tears. I didn't know where we were going, or why she had said we had to leave. I loved my home and my friends. I didn't want to leave. My short legs struggled to keep up with her as she strode onward, not daring to look down at me.

Another blink and we were standing in a small village, on a porch I didn't know. Or did I? It was raining, I could hear it beating down on the roof of houses unlike anything I had ever seen. It was a strange and unfamiliar place. No… I knew that place, didn't I? My mother banged against the door, tears still streaming down her face. The door opened and she knelt down, pulling me into a tight hug. I didn't understand why she was so sad. I looked over at the older woman standing in the doorway. Her face was sad, too. My mother pulled away, saying something I couldn't hear. She placed her hand over my eyes and with a flash of light everything changed again.

I was older in the next memory. My gangly teenage arms reached out to pull weeds from the earth. I glanced around at the bountiful garden I had grown all on my own. Pride filled me. The smell of dirt and flora filled my nose, and the sun beat down on me harshly. I loved it. My grandmother knelt beside me. She looked at me kindly, and her lips moved. I closed my eyes, and I could feel the silent laughter in my throat.

When I opened them again I was lying next to that boy I swore I was in love with. The one I knew I would end up marrying. His eyes were closed, he was sleeping soundly. I brushed my fingers through his hair. I could see my future clearly. I could see us moving into a small house together, raising a family, growing old together. He loved me. I slid closer to him and closed my eyes to sleep.

Tears slid down my cheeks. I sat at a small wooden table, a cup of bitter tea in front of me. Hellen looked at me with sympathy, her mouth moved silently. She was giving me words of comfort I could not hear now. She slid me a jar of dried poisonous flowers. Offering me revenge for the boy who broke my heart. *"Take them,"* Wrath urged. I thought of my grandmother's face and pushed them back to her. I couldn't take another person's life. It went against everything I was.

Everything blurred and the next set of memories came rapidly, in small flashes. Red eyes in the woods. A black shaggy dog. An open window. A white narcissus sitting on my bed. Hecate's cabin in ruins. Hermes' catlike grin, mischief dancing in his eyes. Hecate's face lifted to mine, as her body was bent in a low bow for Hades. A swirl of darkness, the smell of smoke and iron. The first time I had met Hypnos. A rushing river. A three-headed dog. Power crashed through my body as I destroyed the iron earth around me. Another flow of energy through me as a sea of poppies surrounded me. And finally, Hades' face, looking at me like I was his entire world.

He knew the whole time.

The betrayal twisted around inside of me, snarling and growling. It grew and morphed into something ugly and wretched. It snapped its fanged teeth, the desire to consume everything in its path was undeniable. I would no longer sit back quietly while Gods paraded around me like I was some sort of underling. I was angry. I was power. I was Wrath.

No!

I struggled to gain control again, to pry the reins out of Wrath's hands. She fought against me, not wanting to yield to me. She was frantic and hungry to be released. She had waited so long. I could feel her frenzied desperation to dominate everything and everyone in her path. She screamed and thrashed as I chained her deep within.

I gasped for air, my lungs and throat burning. My fingers dug into the crumbling iron earth, my knees barked in pain. Black ichor trailed down my cheeks and dripped onto the cracked and gray ground. Everything had been drained around me. I lifted my eyes. The Goddess of Night stood before me, her eyes narrowed on me. Hermes stood next to her. His skin was clawed and bleeding. I must have done that. Guilt washed over me.

"Have you come back to us, Kora?" Sadness and worry were clear on his face as he spoke.

My eyes drifted back to his torn flesh. I looked down at my own hands. They were covered in blood, it was caked under my nails. His blood. My lip trembled and the ichor turned to salty tears. His sandals crunched along the ground I had ruined and he knelt in front of me. I squeezed my eyes shut, unable to bring myself to look at him again.

His hand lifted my face gently to his and I opened my eyes. As they fell on his, the understanding I found there shattered my already broken heart. I had lost control completely, and he had paid the cost.

A sob escaped my lips and he pulled me in tightly. I wrapped my arms around him and let myself cry. He stroked my hair and whispered to me softly.

"It's ok, Kora. I'm ok, and you're ok."

As my sobbing continued Wrath also whispered to me.

"You liked it. It's who you are. Who you've always been."

TWENTY-TWO

I sat with my knees pulled up to my chest. Hermes sat across from me, staring at me intensely. The Goddess of Night, Nyx I had learned, had left the two of us alone. He waited patiently as I gathered my thoughts. I would have to tell him about Wrath, who lived inside me and goaded me constantly. I only hoped that he would understand.

"Of course, he won't."

My eyes flicked up to his. He was still waiting for my explanation. I would have to give him one. I reached up, rubbing my eyes roughly. Where to even start? Any sliver of trust he might have had for me would surely be gone after I told him the truth.

"I came here to look for The Furies."

My voice was barely above a whisper, I was embarrassed to even admit what I was doing. I waited for the backlash, for him to shout and tell me I was naive and reckless. Silence hung between us instead. I looked up at him again to see he was not looking at me at all. He was staring past me, lost in thought. My eyes dropped to his wounds, which were almost fully healed now.

"Did you hear me, Hermes?"

He blinked, turning his attention back to me.

"Oh, I heard you. I think it's an excellent idea. I can take you to them."

Astonishment contorted my face. It couldn't be that easy, there had to be a catch. I narrowed my eyes on him and he flashed me a wide grin.

"What's in it for you?"

He answered quickly, like he didn't even have to think about it. "For starters, I want to know what's going on with you. You seemed to be completely out of it before. Second, I would like you to make a place for me on the council of Gods once you become queen. I assume that is your goal."

I considered what his demands were. They seemed... oddly reasonable to me.

"What is this council?"

"The Gods come together to discuss important matters, everyone votes. I've never been allowed anywhere near it. Everyone looks down on me until they need me."

There was resentment in his voice, and his face was serious for the first time since I had known him. His second stipulation might prove difficult, but I would fight tooth and nail for him. I owed him that much after what I had done. He watched me quietly, waiting for my answer. He looked collected, but his chest rose and fell rapidly. He really wanted me to agree.

I nodded my head. "Ok."

His eyes widened. Surprise. He had expected me to say no.

"I have always struggled with... myself, I suppose. I have this voice in my head. She's angry and vindictive. She–" I cut myself off. Contemplating exactly how much I should tell him. "I call her Wrath."

He nodded, no judgment on his face. "Does she take control often?"

"No. This was the first time."

I thought back to my first day in the underworld. No… She had been in control for some of that, too. I decided against correcting myself. It didn't matter in the end.

"Very well, then."

He stood, brushing particles of iron from himself. He looked down at me with bright, wild eyes. Eyes that told me he would help me in any way I needed if I was willing to help him. I supposed he and I were a lot alike in some ways. He offered me his hand and I took it. I told myself, as he pulled me to my feet, that I would do whatever it took to make sure he had the respect he deserved.

As long as it put me on the throne.

"Have you been warned of The Erinyes?" he asked.

"I was told they're cruel."

"Good. They are cruel. They're monsters, honestly. But I've always believed there is a place in the world for monsters."

I swallowed, disregarding my anxiety. There was no point in being nervous. He turned from me, looking out at the horizon, and I followed his gaze. There was nothing but black, iron earth as far as I could see. He looked at me and offered me his hand again.

"Ready?"

I said nothing and slipped my hand into his.

"Show no fear, Kora. They can smell it, and they will tear you apart."

The air around us moved. Bright, divine light engulfed us. It felt like time both slowed to a stop and sped up around us. In a flash, it was over. My mind and my body were reeling when we appeared at our destination.

I recoiled in shock. My eyes darted around. I couldn't believe what I was seeing. I had never considered... *People* wandered around us. They kept their eyes down, sorrow on all of their faces. They moved in waves, not going anywhere in particular. I looked up to Hermes, my mouth agape.

"Shades," he whispered. "Souls of the dead."

I looked at them again. How had I never questioned where all of the souls of the underworld were? Sadness threatened to unravel me. This was what waited for all who died– an eternity of wandering quietly in a sea of other souls.

A loud wailing ripped me from my thoughts and I whirled towards the sound.

There, in the distance, three vaguely humanoid beings stood over a soul. The soul shrieked and covered her face with her hands. She was lying on the ground, curled up in the fetal position.

"That's them."

But Wrath's words fell on deaf ears.

My eyes were locked on to the soul. She was a child. Her clothes were tattered and her body was small and frail. My heart shattered at the sight of her lying there screaming. Movement caught my eye. One of The Furies drew her arm back, a whip in her hand. My eyes widened, my face full of terror and disgust. That was a child. What could a child possibly have done to deserve such a thing?

Before I could even react the whip was slicing through the air. I couldn't let them do that. My mind screamed for my body to move, but my feet were planted to the ground. Fire burned through my skin, down to my bones, as I begged myself to help. To do something.

The ground beneath my feet rumbled, and the burning grew hotter. Time slowed as I watched the whip come down towards her.

In a blink I was there, standing in front of The Fury. I threw myself on top of the soul and lifted my hand out towards the whip. Thorn-covered vines blasted through the iron earth, shielding us from the blow. The Furies all screeched in unison. I slammed my raised hand down to the ground, and the vines separated, darting towards all three Furies. They slid their bodies around in a serpentine fashion, evading my attack entirely. They let out another horrific, bloodcurdling sound.

The soul of the young girl was latched on to me, her face buried in my dress. My eyes flicked between The Furies as they circled around us hissing, bearing mouthfuls of sharp teeth. Their eyes were solid black, their skin nearly transparent, it was so thin and pale. Their nails were like daggers, and they all had leathery bat wings. Each Fury had long, stringy black hair. They looked nearly identical.

My eyes darted to where I had left Hermes. He was still standing there, arms crossed over his chest, watching things unfold. For a moment I wondered if he brought me just so The Furies could rip me apart. I brushed it off. I came here for a reason. I pushed myself up on my feet, continuing to hold the soul close.

"Enough!"

They tilted their heads at me, black eyes studying me intensely. They moved slower around us. My skin crawled as one of them leaned in, inhaling my scent deeply. I beat away the fear that tried to grow inside of me. Her eyes shifted to mine. I stared back, refusing to look away.

'Show no fear,' Hermes had said. Her face was inches from me, her musky breath mixing with mine.

"Enough." My voice was quiet but steady this time.

The other two Furies came up to the first one's side. They glanced between themselves as if speaking to each other silently. I moved the soul from my side and ushered her off to join the others.

Their eyes all flicked up to her as she ran off, but turned back towards me quickly.

"Why do you come here and interrupt our fun?" Her voice was high-pitched and shrill. The other two at her side hissed at me, spit flying.

"Fun? You were whipping a child!"

"A shade," one of The Furies corrected.

"Shade or not, she's a child."

"She's ours to do with as we please, as are they all."

Anger boiled and bubbled up inside me. They were wretched, awful creatures.

"By whose decree?" I snarled.

"Hades, King of the Underworld," said the third fury.

Hades. Hades had given them rule over the punishment of the shades. Not full reign to torment them. There was no way he was ok with that. He couldn't be…

"Well, I'm setting a new decree. There will be no torturing of the souls needlessly."

The middle Fury let out a bone-chilling cackle, the others hissed at me again.

"And who are you to change the rules? You come barging into our given territory and tell us what to do. We should rip the flesh from your bones."

They moved as one towards me. I lifted both my hands up towards them, my nails turning long and sharp. Their eyes dropped to my hands and then down to their own. I followed suit and confusion settled over me. Our claws were the same.

Their eyes flicked back up to mine and they tilted their heads again. "I ask again, Goddess. Who are you?"

I lifted my chin, trying to embody the titles I was about to use. Trying to believe them with every fiber of my being. To make it real. To make it *mean* something.

"I am Kora. Daughter of Demeter, Goddess of Spring. The Promised Queen of the Underworld."

Their inky black eyes widened and they glanced between each other before looking back at me. They took several soft steps backward, and then they knelt before me. I watched in awe.

"We bow to you, queen. We will adhere to your decree, but you must offer us a reward for our compliance. Something far greater than what Hades has offered."

I rushed through anything I could promise them. I didn't have much that I could offer without risking Hades' anger. Panic settled over me.

"We will hold a court for the soul's judgment, if deemed necessary you may still punish them. You will not torture them without cause, though."

Their eyes slid between themselves, clearly unsatisfied with what I had said.

"And," I continued. "And I'll bet you miss the upper world. I can make this land look like it does up there. You can have whatever trees or flowers you want. Fresh fruits and vegetables whenever you like."

I had no idea if they cared for what the upper world looked like, or if they had a need for food at all. I should have gotten more information on them before I came. The first Fury narrowed her black eyes on me.

"Tempting, Goddess. But I'm not sure we're sold."

I ground my teeth. What more did I have to offer them? I had nothing. I was nothing…

"You are a Goddess, a queen. Promise them whatever you like."

"If you can keep yourselves under control, you may move through the Underworld as you like."

Their eyebrows lifted. The other two looked to the first, waiting to see what she said. My heart pounded in my chest. Hades would be furious with me for releasing The Furies into the rest of the Underworld. Had I left room for a loophole? Had I made a mistake? I wasn't even sure that would satisfy them.

The first Fury smiled, her sharp teeth gleaming. She stood and then bowed lowly.

"Very well, Goddess. It is done."

Dread filled me where triumph should have been. I hoped that I had made the right decision, but it was too late to second guess myself.

"I am Megaera. These are my sisters, Alecto and Tisiphone. We are at your service."

TWENTY-THREE

"It's just up ahead."

I walked beside Megaera as she led us to their alcove which was tucked away in an iron formation. Her sisters trailed behind us, and Hermes followed behind them. He kept his distance from The Furies, obviously uncomfortable being around them. I understood his hesitation as their whispers found my ears.

"He smells delicious."

"I bet he tastes *divine*."

They snickered amongst themselves like young girls. Megaera kept her eyes trained ahead, unaffected by their remarks. I tried to keep my face straight; to be unbothered as well. I needed them to respect me, and I was sure if I showed any sign of disgust or fear they would view it as weakness. I could not afford for them to see me as weak.

My eyes slid over Megaera's wings. She noticed my attention shift and turned her head to face me as she walked.

"Do you like them?"

There was a sly taunting to her voice as if she expected me to be repulsed by them. I found myself mesmerized instead, though. I shot her a small smile and looked back ahead.

"I was actually just thinking how nice it must be to fly wherever you wish."

She hummed, glancing up to the gray skin.

"It is nice– to feel the wind in my hair, to feel the resistance of the air against my wings as they beat. Sometimes, however... I think it would be nice to simply think of a spot and then be there. Be grateful for the gifts you were granted as a God."

The moment she was about to whip the soul of that child flashed in my mind. I had done exactly that. I had merely thought of where I wanted to be, and then I was there. I hadn't done it intentionally, I wasn't even sure I could do it again. Yet I had done it.

Megaera came to a halt, catching me off guard. She turned towards me, staring down at me with her pitch black eyes. I no longer had to concentrate on keeping the fear at bay. There was none left to ward off. As I stood face to face with the creature that sent a chill down the spine of other Gods, I felt powerful. I felt in control. I didn't care that I had to barter with them to gain my authority, I only cared that it was mine.

"I was beautiful once," she whispered for only me to hear. "We all were. Do not forsake us, Goddess, the way others have."

I didn't understand her request fully, but desperation dripped from her voice as she spoke. They had been slighted in some way I was sure I had not been told. She turned, before I could respond, and continued on. Her sisters passed me, their eyes sliding over me as they did. There was sorrow in their expressions as if they shared the same thought Megaera had.

My eyes met Hermes', inquisition glistened there. But it felt wrong to share what Megaera had said, so I turned and followed the three sisters onward. My heart was heavy, and my body was tired. I thought of what I had learned about Hermes and Hypnos… then The Furies.

"Here."

Tisiphone's voice brought me out of my thoughts. I looked to where she pointed, a large iron formation jutted up from the ground. I could see the alcove. It was different from the cave Hypnos lived in. The entrance to his home was smooth, like it had been carved out of the iron with the utmost care. The opening to The Furies' home was jagged, deep cuts into the formation told me they must have clawed the alcove out themselves. Somehow that only deepened my sympathy for the three sisters. What a life they must have lived.

I turned to Hermes, who had caught up with me. "I appreciate you coming along with me, but I would like some privacy. Can you be back for me in an hour?"

His eyes widened and a warning flashed across his face. I had known, before I ever said the words, that he wouldn't want to leave me alone with The Furies.

But my mind was set. I wanted to speak with them alone.

"An hour," I repeated sternly.

His lips pulled to a tight line, brows furrowed. I could see how badly he wanted to argue with me. He wouldn't, though. We had a deal. I could give him something he desperately wanted, so he would do what I asked. Even if it meant I was killed in the process. He and I were more alike than I had given him credit for.

He nodded and then vanished, leaving me alone with three of the most vile creatures that had ever lived. At least, according to everyone else. I could feel an unsung melody waiting to be heard.

When I turned back to the sisters they stood in a line, staring at me. Their stares were cold and calculated, but also full of respect for my willingness to be alone with them.

"May I ask you something, Goddess?"

"Of course, Alecto." I wasn't sure how I could tell them apart, but somehow they looked distinctly different, whereas earlier they had been nearly identical to me.

"What brought you here to us? What made you seek us out?"

Wrath whispered for me to lie, and for a brief moment, I considered it. But I felt in my heart that the three vengeful creatures could understand my goal more than anyone. I had no desire to lie to them.

"I want to claim my right to the crown here in the Underworld. In order to do so I need powerful allies."

I held Alecto's stare, then my eyes slid to Tisiphone, then to Megaera. The silence that I was met with was painful, as I waited for their reaction. My heart pounded like thunder in my chest. They glanced between each other, then back to me in unison. I could see their decision on their faces without them saying a word.

It was Megaera who replied.

"Very well, Goddess. If you uphold your end of the bargain we will stand at your side. Be aware, however, that we will no longer stand by idly as we are cast aside by the Gods. We are not garbage to be discarded."

I nodded. It was settled then. The Furies would stand with me as long as I stood with them. I had no intention of discarding them. They were strong, feared, and beautiful. And they were mine. They would always be mine.

"Be welcome into our home then, Goddess."

They turned towards the alcove and made their way inside. I followed the sisters, my heart and my mind racing. As I entered the cave, my eyes caught on all of the claw marks across the iron. They had gouged out crude bed shapes in nooks to sleep.

The smell of the rotting food hit my nose like the blow of a fist. Rotted food was strewn about. Vegetables, fruits, and the carcasses of dead animals. I fought the nausea that tried to consume me. I tried to keep my face straight, but the stench caused my nostrils to flare and my lip to curl.

They looked at me expectantly. My stomach would have reflexively emptied itself had I eaten anything earlier in the day. I pushed against the feeling of being sick. I could show no weakness. Not after I had gained their respect.

"May I?" I motioned around vaguely.

I could see the confusion on their faces, but I didn't dare open my mouth again to clarify. After brief glances between themselves, Megaera nodded. Relief washed over me.

I knelt to the ground, placing my palm against the cold iron earth of the cave, and beckoned my power to flow. Death seeped from my skin and skittered through the ground toward all of the decay. It met the remnants of what was once their meals and sucked everything out of it. The rotting corpses and food crumbled into dust at an alarming rate.

I was getting much better at that.

As I watched it happen, the reality of what I was looking at hit me. I wondered where The Furies retrieved their food if they were contained to the land below, if they could not venture above. I turned back to The Furies, their eyes alight with intrigue at my power.

"Where did all of that come from?"

Megaera's eyes flicked to mine. They were the eyes of a ruthless predator. And they were mine. I felt a ripple of satisfaction and pride at what I had managed to accomplish.

"Hades. He brings us food weekly. He has since we arrived here."

Guilt coiled thickly inside of me. I feared he would hate me after what I had been doing. I feared he might kill me. Doubt forced its way into my mind as I wondered again if he would have shared his kingdom with me, had I only been honest with him.

It didn't matter any longer. I had already chosen my path and I knew there was no turning back. When I said nothing, Tisiphone spoke.

"I thought you were the Goddess of spring? What was that?"

"Yes, well… It seems spring is the least of my gifts."

Megaera's eyes were glistening with something akin to love, though I was unsure if they were actually capable of such a feeling. Her mouth twisted into a smile. She would be an invaluable ally, indeed.

"So it seems. We would like to discuss how you plan to overthrow the God of the dead, if you care to share."

I had come so far with honesty, I had no plans to withhold things from them moving forward either. I would share everything with them.

"Of course. But first," I said, placing my palm back to the ground.

I pushed another wave of power into the iron, willing the life that burned in my veins to grow. The ground cracked and opened up. Green sprang from the black earth. Leaves unfurled, flowers bloomed and fell, leaving berries hanging from the bushes. Large, red strawberries. The smell strangled out the stench that had filled the space prior.

I looked up to The Furies, their eyes hungrily locked onto the fruit.

"Eat, and I will tell you everything."

TWENTY-FOUR

I watched as the sisters ravenously devoured the strawberries. They ate like it would be days before their next meal. The juice ran down their sharp claws and dripped from their arms. I imagined the weekly deposit of food Hades brought them probably did not last long, they probably went hungry often.

The thought saddened me. I knew they had been sent below for being vicious towards mortals… but I couldn't imagine how anyone deserved to go this hungry.

I laid my palm on the ground again, willing my power to grow more fruit. I would feed them until they could eat no more. I would make sure they never had to wait for their meals. The iron earth split again, and vines of blackberries and bushes of blueberries sprung forth. The sisters did not hesitate to dive into them.

"My plan is simple."

Their black eyes slid to me as they continued eating. I could tell by their expressions that they were listening intently.

"I will gain as many allies as I can, the more I have at my back the better. I need to make myself seem strong and capable. Especially as I'm… still learning exactly how to wield my power."

They nodded together. Megaera spoke, her mouth full of fruit. Her razored teeth caked in the berries. It would have been comical, had her face not been that of someone poised for war.

"That is smart, Goddess. It is easier to gain control with an army. One ant is vulnerable, it can be crushed effortlessly underfoot. But thousands of ants become a much more complicated problem."

"Exactly. Once I have the support I need, I'll present my claim to the crown to Hades. If he refuses to concede," I paused, watching their faces. "I'll take it. Whatever the cost."

Their eyes grew eager. I wondered if they had perhaps been waiting for a chance to exact their revenge on the Gods. My plan was full of holes, I realized as I spoke. The Furies did not seem to mind my loose-laid scheme or care about all of the ways that things could go awry. Maybe they didn't notice. As I sat there, watching them nod and comply with me, I wondered if we would pull it off.

"You are cunning, Goddess. We admire your determination and fervor. We will fight with you if that is what it takes. Whatever you need, my sisters and I will be there."

"I am thankful for your aid. You three will be invaluable to my cause."

"You sought us out, here in the wastes of the Underworld. You came to *us*, as though we were precious, when others cast us out. For that, we will always be grateful, Goddess."

Her eyes again burned with that love I had seen earlier.

"You've done well," Wrath cooed.

I could feel her pride in my quick accomplishment of winning over The Furies. But somehow I had gone from wanting them on my side to help me gain control, to wanting them because I wished to keep them safe and happy. Even if I didn't end up on the throne, the three sisters would always be mine.

We had just finished our discussion when Hermes appeared in the alcove, wreathed in bright light. He looked antsy. I glanced up at him from my spot on the ground, The Furies were now sprawled out around me, still eating. He looked from me to the sisters, his face full of worry.

"It's time to go, Kora. You've been gone long enough, Hades will be suspicious."

I sighed heavily, pushing myself up. The Furies stood after I did, looking at me expectantly. It felt like the right time to give some sort of speech for morale, but I could think of nothing. I turned to The Furies, the fire of determination burning in my eyes.

"Wait for me here, I need to bide my time for now. I'll see you all soon."

The sisters bowed lowly, their long hair and leathery wings sweeping the ground. When they stood back up their faces mirrored my own.

"Very well, Goddess. We will be where you need us."

I stepped towards them, leaning into Megaera first. She stood frozen as I brushed my lips across her cheek and kissed her softly.

"You are *still* beautiful."

When I pulled away, tears lined her dark eyes. She looked at me like I was already her queen. It filled me to the brim with... something. After spending some time with them, I could not imagine why anyone could throw them away. They were perfect.

I had forgotten all of the anger and disgust I had felt from my first impression of them. I moved to Alecto, then to Tisiphone, kissing both of their cheeks as well.

When I turned back to Hermes, he no longer stared at me with concern, but with a dangerous curiosity. I could not explain to him how things had transpired, because I did not fully understand myself. A kinship burned between the sisters and me in a way I never expected.

I walked up to him, extending my arm. He reached out and took my hand. With a swift breeze and a flash of light, we were swept away from the cave. It caused a hole in my heart to leave them alone. I hoped my plants continued to bear food for them as the days went on.

We appeared outside the front door of Hades' castle. My mind was still on the three sisters I had just left. I tried to slip my hand from Hermes' and he tightened his grip. I turned to him, his brows were furrowed. He shook his head slightly.

"Be careful, Kora. I feel like you are playing a dangerous hand. You trust too quickly. Those three are unpredictable."

I mulled over his words. I didn't think they were as unpredictable as the Gods gave them credit for. They were slighted and I understood how that would make them angry. If I had been discarded… But I had been, hadn't I? I had felt that rage and let that sadness break me as well. Perhaps that was why I latched onto them so tightly, so quickly.

"Be that as it may, they are also exactly what I need. They will be there for me when I need them to."

I would not back down, and I would not change my mind. I had decided already. Hermes shook his head again, clearly uncomfortable with how I was proceeding with our plan.

"Very well. Be careful, though. You're no use to me if you're dead."

There was no playfulness in his warning, no mischievous sparkle in his eyes. I had no fear of being betrayed or killed by The Furies. Hades was the one I was scared of. I nodded once and turned back to the door. I felt Hermes leave behind me and my stomach turned. How would I face Hades when I walked through the door?

"Act normal. Bide your time."

I pushed the door open and stepped inside. The entire manor was freezing cold. The hair on my arms stood, every sense I had screamed at me. My eyes shot to the throne, where Hades sat. He stared at me with anger. I slid my eyes down... To Minthe, who was sitting on the floor at his feet. She was smirking at me, her eyes shone with a look of triumph. I looked at Hades again. He must have discovered what I was doing. My heart sank and fear took hold of me.

I closed the door behind me and stepped up, keeping my chin high and my face flat. If he had figured my plan out I wouldn't go down without a fight. I held his stare as I approached him.

"Hades."

He looked down at Minthe without acknowledging me at all.

"Leave us."

His voice was cold and harsh, his words clipped. She whipped her head towards him, frustration plastered on her face. Her red lips parted to argue but he held up his hand. She sat quietly for a moment before she decided to plead anyway.

"Hades, please. I want to stay."

Her voice was soft and sweet, unlike the tone she always had with me. She batted her long eyelashes at him, flashing her big doe eyes. I felt hatred boil inside me. Everything about her sent me spiraling. I had never had such disdain for anyone. His red eyes lifted back to mine as he spoke again to Minthe.

"I said leave us."

She shot me a snarl and then rose to her bare feet and padded out of the throne room. As she passed me she smiled coyly, dropping her mask of innocence. I didn't take my eyes off of the God of the Dead sitting on the throne, though. I waited until she was gone before I spoke.

"Yes?"

"Where have you been?" His voice was low and raspy.

"Lie."

"I was with Hecate."

His eyebrow arched and he shook his head. I fought to keep myself calm. If he knew where I was and who I was with he would kill me. He tapped his fingers across the arms of the throne. I could feel his impatience from where I stood.

"Why lie to me, Goddess?"

My stomach felt like it was full of lead, and sweat formed on my back. It was physically painful to lie to him. To not tell him everything I had done, everything I wanted. But the Gods were selfish, angry creatures, and I was not ready for death.

"Stand your ground," Wrath whispered to me.

"I was with Hecate," I repeated cooly.

A devilish grin, one that did not meet his eyes, flashed across his face. My feelings of guilt and fear intensified. The lie was bitter on my tongue, and the truth clawed to be released.

"Funny, Hecate came here looking for you."

My eyebrows rose and my eyes widened. I had made a mistake by not confiding in her and telling her what I had planned. She would have sided with me. She would have helped me. Instead, I single-handedly ruined everything. I should have thought things through more thoroughly. I was not ready.

"So I'll ask again… Where were you?"

I opened my mouth to speak, to spin another lie, and he interrupted me.

"Before you say Hypnos, he also came looking for you."

Shit. No point in lying then. I needed to twist the truth.

What if he already knows?

"He can't know. Surely Hermes would have known if Hades had discovered it."

"I was with Hermes."

I saw his anger burn hotter in his garnet eyes. My heart sank, I had said the wrong thing. I waited for him to speak to avoid digging myself into a deeper hole. His fingers tightened on the arms of his chair, but he sat there silently.

I bit the inside of my cheek to keep myself from saying anything as I waited. The seconds ticked by painfully slow. The sweat dripped down my back, my hands were clammy.

"And what, Goddess, were you doing with Hermes?"

TWENTY-FIVE

My eyes were locked onto his, my mind reeling. Lies and truths both swirled in my head, intertwining and melding into a jumbled mess. I had to say something instead of standing silently.

Anything. Anything would do.

"He was just showing me around. I hate being cooped up in here all day."

His eyes narrowed on me like he could taste the pungent dishonesty as well as I could. I swallowed thickly, hoping that my words had been believable. He leaned forward on his throne, waiting for me to continue. I needed to give him more truth.

"I met Nyx."

His eyebrow arched. I could see him contemplating my words. He leaned back again, crossing his legs.

"And?"

He was testing me. Backing me into a corner so that my lies would show themselves. I steadied my breathing, focusing on the image of The Goddess of Night that was burned into my mind.

"And she's beautiful. And Kind. I've never heard such an accent, either."

I watched his face relax as he nodded. Relief flooded me. He believed me. The panic I had felt just moments before started to recede. He stood, descending the steps from the throne, walking towards me.

"She's one of the oldest Gods. She generally keeps to herself, but you're right; she can be very kind. She finds most of the Gods to be bothersome, which is why she resides here now."

I had to keep him talking.

"Ask him a question."

"How many more Gods stay here in the Underworld?"

I was genuinely curious, but mostly I wanted to change the subject. To make him forget about his earlier anger. He walked up, standing just in front of me. I stood there, looking up at his red eyes and his dark skin. My mind flashed to the dream I had, my fingers tangled in his black hair.

Heat crept across my cheeks and my chest rose and fell quickly. I had forgotten my embarrassment within the fear of him discovering my plans, but it was painfully in the forefront of my mind with him standing so close to me.

"There are a handful. Most of the Gods live in Olympus full time, some of them reside in the mortal realm, and fewer still live here. Or split their time between here and the mortal realm."

He was so close to me that the smell of smoke and iron inundated me. It nearly consumed me. My mind, again, drifted to my dream, his face between my thighs. My face burned hotter. I needed to keep talking, to distract both him and myself. I tried to stay focused on the conversation instead of the ache that was now building between my legs. My skin was ablaze.

"And you rule over them all?"

"I rule over the Underworld itself. The Gods have rules while they're here, but aside from those rules, and outside of the Underworld, I usually allow them to do as they wish. The only God who has complete rule over other Gods is Zeus."

I thought of his teeth grazing my thigh and his fingers digging into my hips. His lips pressed against mine, tasting of my own pleasure. I bit my cheek, hoping the pain would distract me.

"And he's your brother?"

My voice came out quiet and breathy. I cursed my weakness, cursed the way he had such a hold on me. He groaned quietly, closing his eyes and shaking his head. He looked annoyed. I pushed my mind away from my fantasies to contemplate what sort of relationship the two of them had.

I had always wanted brothers or sisters.

"Unfortunately, yes. He's a thorn in my side most days."

"Do you have other siblings?"

His eyes brightened at my question, and his face softened. He offered me his arm. My mind warned me not to touch him, but my body moved against my will. I slid my arm through his gently. He led me towards the dining hall as he spoke.

"We have another brother, Poseidon. He rules the seas of the mortal realm."

"So he lives in the mortal realm instead of Olympus?"

He smiled softly, glancing down at me. I didn't understand why my questions had eased his anger so much. As long as our conversation kept him from prying into my sneaking, and kept my mind from wandering, I would keep asking them.

"Precisely. Poseidon rules over the oceans of the earth, Zeus rules over the skies and I rule over the hells. Zeus is the king of the

Gods, but the three of us stand on equal grounds. He cannot control us any more than we could control him."

I tucked away the information as we entered the dining hall. Those details could be useful later.

The smell of cakes and chocolates filled my nose, drawing my attention to the table. Amidst the sweets adorning the table sat dozens of potted flowers. Peonies and lilies in full bloom, nestled in with heather and babies' breath. Red dahlias mixed with white daisies and roses of varying colors.

My eyes widened, and I turned to Hades. His smile widened at the pure joy I could feel painted across my face.

"I'm sure they won't survive here without your help, but I thought you might like to have them."

Suddenly my heart ached. His words and his gestures were so gracious. I was sneaking around behind his back, lying to him… And he was showering me with gifts. Things he knew that I liked. Guilt dampened my joy, and my face fell as I looked at the flowers and cakes on the table once more. He brushed my hair behind my ear, pulling my attention back to him.

"Do you not like it?"

The concern in his voice threatened to break me. I felt like a terrible person for lying to him. I should have just been honest about what I wanted from the beginning. Maybe he would have shared his rule over the Underworld with me after all.

"But why would he?"

I forced a smile and shook my head. I placed my hand on his arm, looking into his eyes. "No, I love it. It's very kind."

He nodded once and then glanced down to the floor. When he looked back at me his eyes held the same look they had when he was kneeling in front of me. He was intoxicating. My body threatened to betray me.

"Kora, I wanted to talk about last night–"

All of the guilt I had felt just moments earlier evaporated like morning dew, as embarrassment took its place. My face burned so intensely that I worried it would catch fire. I ripped my hand from his arm, my eyes wide with mortification.

"Absolutely not!" My voice came out shrill.

The corner of his mouth turned up in a half smile. I took several steps back, I needed to put distance between us. He held his hands up, fighting away a smile.

"I just wanted to apologize."

I crossed my arms tightly across my chest, frowning at him deeply. I tried to be angry with him, but no matter how much I wanted to be, I wasn't. My scowl cracked into a grin.

He shook his head, smiling. I watched as he walked to the table and pulled out a chair to the right of where he usually sat at the head of the table. I moved to follow him, expecting that it was for me. As I drew near he sat in the seat that he pulled out and glanced up to me. I looked from him to the large, ornate chair. His eyes followed mine and then flicked back to me.

"Sit, enjoy your food."

I moved cautiously towards the head of the table, still unsure if he wanted me to sit there in particular. I laid my hand on the arm and he turned his attention to the desserts. He filled a plate with dark chocolate morsels and cake that smelled like coffee. I slid into the chair and filled my own plate with various chocolates and fruits. The sweets and cakes were more rich than anything I had ever eaten, the fruit was perfectly ripe.

I glanced up, watching him pour a bottle of deep red wine into two glasses. He sat one of them down in front of me. I lifted the glass to my nose and smelled it. It smelled exquisite. I took a sip, expecting it to be as sweet as the food on my plate. My tongue was hit with a dry bite I was not expecting. I had come to appreciate a more bitter flavor to my drinks rather than the sugary ones I had known growing up. Courtesy of Hecate.

"That has a very intricate flavor."

He raised his brows at my observation. I wondered if maybe I had said the wrong thing. Growing up in the mountains had left me inexperienced with many of the finer things in life. I had noticed immediately upon my arrival that Hades didn't spare a second thought to frivolously spend his coin. If he even needed to purchase things. Perhaps the Gods could just create things out of thin air.

"Indeed. It's an aged wine."

There was pride there in his eyes. I had said the right thing, then. I straightened myself, going back to my food. After a moment of silence, I decided to test the waters with him.

"I was thinking…"

He looked at me, waiting for me to continue. I stared back at him. I regretted speaking at all. I wasn't sure where my audacity had come from to request anything of him. Especially after he had given me so much already. It was the wine. And it was the wine that caused me to finish my request.

"Perhaps we could have a gathering?"

Surprise flashed across his face. I waited for him to dash my dreams of filling the dining hall with joy. He tilted his head and pursed his lips. As soon as I had asked I felt silly. I wouldn't even know who to invite to any sort of function.

"If that would make you happy, I think it's a great idea."

"Oh." I hadn't expected him to say yes.

My eyes dropped to my plate as I contemplated how sad any sort of party I threw would be. I didn't know many people in the Underworld. Maybe he would invite other Gods that I had not met yet. Perhaps I would meet his brother. I wondered if my mother would come.

"What sort of gathering are you thinking about?"

I sat back in my chair. I had no idea. The Garden was definitely not ready for the tea party I had discussed with Hypnos.

"I'm not sure, really."

"We could throw a ball."

My eyes shot up to him. A ball… I had certainly never been to anything like that before. I imagined music filling the space, and people in large gowns dancing. It sounded magical. A small smile bloomed on my face.

"That sounds fun."

He returned my smile and nodded. "It does. I've never hosted anything like that here before."

"Who would we invite?"

He smiled wider. "I can think of a few people."

TWENTY-SIX

I slipped from the manor early in the morning, eager to meet with Hecate. Power thrummed through my veins, feeling as though it was scorching me from the inside as it moved. I thought I might burst if I didn't expend some of it. Training with Hecate was exactly what my body needed.

    I opted for comfort with a sage dress and my boots, which were starting to show how often I wore them to trek through the waste of the Underworld. My hair was left unbound and hung in tight curls down my back.

    I glanced towards the narcissus I had grown days before. The blooms were still as fresh as when I made them and new buds were forming. My face beamed with pride. I still couldn't believe that not only had I grown something where life did not come freely, but it was thriving. I hoped the poppies I had grown for Hypnos were doing just as well.

    I was still admiring the flowers when I felt power ripple behind me. I turned back and saw Nyx standing there. Her long braids were decorated with gold clasps and crystals. Her black feathered wings were tucked in closely. The dress she wore looked like she had captured the night itself in it. It was a deep color I could not place, and had what looked like stars sparkling inside it. She was staring at Hades' castle. I couldn't fight off my curiosity. I raised my arm over my head and called to her. She turned to me and her face lit up.

"Goddess! How lovely to see you today."

She made her way toward me, her movements were fluid as if she were gliding across the earth instead of walking. Her dark eyes slid from me to the sad excuse for a garden. I tried not to let the embarrassment of it eat me alive. It was a start. And more than anyone else had ever done for the Underworld.

"That is a beautiful change, Goddess."

"Thank you, Nyx. What brings you here today?"

Her focus moved from the narcissus to me. There was a sadness in her eyes that hurt my heart to see. She forced a smile, but her eyes still held that same sorrow.

"I was hoping my son would see me today."

Shock blasted through me. Her son... My jaw fell slightly ajar, my eyes were wide. I opened and closed my mouth several times, trying to think of something to say.

"Hypnos," she clarified, noticing my surprise.

My confusion only deepened. He looked nothing like her at all. My mind drifted to the God I had seen who resembled Hypnos.

"Thanatos?"

"My other son," she said softly. "They are twins."

"Oh. Well, I don't think Hypnos is here today."

Her face fell. She looked back to the castle as if she could make him appear with only her aching heart. I glanced down at my feet and shifted. When I looked back up her eyes were on me again.

"He has refused to see me for a long time now. I wronged him and he has not forgiven me."

Again I found myself at a loss for words. I could not imagine someone who radiated kindness the way Nyx did wronging anyone. And I could not imagine Hypnos refusing to forgive someone for as long as she eluded. I wanted to pry. To ask what had transpired between the two of them. But it felt rude, with such sadness shadowing her face.

"I'm sorry."

I was sure there was nothing I could say to help ease her pain. I felt sympathy for her, but a sliver deep inside of me wondered what she had done to him. It must have been something truly atrocious if he refused to see her.

"If Hypnos hates her, we should too."

She's done nothing to us.

"That matters not. Hypnos is ours."

I nearly invited her to the ball Hades and I were planning, but I didn't want to risk Hypnos not coming. Wrath was right. He had been a good friend to me, and I did not want him to feel slighted.

"I'm supposed to meet Hecate today. It was nice to see you, though."

She nodded to me, smiling.

"Yes. It was nice to see you as well, Goddess. If you see my son tell him I would love to see him."

"Of course."

Without another word, she was engulfed in a night sky, and then she was gone. I sighed in relief. My power pulsed inside me and I winced. I needed to get to Hecate quickly. I looked in the direction of her hut and rolled my shoulders. I had decided before going to sleep that I was going to try it. I had done it before, surely I could do it again.

I spread my feet and planted them in place, then squared my shoulders. I closed my eyes and focused on the pounding magic in my body. I pushed into it. Willed it to mold into what I needed. I pictured Hecate's hut, the worn boards, and the stone chimney on top. I envisioned the smell of dried herbs and steeping tea. And Pie. I felt the power rip its way out of my body, swallowing me entirely. As it enveloped me I felt like I was tumbling through the air.

I opened my eyes as the magic dissipated. The air stung and my hair whipped around violently. The ground was far away but was getting closer very quickly.

I *was* falling.

Fear filled every part of me as I tried to coax my power back out, to wield it enough to stop my fall.

"You're going to get us killed!"

I tried to respond to Wrath, but I couldn't. I couldn't think, I couldn't speak, I couldn't even get a proper breath. My arms flailed and I kicked my legs. My movement caused my body to twist me until I was facing up to the gray sky. I imagined my body broken on the iron ground. Would this fall kill a God? I was a halfbreed… I was definitely going to die.

My body stopped fighting against the fall and my vision flickered in and out. My lungs burned as they tried to fill. Maybe I would die before I even hit the ground.

"Don't just give up!"

Black and purple magic swirled around me, hugging me tightly. It slowed my fall enough that I was able to gasp for air. I coughed and choked as I was lowered to the ground safely. It placed me down on my feet and held me in place as I caught my breath and oriented myself. I straightened and took several ragged breaths, my throat burning.

When I raised my eyes they fell on Hecate's hut. And Hecate. She was snarling at me, her eyes burning with rage.

"You!" She growled.

The relief and adrenaline that pounded through me drowned out any fear of her anger. I huffed a laugh, still struggling to breathe properly. My laughter only fueled her rage further. She stomped up to me, her long twin braids trailing behind her.

My laugh turned wild and I bent over, grabbing my knees to keep myself from losing balance. Tears lined my cheeks. I couldn't tell if it was from the air burning them or the hysterical fit I was having. My laughter finally died down and I looked back up to her. Her eyes were narrowed and she was snarling at me again.

"What the hells were you thinking?"

"I did it!"

Her face twisted with shock. She shook her head feverishly, grabbing my shoulders.

"No, Kora. You did not *'do it'*. You nearly killed yourself! What if I had not been here?"

"She's right. That was idiotic. You could have killed us both."

I forced my face straight, though there was a ghost of a smile still on my lips. "You're right, Hecate. I'm sorry."

She released her grip on me and stepped back. She crossed her arms and stared at me like I was a child. I brushed my fingers through my tangled hair and smiled at her brightly. I was still high from the excitement of it all. I had nearly died.

But I *had* done it.

"Thank you."

She scoffed and rolled her eyes, then smiled at me softly.

"If you're going to try something like that again, at least let me know first. Hades will have my hide if he finds you flattened on the ground."

"Yes, yes. Of course."

She turned to her hut and then glanced over her shoulder to me. She had a mischievous grin on her face. I looked past her to the hut, her strange dogs with their unusually long noses were waiting at the door for her. Their tails wagged slowly as she started walking towards them.

"Come," she said as she motioned me to follow her. "I have a guest I would like you to meet."

I stepped into her home and the dogs surrounded me. Hecuba pushed past the other dogs to lean against me. Her bushy tail wagged and her tongue was lolled out. I brushed my fingers through her thick, black fur as I walked through the space.

When we entered the kitchen my eyes fell on the guest Hecate had mentioned. Surprise contorted my face as I took her in. She was unlike anything I had ever seen.

There was a slight green hue to her skin, and it had a serpentine sheen to it. Her face was beautiful. Her features were sharp and elegant, but her eyes… Her eyes had been crudely carved out. The flesh where they had been was marred with scars from the act. It was harsh against her very feminine face. She wore a simple black dress that fit loosely around her body, concealing any curves she might have.

There was no hair atop her head. In its place was a tangled mess of snakes. The snakes were solid black. They looked at me as I approached and several of them hissed loudly, revealing sharp fangs. The inside of their mouths were also black. I gasped, taking a step back. Her lips curved up into a small smile.

"Oh dear," the woman said softly, reaching up to pet the snakes. They calmed immediately. "Don't mind them. They're temperamental with new people."

TWENTY-SEVEN

Hecate urged me to sit and served me a steaming cup of tea. My eyes bore into the woman who sat across from me. Her snakes continued to watch me intensely. It was unnerving, to say the least.

She reached out in front of herself and grabbed her own cup of tea with ease. She turned her head to Hecate like she could still see her clearly.

"This is your Goddess, Hecate? The one you've spoken so highly of?"

Her voice was low and airy. Her words came out in a near hiss as she spoke. I fidgeted in my seat, everything about her had me on edge.

"She's no more unusual than The Furies."

Wrath was right. There was something vaguely similar about the way their bodies held a very human femininity as well as beastly features. I wondered how they had all come to be and what had happened to them. And her eyes… Who would do such a thing?

"Yes, dear. This is Kora, the Goddess of Spring." Hecate's eyes beamed with pride as she spoke of me. "And this, Kora, is Medusa. She's a good friend of mine."

I looked from Hecate to Medusa. She was already turned towards me. Her empty eye sockets pierced me sharply. I forced an awkward half smile, though I wasn't sure why I did it. It wasn't like she could see me anyway.

"It's very nice to meet you."

"Likewise, Goddess. I've heard great things about you."

"Well," I glanced up to Hecate who was leaning against the counter, grinning. "I'm not sure what all I've done that could be so great."

Medusa smiled brightly, revealing fangs that matched the snakes crowning her head. I wondered if both the snakes, as well as Medusa herself, held venom in those fangs. The thought sent a shiver down my spine that felt more like jealousy than fear.

"Nonsense. I heard you nearly tore Minthe limb from limb. I can appreciate that just as much as the next person."

"Ugh!" Hecate blanched, throwing her hands up. "Don't even say that dreadful Nymph's name. It makes me ill just hearing it."

Medusa let out a quiet chuckle and a smile spread across my face. Hecate shook her head, still giving us a disgusted expression. It brought me joy to know Minthe was equally as disliked by others as she was by me. I turned my attention back to Medusa, and her face turned to me quickly. My eyebrows raised reflexively.

"The snakes," she murmured. "I see through their eyes."

I blushed, clasping my hands in my lap.

"Oh. I'm sorry, I didn't mean to stare."

"Not at all, Goddess. I get that a lot. Fortunately for you, Hecate removed my eyes. Otherwise, you'd be stone dead right now."

Hecate barked a sudden laugh, making me jump. I glanced from Hecate to Medusa. I had missed the joke somehow. Hecate sauntered up to the table and pulled out a chair.

"Her gaze turned anyone who met it to stone. Helpful in some instances, but hindering in others."

"Indeed," Medusa interjected. "It's hard to gossip with someone made of rock."

I closed my mouth abruptly, realizing it had fallen open again. My eyes shifted between the two women across from me. They joked about the horrendous action as if it had been a normal thing, instead of the mutilation that it actually was. I could not see the humor in it the way they both clearly did.

"Were you always…"

"A monster?" Medusa finished.

"So different," I corrected.

I didn't like that term. Monster. Was someone's physical appearance enough to categorize them as such a strong term? I had made assumptions about many things since I had arrived in the Underworld. Most of them were wrong.

"No. I was human once. A devotee of Athena. I spent my life dedicated to her, I gave… everything to her. And then *everything* was taken from me."

The emphasis she gave, combined with the fall of her face, implicated a very woeful painting in my head. Again I found myself wondering how everyone seemed to have such a sad story. I supposed if one lived long enough there was bound to be heartbreak along the way. Medusa continued her tale as I sat in silence.

"When Athena found out what had been taken from me, she was angry. She blamed me for it, so she made sure I could never use my body to seduce anyone ever again. She didn't hear my cries, paid no heed to the fact that I had been soiled against my will. It didn't matter to her in the end, anyway. I had been ruined in her eyes, regardless of the details."

"That's horrible," I whispered.

I had no idea who Athena was, but her actions made me sick to my stomach. Medusa had been the victim of a horrific crime, and she had been punished for it. The more I learned of the Gods around me, the worse some of them seemed. My grandmother had been right, indeed.

"So," Medusa said matter of factly. "I was banished here to the Underworld. Hades was kind enough to accept me, and after a time Hecate remedied some of my woes."

"And this Goddess, Athena. Who is she?"

The two of them exchanged glances before Hecate answered.

"She is Zeus' daughter."

The pieces fit together for me quickly with that information. After the things I had heard about Zeus, it made sense that his daughter would be equal in his cruelty. I shook my head and rubbed my forehead.

"And this ghastly man who harmed you. I assume he was punished as well?"

A sad smile spread across Medusa's face. I knew before she even spoke that he had not. How unjust Athena had been in her judgment. It was unfair.

"No, Goddess. Athena would not dream of confronting her own uncle with such accusations."

Her words stabbed me in the chest. My face twisted with horror, and my stomach turned. It could not have been Hades, I refused to believe he was capable of that. That left Poseidon. Poseidon had done that to her. My heart broke for what the woman had been through.

When the crown of the Underworld rested on my head; when I sat upon that throne… I would make sure that sort of thing never went on without reprimand. I would be a just ruler in the way the other Gods had failed to be.

"Weep not for me, Goddess. I am here, despite what they have put me through. And I am stronger for it."

Hecate cleared her throat loudly. "Well, that's enough sadness for one day. Tell me, Kora. What have you been up to? I went looking for you yesterday and Hades said you were out."

I turned to Hecate, unable to hide the guilt that washed over my face. She saw it instantly and narrowed her eyes on me. I stammered, trying to think of something to say. I was not good at lying, and even more so with her. She had been my closest friend for so long. She knew everything about me.

"Kora, where were you yesterday?"

I took a deep breath, glancing between Hecate and Medusa. I would have to tell her. I only hoped that the two of them would keep my secret. Medusa had trusted me with her dark past, and now I would have to trust her.

"I went to see The Furies."

Medusa gasped loudly, her snakes drawing back with a hiss. Hecate's face stayed flat, like she suspected where I had been all along. I waited quietly for her to say something. Anything.

"The Erinyes?" Medusa asked incredulously.

"And how did that go?" Hecate asked.

I shrugged slightly, keeping my lips in a tight line.

"Oh no," she said sternly. "You will not leave it like that. I want to know *everything*."

I took a sip of my tea before speaking. "They're not as bad as everyone made them out to be."

"Not as bad–" Hecate held up a hand, silencing Medusa.

"They're awful, Kora. I'm sure you know that as well as I. So what aren't you telling me? Why did you even go looking for them?"

Her harsh tone made me wince. I hesitated, unsure still if I wanted to tell her everything.

"She must know."

What if she tells Hades?

"She's more likely to tell him if you keep her in the dark."

I cursed Wrath for being right. Hecate was much more inclined to go to Hades if she had no idea what I was doing at all.

"Nyx told me–"

"You spoke to Nyx?" There was an edge to Hecate's voice that told me she did not like the Goddess of Night. Curious how Hades had seemed to like her, yet both Hypnos and Hecate seemed to not.

"I did. She told me that I had a claim to rule the Underworld."

She raised her brow and shook her head. I felt then like I was missing a very crucial piece of information. She rolled her eyes and sighed deeply. She slid her eyes to Medusa, who shook her head as well.

"Of course, Nyx would stir trouble. So you went to The Furies, why?"

"Because if I'm going to rule the Underworld I need people to stand behind me."

Hurt flashed across Hecate's face as I spoke. She sucked air through her teeth and closed her eyes. I had been wrong to not come to her with everything at the very start. Guilt curled around inside me.

"I told you," Wrath chastised.

"And you went to them before you came to me?"

"Hecate I didn't..." My words fell, as did my face. I didn't know how to remedy the mistake I had made.

"Well," Medusa clipped. "What's done is done. Hades is a fair ruler. He's been kind to me. To all of us."

I put my face in my hands. I should have known they would not side with me. Hades had ruled for so long.

"That being said," she continued. "I stand with you, Goddess. You can bring things to this land no one else can, if what Hecate says is true."

I looked up to Medusa, surprise on my face. My eyes drifted to Hecate, who still looked bruised by my actions.

"I will always stand behind you, Kora."

My lip trembled and tears threatened to fall. I sat back in my chair and wiped my eyes. My heart was both broken and full. Hecate reached over and laid her hand on my knee.

"Always."

"I'm so sorry, Hecate."

"As Medusa said, what's done is done. You tell us what you need and we will be there. Tread carefully though, Kora. Hades is powerful and though he is kind, he has a cruel streak."

I had nearly forgotten over my weeks here, the cruelty that was buried in the God of the Dead. He had destroyed Hecate's home in the upper world. I could not help but wonder what he was actually capable of.

My power rippled through the air. The plants Hecate had scattered about shook and grew slightly. I winced at the accidental release of magic. I had apparently not used enough when I jumped space to get to Hecate's hut.

"It looks like you need to burn off some steam," she teased.

TWENTY-EIGHT

We spent several hours outside as I grew and destroyed fields of wildflowers. My reserve of power seemed neverending. The more I used it over time, the more it built and strengthened. I could feel it humming through me, filling me to the brim.

Hecate held up a hand to end our session before I had even broken a sweat. I could have continued for hours more.

"I think that is quite enough for today. We don't need you burning yourself out. I would never hear the end of it from Hades if your time here resulted in you stuck in bed for days again."

I shrugged, standing up from the ground. She was right. I had things to do over the course of the next few days, including preparing the castle to host our ball. The rooms and halls were decorated with fine art and furniture, but it was not presentable for such a gathering. His manor had always held a certain coldness that was uninviting, to say the least. I turned to the two women, who lounged on the natural formations of iron jutting from the earth.

"I forgot to mention earlier, I'm throwing a ball in a couple of weeks. I would love it if you would both attend."

Medusa's face lit up with excitement. The snakes atop her head bobbed and flicked their tongues. Hecate narrowed her eyes on me, her expression suspicious. Medusa turned towards her, grabbing her arm.

"We're going, yes?"

Hecate continued eying me apprehensively. Disappointment constricted my lungs as I held her stare. I wanted her there with me. I wouldn't be able to enjoy myself if she did not come.

"Did Hades agree to this, or is this another of your schemes?"

I shot her a playful glare, crossing my arms.

"He said it was a great idea!"

"A 'great idea', hm?" She arched her brow at me.

"Yes. And I think it will be nice. He has all of that space in his manor, he might as well make good use of it."

"I also think it's a great idea," Medusa interjected happily. "I've never been to a ball before."

"I cannot imagine Hades throwing a *ball*."

I rolled my eyes, groaning. She acted as though the party was a bigger inconvenience than my plan to upheave the entire Underworld. I stalked up and knelt in front of her. I placed my hands gently on her knees, looking up. I feigned a doe-eyed expression, batting my eyelashes.

"It would mean so much to me if you came, Hecate."

"Ugh!" She waved her hand at me as if to shoo me away. "You know I hate that. Very well, Kora. No need to beg. If it's that important to you, I'll be there."

I smiled, standing back up. I looked towards Medusa and flashed her a smile as well. She returned it and laughed brightly. Watching the joy on her scarred face made me wonder how she had kept her light after going through so many awful experiences.

"Perfect. The ball will be in two weeks' time."

Medusa absentmindedly stroked her snakes. "Wonderful!"

"Indeed. Who else is coming, Kora?" Hecate asked flatly.

I turned to her, my face full of uncertainty. She closed her eyes and rubbed her forehead.

"Well…"

"Kora, please tell me that Medusa and I will not be the only ones there."

Medusa's face fell as she turned from Hecate back to me. I shook my head at her, shooting a scowl at Hecate.

"Of course not! I plan to invite Hypnos, and Hades said he had some people in mind to invite."

"*Hades* is inviting people to a *ball*?" She said incredulously. "Honestly, Kora, I have no idea what you have done to him. I never in my life would have expected that out of such a dull God."

I scoffed, and the words flew from my mouth before I even realized what I was saying.

"He's not dull. He's been rather enjoyable at times."

She raised her eyebrows, grinning mischievously at me. My face flushed and I stammered on, trying to clarify what I meant. Unable to form anything coherent, I clamped my mouth shut. She chuckled and then turned to Medusa. Her snakes swiveled towards Hecate.

"I think it's time to get you home, darling."

Medusa smiled, then leaned in towards Hecate. Their faces were inches apart. The way Hecate gazed softly at Medusa had me feeling suddenly very out of place there with them. I turned away, trying to concentrate on a crack in the iron. I felt the swirl of Hecate's power building around us.

"It was so nice to meet you, Goddess."

I flicked my eyes to Medusa. "You as well."

With that, the power coursing in the air around us became tangible. It wrapped around Medusa, swallowing her completely. Then she was gone. Hecate and I stared at each other. There was determination burning in her brown eyes.

"So you know, Kora, this thing you're planning… It may very well cause an all out war. Hades has ruled these lands for a very long time. He will not concede easily."

I sighed deeply, looking up to the gray skies I had come to love. The air was thick and heavy, it smelled of iron. I still could not believe how my life had changed so drastically in such little time. Was it all the work of The Fates? I had never believed in fate, but it was no longer an idea. It was the work of Gods weaving webs around us all. I had no choice but to believe it now. Somehow the idea of ruling the Underworld took over my entire life. I craved it in a way that could be nothing short of the work of The Fates.

"I know," I whispered. "I can't imagine it will go well for me, but I cannot let this go. It's something I have to do. This place could be so much more."

I turned and met her stare. Her face was straight, her eyes still burning. She was a force to be reckoned with, I had always known that. Long before I even knew she was a God. She had always been the embodiment of strength that I wished I had.

"You will do great things here, Kora. Hades has done well, but you're right. You will bring changes this place needs."

"The souls deserve a better eternity."

She smiled at me, her eyes softening, then nodded solemnly.

"Indeed, they do."

"I want to make an oasis here for them. Something beautiful to enjoy."

"I look forward to it. The Gods of old have sat stagnant for far too long. It's time for a change."

A sharp pain shot through my skull. I cried out, clutching my head. Hecate was on me in a second, grabbing my shoulders. She spoke to me, but her words were muffled. There was a rush in my ears like I was underwater. And the splitting pain in my head was debilitating. I felt my body convulse and crumble, but I couldn't stop it. As my body hit the hard ground my vision went black.

***

I was looking down at my garden. All of the vegetables and flowers were black and rotting away. The earth that they had sprung from was dried and cracked like a desert. I reached out, running my fingers through the dirt. Pain had torn through my body and twisted into the ground, strangling the life out of my garden.

I heard footsteps crunching across the ground behind me. I turned to see who was approaching. Fear and shame filled me, both from what I had done and who might see.

A tall man approached. At that moment I didn't know who he was, but… I would know those mischievous green eyes and that red hair anywhere. It was Hermes. He knelt on the ground next to me.

"Quite a mess you've made here, Kora."

His voice echoed through my mind. It was a memory. He had come to me before. Why had he said nothing to me about it? How had I forgotten?

"Who are you?" I had asked.

His green eyes slid to mine. I felt a shiver go down my spine.

"Hermes. And you," he whistled, turning back to the wreckage I had caused. "You really can't keep yourself under control, can you?"

I turned towards my ruined garden, my voice shaking. "I didn't mean to do this."

"I know," he whispered to me softly. "Don't worry. You won't even remember this."

Fear flooded me. I tore my eyes from the death and decay towards Hermes.

"What do you mean?"

When he looked back towards me, there was sadness in his eyes. He placed one hand on the back of my head and the other over my face. As my vision was blasted with a blinding white light his words rang through my head.

"I'm sorry, Kora."

***

I sat up, gasping for air. My eyes darted around the space. Hecate knelt beside me, her eyes wide with fear. I could feel the black ichor staining my cheeks. I scanned her, looking for any sign of harm I may have brought to her. She was unscathed. I gulped several large breaths down, relief filling me.

"What the Hells happened?!" she demanded.

Anger took the place of the relief I had felt just seconds before. It burned through me hotter than anything I had ever experienced. It threatened to sear the flesh from my bones. It scorched every fiber of my being like a wildfire in the woods.

I had been tricked. Deceived. Lied to. I had trusted Hermes. Told him things that could get me killed. And he had wiped my memories, how long ago? How many times?

"Kora?" Her voice trembled, as did her body.

When I lifted my eyes to meet Hecate she pushed herself back away from me. Fear replaced the worry that lay there before. She held her hands up in surrender as if I might rip her apart where she knelt. But it was not her that my hands itched to tear into, it was not her that my Wrath ferociously begged to end.

It was Hermes.

I bared my teeth and pushed myself off the ground. I held her stare the whole time. She looked up at me like I was death incarnate.

And maybe I was.

Wrath writhed around inside me. She wanted to take the reins. She wanted revenge for the secrets he had kept from us. I considered releasing her, letting her wreak havoc and have her retribution, but kept myself steady because I didn't want it to be her hands that cleaved Hermes' body apart.

I wanted it to be mine.

And once I was done with him I would give him to The Furies. I would let them torture him for all of eternity. He would never lie to anyone else.

I focused my attention back on Hecate.

"Hermes."

TWENTY-NINE

My boots crunched along the iron earth. I was marching ahead, still fueled by my Wrath. Hecate followed along behind me quietly. She had asked no questions. She knew where I was going as well as I did. I headed straight for the wastes beyond her hut. To The Furies. Still, she followed, not daring to utter a word, ignoring her disdain for The dreaded Erinyes.

    I entered their territories, the shades parted and scurried away from me. The sound of beating wings filled the air. I didn't glance up to the sky to look for them, I planted my feet firmly on the ground and waited for them to come to me. It was mere seconds before they landed several feet away, their large wings spread open wide. The three sisters walked up to me, Megaera leading the way. As they approached, their black eyes slid to Hecate. I could feel her hesitation without even looking at her.

    The three sisters turned their attention back to me, and then they knelt. I watched them, my anger still burning hot. When they lifted their eyes to meet mine, I spoke.

    "Tell me, sisters; what do you know of Hermes?"

Alecto hissed quietly. Megaera lifted her hand to silence her sister, while her eyes pinned me inquisitively. When she spoke her words were slow and deliberate, like she feared I was testing them.

"You came here with him before, Goddess. Why ask us, instead of him?"

My lip curled into a snarl. My tone came out clipped, more harsh than I had intended. "I asked you a question, Megaera."

She studied me intensely with her predator's eyes. Before my time in the Underworld, she would have sent me running with those eyes, but no longer. I had changed.

Tisiphone answered me before Megaera could. "A trickster," she hissed.

"God of lies," Alecto said.

I raked my eyes across both of them, and then they fell back on Megaera. I waited for her to speak again. I wanted to hear it from her mouth, too.

"Indeed he is a trickster God, a weaver of lies."

I nodded, satisfied with their responses. I turned back to Hecate, who looked as though she might vomit at any moment. Everyone had let me trust him. But not her, she had warned me. I should have heeded her words from the start. Instead, I let my naivety shroud my judgment. I wouldn't make that mistake again.

I marched back to Hecate, meeting her terrified eyes, and called over my shoulders to The Furies.

"If you see him, sisters, I want to know immediately. I don't know what he's up to, but I plan to find out."

I couldn't see them, but I heard them take off into the air again. Alone with Hecate I finally felt my rage simmer down. Her face relaxed.

"Can you tell me, now, what happened?"

I shuffled through the memory, recalling every detail. Every freckle on his fair skin, the way his hand felt against my face. The smell of dirt and rotting vegetation. It curled my stomach to think how often I had been alone with him. How I had taken his word as truth. I was a fool.

"Hermes… He was taking my memories."

Her mouth fell open. I could see the confusion in her eyes and could feel her processing what I had said. Her lips clamped shut in disbelief. She was feeling what I had felt when I realized. Slowly her face twisted in anger. Yes. She understood exactly why I was so enraged. He had played us both like a fiddle.

"That bastard! Why would he do that?"

"I don't know. But I will find out. One way or another."

She nodded, her eyes mirroring the fire in mine. Her mouth turned up in a wicked grin. "He'll be at the ball?"

"Oh, yes. Yes, he will." I would make sure of it.

My eyes slid across the crowd of souls around us. They wandered aimlessly, but they gazed nervously towards me. I realized then, how aware they were. I remembered the terror the small child had in her eyes the first time I had met The Furies. They now looked at me with that same fear. My heart fell.

I knelt to the ground, pushing my palm against the iron ground. The earth beneath us shuddered. The souls looked around in panic. They all froze, their eyes locking onto me. I coaxed my power up, coursed it through my body and into the iron.

More. I needed to push more.

A large pulse blasted out of my hand, snaking through the ground. The surface cracked like glass, thousands of paperwhite narcissus sprang up from the crevices. They grew tall and strong, blooms and leaves unfurling.

I lifted my gaze, and saw the fear leave the souls' eyes. Instead, they stared at my creation in awe. They moved about the large flowers, running their fingers over the petals. The souls of children slipped from behind the older souls. They ran through the flowers, bright laughter filling the air.

That was what I wanted. For them to have unbridled joy forever.

When I turned to Hecate she was smiling down at me softly. Her eyes held a pride that snuffed out the last of the fiery anger that had been bubbling around deep inside of me. I would handle Hermes. But I would keep my eyes locked onto my goals in the process.

"You are truly magnificent, Kora. I will see you on that throne. Even if it kills me."

"I have no plans to let you die, Hecate."

"Indeed. But even still, I want you to know that I will be with you until the end."

Her words sparked my curiosity. She could see it there in my face as we held each other's stares. She narrowed her eyes on me and crossed her arms. I stood, placing my hand on her shoulder. The souls around us continued to frolic in the narcissus, some weeping. She leaned in, whispering to me quietly.

"What are you thinking, Kora?"

A smile broke across my face. It was not one of glee or delight. But of a cold, calculated, murderous intent. If the version of myself before the Underworld had met the new me, I didn't think she would recognize herself. Some crucial part of me had changed somewhere along the way. It had been broken and crushed under the foot of fate. I was no longer that scared little village girl, desperately seeking the approval of her grandmother.

No, I was a God. Everyone else should be seeking my approval. And if they didn't? Well, then their souls would be mine forever, anyway.

"How exactly do you kill a God?"

THIRTY

Sweat dripped from my brow. My arms trembled as I fought to keep them lifted towards the tree. Power flickered through me like a weakened flame, struggling to force its way through the iron earth.

"More!" Hecate's shout cut through the air.

"You can do better than this. Why are you distracted?"

I wasn't sure why Wrath asked. She knew every thought that crossed my mind. It was infuriating to not ever have a single thing for myself. She was always there, always with me.

"Perhaps if you acknowledge it then you can let it go and focus on your training."

"More, Kora! What are you doing?"

But I couldn't do more. My mind was indeed elsewhere.

I let my hands fall slack at my sides and kept my eyes glued to the large oak tree. For days we had worked on fields of flowers, growing and destroying them. Then Hecate had declared I was ready to move on to bigger things. *'Grow a tree,'* she had said. I had grown one once before so I felt confident it would be effortless.

How wrong I had been. The first tree was a challenge, but three trees in I was exhausted and tired of the repetition. At the very least I had become flawless at controlling which side of my power I drew from. It was no longer like flipping a coin, only able to hope it landed where I wanted it to.

"What is wrong, Kora?"

My eyes flicked to hers, then drifted back to the tree. "I'm angry. About Hermes. I feel betrayed."

She was silent for a beat before responding. "Hermes has always been full of secrets. I think he thrives on it."

"It's hard to know who to trust anymore."

She flashed me a sympathetic smile. "That holds true for us all."

"I stay awake at night thinking about how badly I want to rip him apart." I glanced back at her. "You're sure there is no way to kill a God?"

She huffed a laugh. "When you live as long as some of us have you'll understand there are far worse fates than death."

I lowered myself to sit on the cold ground. "How long will I live, being a half-breed?" It was a question that I had not yet dared to ask.

"Demi-God," she corrected, her tone insinuating she hated the term I had used. "I'm not sure, Kora. It seems to vary from person to person. Along with the very human quality of being able to be killed by mundane things."

I hated not knowing.

"We have immortality," Wrath promised.

You cannot know that.

"I can feel it. Can you not?"

The only thing I felt was anger and exhaustion. Wrath scoffed and then retreated into the dark corners of my mind. If only she would have stayed that way.

"Why do you ask?"

"It would be nice to know how frail this body is." Especially if we would end up in a war.

"Just be careful with yourself. I'd rather us not have to find out."

A deep sigh left my lips and I raised my aching arms back up the tree. I did not bother to stand. I could do it from the ground just as well as I could standing. I pulled on the darkness deep inside of me. Willed it forward. I sent it pulsing through the iron towards the tree. Slowly it took hold of my creation. Little by little the tree was sapped of its life. I watched as it turned black and rotted, then dried and crumbled to dust. There was nothing left of the tree after my power slowed to a stop.

"Good." She paused. "Again."

I bit the inside of my cheek and reminded myself that she was merely trying to help me. I pushed once more into the other side of my power. The one that wanted only to grow and create. It coursed through my body in small waves and came to a halt as it met iron. My eyes closed and I breathed in deeply. I could still feel plenty of power inside of me. I knew I had more to give.

"How is the preparation for the ball going?"

I silently thanked her for the change of subject and the break in training. "Hades is filling the manor with even more art and sculptures. Everything looks very nice."

She rolled her eyes. "Yes, he has always been enamored by fine art. I don't understand it, personally."

A smile spread across my face. "There are worse things, I suppose."

"Indeed. Do you know who he is inviting?"

"I do not."

She shrugged and reached inside her coat pocket, pulling out a large toad. I stared at her, my lip slightly curled and my nose scrunched. I narrowed my eyes at her as she patted its fat body and tucked it back into her coat.

"Why on earth do you have a toad in your pocket?"

"Well if I leave him home the dogs will torment him!"

She said it as if that was truly an answer to my question. I grinned and shook my head. I wasn't sure why I was surprised after the weasel on her table.

"I call him Little Zeus," she teased.

I barked a laugh before I could stop myself. "I highly doubt he would appreciate you naming a toad after him."

She flashed me a wicked smile. "Oh, indeed. Which is precisely why I've done it."

"Is he really as bad as you've said?"

Her face became serious. All of the humor she held before was gone. My heart sank before she even answered me.

"Yes, he is. Several of us have had our fair share of spats with him."

I nodded solemnly. "Will I meet him?"

"Only if you are very unfortunate. Zeus has tried to convince Hades to let him meet you many times already."

"Hades told you that?"

She shook her head. "No, Kora. Believe it or not, I know people in Olympus. You're not my only friend."

I shot her a playful look, but my heart was heavy. Everyone I had met so far was so kind, but the Gods residing in Olympus appeared to be very different from the stories I was being told. Zeus, Poseidon, Athena... I didn't know much beyond that, but it felt like enough to give me a clear picture of what they were like. I found myself fretting at the thought of meeting them. I wondered who might be among them that Hecate would consider a friend.

"Well, I think we have done enough for today. You should head home."

I stood and brushed myself off, then began pulling at my powers to send myself back to the God of the Dead's castle. I was far too tired to walk.

"Absolutely not!"

I whirled to look at Hecate. "I'm sorry?"

"I will not have you killing yourself by trying to travel on your own. I will send you home."

I could tell by the look on her face I would not win an argument with her. I decided it would be best for me to concede, so I gave her a small nod. She smiled at me softly.

"I'll see you soon, Kora."

Power swirled around me in thick black and purple smoke and swallowed me entirely. Her magic had a pungent smell. It reminded me of the tea she had always served me.

I appeared just outside of the manor. Habit nearly took me straight inside, but I needed to plan more of the garden that I had promised Hades. I trudged over to the small area where I had grown the narcissus and I took a seat on the ground. I glanced around the space, I still had made no progress on it. It was nearly impossible to commit to anything, even though I knew I could just destroy it and start over. I wanted it to be perfect.

My mind drifted from the garden to Hermes. I had not seen him since he had taken me to The Furies. Part of me was thankful for the time to process the memory that had resurfaced. But it seemed the longer I had to stew on it, the more I wanted to tear him apart. I had tried to reason with myself. To rationalize what had happened, and give him a chance to explain.

"Foolish. It would be foolish to trust him again."

Maybe he has a good reason.

"There can be no justification for his grievance."

I knew in my heart that Wrath was right, but I still wanted so badly to believe that there had been some grave misunderstanding to my fragment of a memory. Perhaps I was more naive than I had even given myself credit for. He was a liar. I would only end up hurt again if I continued to blind myself to it.

I felt a wave of familiar power from behind me and the smell of the Lethe river fell over me like a blanket. I felt a smile creep across my face as I turned to see Hypnos standing there. He strolled over, taking a seat on the ground next to me. His eyes were bright and he looked well rested.

"How have you been, Kora?'

"It's a long story. How have you been?"

"Well, I just woke up from an incredible nap. I have some time to kill."

He winked at me and bumped his shoulder into mine. A soft laugh escaped my lips. I had so many things I wanted to ask him, to tell him. A sliver inside me questioned whether I could trust him, or if he might betray me the way Hermes had. When my eyes met his I knew he wouldn't. He was too good for the world of games and lies that the Gods played.

"A secret for a secret?" I proposed.

He considered it for a moment, then conceded. "Very well."

"I met your mother. Nyx." I watched as a shadow flashed across his eyes. "She told me that she had wronged you a long time ago. What did she do?"

He looked down at the ground, his face crumpling. I regretted asking. I wanted to take it back. To undo the hurt that I had rekindled.

"I was in love once, a long time ago. Her name was Cassandra. She was mortal, and the most beautiful woman I had ever laid eyes on. She was kind. She had so much love for everyone and everything. We were happy together, even though I knew it would only last so long. Mortal lives are a flash compared to the lives of Gods. Nyx… She didn't approve of the relationship. She said it was pointless to waste my time with a mortal who would grow old and whither away."

I turned my body towards him. I had a sinking feeling that I knew exactly where he was going with his story. I placed my hand on top of his, and his eyes flicked up to mine. The pain that had settled there broke my heart.

"She tried to convince me to leave her," he continued. "I should have just listened to her, but I was blinded by my love for Cassandra. Nyx was enraged by my *insubordination*, as she called it. She went to Cassandra in the dead of night, and she took her life. I found her the next morning. I will never forget the carnage that Nyx left her in…"

As his voice trailed off, tears streamed down my cheeks. He smiled sadly at me, reaching up to dry my face. My lip trembled. I wrapped my arms around him tightly, more tears replacing the ones he had wiped away. I was ashamed that I had been so kind to Nyx when she had caused him such heartache.

He pulled away gently, his eyes meeting mine again. "Your turn, Kora."

For a moment I stared at him, confused. *That's right. A secret for a secret.*

"I…" My words caught in my throat. How childish mine felt after hearing his tale. I wondered if he would think me immature for falling into such an unnecessary game, or if he would go straight to Hades. I wasn't sure which I feared worse.

"You can tell me anything," he promised, wiping the remnants of my tears from my cheeks.

"I want to rule the Underworld. I think I'll have to take it from Hades. I plan to."

He stared at me with wide eyes, his mouth ajar. Regret crashed over me. The shock I saw on his face made me question my decision to tell him.

"I must say, I did not expect that."

He looked around us, to the narcissus. Then to the natural iron formations. When his eyes slid back to mine, the surprise was gone. Instead, I saw that same burning determination I had seen in both The Furies and Hecate.

"I have stood by Hades for a long time, but if it comes to choosing sides… I will choose yours without hesitation, Kora."

I should have felt relief from his words, but it was guilt that wound itself inside of me. Guilt for dragging him into the mess I knew it would be. He had been through enough already. He deserved better. I would just have to make sure that I gave him better.

"I want to make this place great."

"You will. If anyone can do it, you can."

We sat there, face to face, with clasped hands. I made a promise to myself right then; that I would do whatever I could to make sure that he got the life he had earned. My eyes stung as tears attempted to fall again.

I was ripped out of my thoughts abruptly by Hades clearing his throat behind Hypnos. I hadn't even seen him approach us. My fear-filled eyes shot up to him as panic held me. If he had heard us…

Hypnos twisted around to look at him, releasing my hands quickly. Hades was glaring down at him angrily. He slid his eyes from Hypnos to me and crossed his arms.

"Am I interrupting something?"

Hypnos scrambled up to his feet, dusting himself off. "Of course not." He glanced down at me. "I was just leaving."

Hades did not respond as Hypnos nodded his farewell to me and vanished in a swirl of dust and power. My eyes were locked onto the God of the Dead, and his on me. The silence in the air between us was sharp and painful. I waited for him to bring up anything he might have heard.

He moved his gaze from me to the narcissus. His face softened. "Will you be doing anything else with this space?"

His question caught me off guard. I stood, trying to recover from my surprise. Even with Hades' gentle expression, I worried that he might have overheard my conversation with Hypnos. I glanced around the space awkwardly.

"I would like to. If I'm being honest, I'm not really sure where to go from here."

He hummed, settling his attention near the stone bench. "I think a tree there would be nice."

I followed his gaze. "What sort of tree would you like?"

His red eyes flicked to me, causing my stomach to clench. Fear tangled with the arousal that always taunted me any time he was near. I became distinctly aware of how little space there was between us. It was suffocating. It infuriated me that I had no control over my body with him so close. I took two steps back.

"A magnolia tree, I think."

A magnolia. My mouth turned up in a small smile. Magnolia trees had always been one of my favorites. I brushed past him and took a seat on the bench. I glanced over my shoulder to the spot where he suggested the tree should be grown and with my hands flat on my lap I willed the power into the ground beneath us.

The earth shook and the surface split and cracked. A sapling sprang up. Its thin stem grew and thickened quickly. Within seconds it was a full-sized magnolia tree. I willed another wave of power into the tree and flowers bloomed throughout the leaves.

I glanced back to Hades. He was staring at the tree, his eyes gleaming. He turned to me and smiled widely. "It's beautiful."

I tried to ignore the heat creeping across my face. "I'm glad you like it."

He opened his mouth to speak, when Cerberus came bounding around the corner. All three sets of ears were erect, posture stiff. He looked at Hades, then the tree, and finally me. He walked up to me cautiously, still eyeing the tree. I reached out, stroking his coarse fur.

"Do you like it?"

His heads turned to me, eyes full of curiosity. He leaned into my touch, nub tail wagging. I smiled down at him. I felt peace, then. The smell of narcissus and magnolia filled the air, Cerberus leaned against me… I looked at Hades, his eyes were locked onto me. My smile faltered.

The longer I stayed in the Underworld the more confused I grew. Everything and everyone was becoming an integral part of my life. I was starting to feel doubt as my eyes lingered on Hades.

"There's no room for that."

Maybe he would let me rule alongside him.

"After all your scheming? He wouldn't. You have no choice now, you've made your decision."

My expression hardened at Wrath's words. She was always right. I couldn't let myself turn soft. I would be killed if I did that.

Hades frowned slightly, seeing the change in my face. I tried to recover, but it was too late. He walked over and sat next to me on the bench.

"Does something trouble you?"

I averted my eyes, fearing if I held his stare I might tell him everything. I had no control over myself around him. I cursed The Fates for their meddling.

"I'm fine." I tried to focus on the petals of the narcissus. Tried to memorize every curve, every vein running through them.

He placed his hand gently on mine. I whipped my head towards him, our eyes locking again. I felt a buzz through my whole body. Images from my dream flashed in my head. My face warmed.

"If you need to talk, I will listen."

His tone was soft; understanding. Like he knew what it felt like to hold tightly onto secrets. I wondered what he might be clutching onto deep inside. Everyone I met had something they kept hidden. Why would Hades be any different?

I leaned closer toward him, fighting the thrum of power that hung heavily in the air between us, begging me to close the distance completely.

"Tell me something," I whispered.

His eyebrows furrowed. "What do you wish to hear?"

"Something no one knows."

I saw the conflict flashing across his face. I wanted him to tell me no. To tell me that I should mind my own business. I wanted him to give me a reason to not feel the guilt that crushed my lungs in my chest.

Instead, he spoke to me with a sadness in his voice that would have brought me to my knees, had I not been sitting.

"I'm lonely. I have been for a long time."

"Don't you have friends here?"

He broke his eyes from mine, settling them on the magnolia tree. I could feel his emotions swirling darkly around him. Like a rain cloud. There were layers to him that I had not considered before.

"They look at me differently because I rule this place. They respect me, yes, but they do not see me as a friend. Not really."

I longed to reach out and embrace him. To tell him that I would be his friend, that it didn't matter to me if he was a king or a peasant. But it did matter, didn't it? Because he had exactly what I wanted. I could no sooner be a friend to him than anyone else could. His eyes flicked back to mine.

"Tell me something," he said, echoing my earlier request.

A lump formed in my throat. Telling him anything felt like I would be exposing my soft underbelly for him to later rip open. How could I be vulnerable with my enemy? An enemy who had no idea I was priming myself for war.

"I fear that I've hidden myself away for so long that I do not know what I really want. Or who I really am."

He nodded, a sad understanding on his face. Our eyes ripped from each other and focused on the narcissus. We sat there for a long while, in silence.

I imagined he felt the same as I did to some degree. Unable to force out anything else that was buried deep inside, but dreading going our separate ways to be swallowed by loneliness. The quiet that hung between us was not uncomfortable.

It felt like…home, somehow.

THIRTY-ONE

I stepped into my room, closing the door softly behind me. Sadness and guilt still pulled at me from my earlier conversation with Hades. I was a terrible person.

"You're doing what you must."

But it didn't feel that way.

My eyes fell to my bed, or rather, the large gown laid across it. There was a small box sitting with it, and a note. I strode over and grabbed the letter first.

I picked these out for you to wear to the ball. I hope you like them.

— Aidoneus

My cheeks burned. I folded the letter up and slid it under my pillow, then turned back to the dress and the box. Guilt threatened to engulf me, to tear me into pieces.

I gently opened the box and my eyes widened. It was too much. I did not deserve his kindness. I closed the box and left it on my vanity. I left the dress draped over the bed and stalked to the closet to change into my night clothes.

After I was dressed for sleep I tucked myself under the blanket, curling into a ball. My eyes slid to the black gown.

I should abandon my plans for the crown. I should talk to him.

"He won't understand."

With guilt eating me slowly from the inside, I drifted off to sleep.

THIRTY-TWO

I sat alone at the foot of my bed, staring at the black dress he had gifted me. It was low cut and covered in a delicate overlay of lace. It was the most intricate article of clothing I had ever seen.

It's beautiful.

"Befitting a queen."

I am no queen...

"Yet."

A rapid knock jolted me from my thoughts. I hadn't been expecting anyone to show up so early. It was still a while before guests were set to arrive and the ball to begin.

I slid from my place on the bed and padded over to the door. When I opened it I saw Hecate standing there, donning a bored expression. Her hair was down, hanging in loose inky curls. She had also opted for a black dress. Hers was much more modest than the one lying on my bed, though. The collar touched her jawline, the sleeves reached her wrists, and the hem hung just high enough to see her boots. A silver skeleton key hung from her neck, and a large, black, pointed hat sat atop her head. She looked every part the Goddess of magic and witchcraft that she was.

"Hecate! Please come in."

She flashed me a smile, which faded quickly, then glided into the room. The smell of incense and honey hit me as she passed. I closed the door and turned to find her running her eyes up and down my body. I was still in my night clothes. My hair was a wild mess.

"Were you planning to attend your own ball, or stay cooped up in your room all night?"

I shot her an unamused look. I still hadn't convinced myself to try on the gown. It felt far too extravagant. I was worried I would feel silly wearing it. Like someone playing pretend.

"Hades gave me something, but I'm not sure if I'm going to wear it."

She followed my gaze to the lacey dress strewn across the bed. Her eyes brightened with mischief, and she flashed a wicked grin over her shoulder at me.

"I'd think it rude to decline such a generous gift."

I frowned deeply, examining it. It *would* be rude to attend wearing something else. It would probably offend him.

"Just try it on," she pushed.

I released a deep sigh of defeat. "Very well."

I undressed quickly, tossing my night clothes to the side. She helped me slide the ornate gown over my head. I looked at myself in the looking glass as she smoothed out all of the wrinkles and made sure it was falling perfectly.

It *was* a beautiful dress. The neckline swooped across my chest and hung off of my shoulders. It clung to my waist and fanned out at my hips. There was a high slit that reached the top of my thigh. It was definitely more skin than I was used to showing.

She stepped back, admiring the ensemble. "You look incredible."

My face flushed at her compliment. I turned my attention back to my reflection. The dark material complimented my complexion and made my green eyes appear even more vibrant.

"You don't think it's too much?"

"I think it's perfect." She walked up behind me, running her fingers through my tangled hair. "We'll have to do something about this, though."

A smile tugged up on my lips.

"Have you picked any jewelry to wear?"

I sighed heavily, gesturing to the intricately carved box Hades had left with the dress. She wasted no time scurrying over to open it. She let out a soft gasp as her eyes fell on the set. She looked at me with surprise on her face.

"Kora, this is very nice."

I nodded. It was all nice. I hadn't expected Hades to give me anything. He had filled my closet and vanity full of exquisite things already, things that would have sufficed for the ball and more. The guilt I felt was sickening. He had no idea that I planned to pull the rug from under his feet. I still so desperately wanted to change my mind. But Wrath was right, I had made my decision. I would have to live with it.

"I've never known Hades to be quite so openly generous."

I shrugged. I certainly hadn't known him long enough to agree with her. He had mostly treated me well, despite my outburst when I had first arrived. I imagined everyone just hadn't given him the chance to show that side of himself.

She pulled the necklace and earrings from the box and walked back to me. She handed me the earrings, then gently clasped the thin gold chain around my neck. A single garnet hung from the chain, laying against my chest. I slipped the earrings into my ears. They were small clusters of matching garnets.

I didn't deserve the kindness he was showing me. I wasn't sure how I would live the possible eternity of my life riddled with guilt. All of the sneaking and lying was not how my grandmother had raised me. Somehow I had slipped so far away from who I had been before.

"I think we pull the top section of your hair back and leave the lower down."

I nodded my approval, my mind far away, and she started working. She detangled my curls and braided the sides back, joining them in the middle and twisting the hair into a bun. It took her several tries to get my hair the way she wanted it, and she fussed the whole time. When she was done she stepped back, admiring her work.

"Perfect. Now, let us head down," she said, making her way to leave. "I want to look at everything before everyone shows up and ruins it all."

"Hecate…"

She stopped just before the door and turned back to me. I felt tears sting my eyes. I was starting to feel like I had made a massive mistake. How could I say I would rule the Underworld better than he had? I had no idea what I was doing. I wasn't even sure I belonged below the earth forever. I thought of the sun and the smell of dirt… Things I would never see again if I stayed in this realm.

"Yes, love?"

"I'm having doubts."

I watched the realization sink into her face. She knew exactly what I meant. She stepped back over to me, running her thumb along my cheek. Her brown eyes locked onto mine. There was a fierceness there that I had felt before, but it was long lost to me now. I wished that he had never spoken so softly to me. Had never shared any intimacy with me. I wished he had been cruel, and cold. It would make my choices so much easier. He was nothing like how I had imagined he would be, though.

"Dear child, I cannot imagine the struggle you must have endured over your time here. Your whole life has changed and melted into something new entirely. You have been strong because you are strong. The Fates brought you here for a reason. You must believe that. I do."

I nodded, forcing a tight smile. I didn't believe it though.

A single tear streaked down my cheek and my lip trembled. She reached up and brushed it away. I wanted so badly to trust The Fates the way everyone else seemed to. But I had spent my whole life disregarding fate and tales of Gods and monsters. It should have been easy to see the Gods, to be a God, and to let go of my doubts in fate.

But I couldn't. It still felt like a child's bedtime story. Some fable spun by mortals.

"I worry I'm not ready for any of this. It may all be too big for me."

"You chose this path because you believe that this place can be so much more. If you have changed your mind I understand, but if this is what you want just know that you have people on your side, willing to fight for your vision."

"Is it enough?"

I saw her contemplate my words. I watched her thoughts flicker across her face. There was reservation in her eyes, though she tried to hide it.

My face fell. She was willing to fight for it, yes. They all were. But did that matter if it wasn't enough to win?

"It will have to be."

Then I saw it. That same willingness to die for my cause that I had seen before. She did not believe we would win that war. But she didn't care. She would put her life on the line for me, knowing it would be her end.

How could I lead them, the people most precious to me, to their deaths?

My grandmother would be disappointed in who I had become.

THIRTY-THREE

My heels clicked along the marble floor, echoing across the spacious hall. Hecate hurried down the stairs ahead of me. I had a moment of envy for the boots she wore as I watched her. The shoes on my feet were unlike anything I had ever owned, and the structure of them threw off my balance. It was a hindrance more than anything. Hecate had argued that it would be distasteful to wear the boots with my gown. I wasn't sure that I cared much.

Slowly I made my way down the stairs after the witch. The dining hall was empty, the guests having not yet arrived. Or… mostly empty. My eyes caught on Minthe. She was glaring at me as I descended. A pang of jealousy hit me when I saw her. She was beautiful, as usual. Her long blonde hair was twisted and braided around her head like a crown, showing off her pointed ears. She wore a red dress, and the collar dove deep down her chest, exposing nearly all of her breasts. Her sleeves were sheer and the rest of the dress shimmered like it was crusted with diamonds.

I was plain compared to her.

"She's trying too hard," Wrath sneered.

Be that as it may, she is still beautiful.

I hated her for it. I averted my eyes quickly, turning my attention back to Hecate. I didn't want the Nymph to see my green envy. The witch was looking at Minthe as though she could set her ablaze with her eyes alone. And maybe she could.

"One could only hope."

I fought the urge to grin at Wrath's remark as I stepped down into the dining hall and Hecate turned towards me.

"Come, we should make sure everything is in place."

I nodded, making to follow Hecate into an adjacent room. As we passed Minthe, I heard her snicker. Embarrassment and anger blasted through me. My legs stopped moving against my will as if they were full of lead. I wanted to rip her into pieces. Hecate looked over her shoulder at me and when our eyes met fear flashed across her face.

"Kora…" Her voice was laced with alarm.

I paid her no heed, turning on my heel to face Minthe. She stared back at me, challenging me. How many times would we have to play this game before I snapped?

"Just kill her, already!"

I let Wrath hang in silence. I could feel her frustration building… Or was that my own?

"No one will miss her. She deserves it."

The doors to the throne room swung open, drawing my attention and saving Minthe's life. It was Hypnos. His eyes beamed and his face lit up when he saw me. I returned his smile as he approached, and threw my arms out to embrace him. The thought of Minthe slipped to the back of my mind.

He looked exhausted, dark circles thick under his eyes. I would need to check on the field of poppies. My eyes flicked down to his wardrobe. He had dressed in a nice suit and had tied his hair back. He pulled me away at arm's length and ran his eyes over my dress.

"Kora, you look amazing."

"Speak for yourself. I didn't know you owned such nice clothes!"

His laugh cut through the air as he released me. "I do not. I borrowed these."

I let out a soft laugh which elicited a moan from Minthe. Hypnos and I both turned to look at her. Her eyes were narrowed on us, and she was grinning like a cat.

"You two look *adorable* together. Does Hades know?"

I glared at her, my thoughts of murder resurfacing.

"Does he know *what*, Minthe?" I snapped.

"That the two of you are sneaking around under his nose?"

My heart dropped into my stomach. Panic caused bile to rise to my throat. If she had figured out what I had been planning…

Hypnos scoffed loudly, and I turned to him, trying to smother the anxiety in my face. "You're disgusting Minthe. Just because you don't have friends, doesn't mean other people are incapable of a platonic relationship."

My face burned bright red. Her insinuation had gone over my head completely. I whirled around to her, shooting her a look that could kill. Every time she opened her mouth my disdain for her grew deeper. A small part of me worried she would go to Hades with those accusations. The last thing I needed was for his sour mood to spoil my night.

Hypnos shook his head. "You're delusional, Minthe."

Her grin only spread wider. She definitely planned to cause problems for me. I could feel it radiating off of her.

"Just kill her now. Be done with it."

Yes, I'm sure murder before the ball will ensure Hades stays pleasant.

"It would certainly make for an interesting night."

Thank you, that's very helpful.

I felt Wrath's amusement as she settled within me. Minthe examined her nails, shrugging her shoulders.

"I'm sure I'm not the only one who sees it. Poor Hypnos is smitten with you, half-breed."

I snarled at her, then turned to Hypnos, waiting for him to fire a snide remark back. Shock fell over me instead. His cheeks were flushed and I saw embarrassment on his face. My shoulders drooped. I had missed it somehow, his feelings for me. I had clung to him so hard when I arrived, in desperate need of a friend, and I was blinded by that. His eyes slid up from the floor and met mine.

"Be gone, you dreadful Nymph! We tire of your childish games."

I turned to Hecate who looked mere seconds from snapping Minthe's neck. Minthe, to her credit, must have also seen the expression on Hecate's face. She scurried off like a rat. My eyes drifted back to Hypnos.

"Kora, I would never…" His voice drifted off. "I value our friendship above all else."

My heart fell. Guilt crashed into me again. I did not return his feelings, that much I knew. He was no more than a dear friend to me. Was that the reason he had sided with me when I confided in him?

He must have seen the thought cross my face. He grabbed my hand firmly.

"No…"

"Enough!" Hecate snapped. "We will not speak of this again. We don't need Hades to kill us all before we ever get a chance to make our move."

I ripped my eyes from his and dragged them to Hecate. I pulled my hands from away and let them fall to my sides. Hades didn't seem to like me spending time with the other Gods, but it was surely because he worried they would turn their backs on him. He had made that clear at our first meeting. He had no reason to kill anyone over me having any sort of romantic relationship.

"Or maybe he does. Perhaps we gravely miscalculated?"

No. There's no way that's true.

A booming voice cut through the air, causing my whole body to jump. "Hecate!"

I whipped around to see a large, muscled man standing in the doorway to the throne room. His blond hair hung down to his shoulders and he had a thick beard. His burgundy suit was delicately embroidered with gold, but he had the air of a warlord. His hands and neck were marked with intricate inked art.

Hecate smiled softly at him. "You big brute. What the Hells are you doing here?"

His piercing blue eyes slid to me. I squirmed under his hard gaze, as I watched his smile fade away.

"I heard there was a ball in the Underworld. How could I miss such a monumental moment in history? I had to come see for myself what, or who it seems, has softened the Lord of the Dead's cold heart."

Hecate laughed, placing her hand on my shoulder. My eyes darted between her and the God I did not know, then to Hypnos. He looked slightly perturbed to see whoever the God was. Hecate seemed friendly enough with him, though.

"Kora," Hecate said, pushing me towards him slightly. "This is Ares."

THIRTY-FOUR

Ares. I had not heard his name before. I plastered a tight smile on my face, feeling extremely uncomfortable standing there in front of him. He had a boisterous aura and was by far the most intimidating God I had met.

"Hello." My voice came out cracked and hushed.

Hecate's elbow jabbed into my ribs and she coughed loudly. I scrambled to give a small curtsey, my movements sharp and awkward. He laughed loudly, catching me off guard, and a blush crept across my face. He reached out and took my hand, brushing a soft kiss along the top of it.

"Pleasure to meet you, Kora. I have heard much about you."

I tore my eyes from his to glance at Hecate. She was frowning at him playfully. She moved her attention from him, peering around behind him. I followed her eyes, seeing nothing there.

"Did you bring her?"

He released my hand and smiled at Hecate. I looked at Hypnos nervously, who gave me a slight smile. Suddenly every glance, every interaction, made me feel ill. I felt like I was to blame for how things had gone between us. Perhaps I had led him on in some unintentional way.

"Do you really think I could slip away to something like this without her finding out? She's here. In the drawing room with Hades."

Hecate snatched my hand, pulling me through the throne room. I looked over my shoulder to see Ares and Hypnos following along slowly behind us. They were whispering in hushed voices. I didn't have time to strain my ears before we passed into the drawing room.

Hades sat on the settee, legs crossed and a cup of wine in his hands. He had a bright, carefree smile on his face. Happiness suited him. There was a woman perched on the arm of a chair across from him. She had layers of gold jewelry around her neck, which sat brightly against her mahogany skin. Her hair fell in tight rings around her face, cascading down her shoulders. She wore a pale pink dress, it was tight-fitted and drew attention to her voluminous curves. Her black eyes slid to me and she smiled widely.

"You must be Kora!"

She launched herself from the chair, gliding over to me. Without warning, I was pulled into a tight hug. I gently placed my hands against her back. The smell of her sweet perfume cut through the air. My eyes drifted to Hades, who looked clearly amused by the exchange. She pulled away, looking me up and down.

"You are more beautiful than he mentioned!" She shot him a glare and he averted his eyes. "Where are my manners? I'm Aphrodite. It's so nice to finally meet you, Kora."

"You as well."

Her eyes drifted past me. "Ares, love! Did you meet Kora?"

I turned to see Ares and Hypnos stepping into the room. Ares was looking at Aphrodite like she had hung the moon. I couldn't blame him. She was the most alluring woman I had ever seen. He flashed her a smile and nodded his head, then looked at Hades.

"Hades."

"Ares."

Ares brushed past me and walked up to Hades, who stood and extended his arm. Ares took it and pulled Hades into a partial embrace.

"How are you, uncle?"

My eyebrows shot up, and I shifted my eyes to Aphrodite who just smiled at me. I had known Hades had brothers, but I hadn't considered he might have nieces and nephews.

"I've been well. How are you?"

"Glad to hear it. I've been the same."

Commotion from the throne room drew all of our attention. A dozen or so Nymphs started flowing in, musical instruments in their hands and strung across their backs. Their skin had a faint blue tint, their hair only slightly darker. Their dresses, if you could consider it such, were drapes of sheer cloth wrapped around their bodies. Extravagant gold and gems adorned their necks and wrists.

Behind them followed a group of people I had never seen before. They were shorter, their hair varying shades of brown and blonde. They all had sunkissed skin, some with a splatter of freckles across their faces and arms. Their legs were furred, and their feet were hooved. They had large horns which curved around their heads like a ram.

Aphrodite leaned in and whispered in my ear. "Satyrs."

I turned and gave her a surprised look. I had heard stories of Satyrs as a child but hadn't expected them to be real. Hecate placed her hand on my lower back and I looked at her, awe still plastered on my face.

"I'm going to go get Medusa. You're ok?"

I nodded slowly. She stepped away and vanished in a puff of black smoke. I moved to sit in one of the cushioned chairs. The other Gods settled into seats as well, slipping into mundane conversation. I sat with my hands clasped in my lap. My eyes slide from Hades and Ares to the Nymphs and Satyrs. Cerberus slinked into the room and laid down at my feet. All three of his heads slumped to the floor, then his noses twitched softly as he drifted off to sleep.

"Will Zeus be coming tonight?"

The mention of his name from Ares snapped my attention back to their conversation. I couldn't tell if I was more curious or scared by the idea of Zeus showing up.

"No." Hades' reply was clipped.

"Good. He's been in quite the mood lately, with–" Ares' eyes flicked to me and he cut himself off.

I had nearly forgotten the fit my mother was apparently throwing in the world above us. Unease snaked its way through me as I wondered if she would show up unannounced and cause a scene. Part of me wanted her to, just so I could meet her.

"Yes, well… That's good," Ares continued.

Hades gave him a look of annoyance, clearly displeased with his attempt to recover from his near slip of the tongue. Neither God had any idea that it was fruitless to hold their words back anyway. I already knew. Thanks to Hermes.

Hells. Hermes will no doubt show up tonight.

"This night may prove worthwhile after all."

I shoved my bloodlust down, keeping my face neutral. As soon as the thought swept into my mind Ares' eyes flicked to mine. He raised a brow, an intrigued expression painted on his face. I quickly buried the thought under the musings of my garden, worried he had read my mind. Certainly, someone would have warned me if there was going to be a God present with that sort of ability.

"Kora," Ares said loudly.

My heart dropped like a rock in the ocean. I smiled slightly, hoping that I had been successful in my efforts to conceal my fear.

"Yes, Ares?"

"I'm afraid I haven't had a chance to find out yet; what exactly are the gifts of power that were bestowed to you?" There was something in his voice I could not place. I fought to keep the worry from reaching my eyes.

The confusion that flashed across Hades' face at Ares' question did not slip past me. I had a feeling that Hades had already shared my powers with him. I glanced at Hades, who wore a concerned expression. I assumed then that he left out the part where I could draw the very life out of things. I could play along.

"It's nothing truly special. I can grow flowers and vegetation, that's all."

The tension in Hades' face subsided. I had bet correctly, then.

"And you?"

A knowing smile crept across his face. The sight of it unnerved me, but still, I kept my face unaffected and pleasant. He sat back, crossing his legs.

"I'm the God of war." My mouth suddenly became very dry. "One of my many gifts is sensing the insatiable need for blood."

There it was. He was no mind reader, but I had been caught just the same. I felt the color leave my face and bile worked its way up my throat. I was to be the Goddess of Spring; a quiet, mild-mannered woman. Ares feeling me yearn to rip the life from anything put a damper on that image.

Hades groaned loudly. "For the sake of us all, spare us your war stories."

He had missed that exchange of looks between me and Ares. He'd been unaware of the two of us standing at a crossroads right beside him. I felt the panic threatening to consume me. Ares could ruin every plan I had. I wouldn't be able to do anything about it.

He looked from me to Hades and nausea turned my stomach. I waited for him to tell Hades what he had felt. Instead, he laughed and flew into one of the war stories Hades had asked him not to tell.

I was safe. For the time being.

THIRTY-FIVE

Music bounced off of the walls, echoing through rooms and down halls. The air smelled like food and cakes. And wine. I was several cups into the night. Candles scattered along the stone walls and tables burned brightly, lighting up the manner in a way I had yet to see.

    The Nymphs and Satyrs strummed their stringed instruments and blew into flutes. Ares and Aphrodite danced around the room. They looked at each other with a love I had only ever dreamed of. Hecate had arrived again with Medusa in tow. The snake-haired woman was dressed in a loose, flowing gown. She and Hecate hovered over the table filled with desserts. Hades and Hypnos stood near the fireplace talking. I had made my rounds conversing with everyone before settling into a chair at the table. I was content watching everyone.

    I found my eyes drifting back to Hades often. I was looking for signs of suspicion, or so I kept telling myself. Making sure he was not catching on to me. I scanned the room, looking for Minthe. I hadn't seen her since she confronted me and Hypnos. Her accusation still stung, as did my naivety.

Ares spun Aphrodite around before pulling her close. Hecate held a piece of chocolate up to Medusa to taste. Her snakes were curled up on top of her head, perfectly at ease.

I looked down at Cerberus, who had been following me around from place to place. He was now lying at my feet. He watched the party just as intensely as I did. I smiled at him and all three heads swung up to look at me before flopping to the floor. I sipped my wine, my eyes sliding back to Hades.

He was already looking at me. For a moment I let myself imagine what life might have looked like for us if we had been able to rule the realm together.

Movement caught my eye from across the room. It was Hermes. Anger flared up within me. It burned bright and hot while Wrath writhed around. I stood, my eyes still locked onto his. He saw my expression and his eyebrows knitted together, his head tilted. As if he had no idea what I could possibly be so angry about. As if he had no idea what he had done to me. I took several steps in his direction when a hand grabbed my arm firmly. I whirled around and met Ares. A warning burned there in his eyes.

"Careful, Kora."

The waves of my rage calmed slightly. "I don't know what you're talking about."

"Even without my divine power, I would be able to see the look of slaughter on your face."

My lips pulled into a tight line and I squared my shoulders as I spoke. "I'm just going to speak with Hermes, that's all."

He pulled me closer and spoke in a hushed voice. "Perhaps you could try a smile, Kora."

Our eyes stayed locked onto each other as I pried my arm free from him. I turned without another word, plastering a smile on my face, and marched towards Hermes. He was leaning against a doorway. I could tell by his face he had no idea what he had just walked into. As I approached my eyebrows pulled together and a frown replaced my smile.

"You look like you're having a good time, Kora."

"You're a lying coward," I seethed quietly.

"You need to be a little more specific."

My anger grew hotter. I reached out, my fingers digging into his arm, and drug him away from the party. We slipped into a darkened hallway and I shoved him against the wall, a snarl on my face. He arched his brow, smiling coyly at me.

"If you wanted to get me alone, all you had to do was ask."

"I know you were erasing my memories!"

Silence. Silence filled the space between us. Silence whirred in my ears. His face became serious. He leaned his head back against the wall. I stared at him, Wrath raging inside me. She begged me to rip his throat out. Begged me to end his life right in the hall. My eyes dropped to his neck.

"You might want to give me a chance to speak before you go ripping me to shreds."

My eyes flicked up to his. "Go on, then."

"Your mother enlisted me to lock your memories away. She didn't want you to know who you were. Didn't want you to end up," he gestured around us, "exactly where you are now."

"And why is that a good enough reason for me not to kill you right where you stand?"

His head tilted to the side. "We had a deal, Kora."

"That was before I knew you were sneaking around behind my back."

"That was before I knew you."

I scoffed, rolling my eyes.

"You know I'm right. And," he grabbed my arm gently, "I can give you back all of those lost memories. Every single one of them. I'm the only one who can give them back to you."

I froze. All my anger rolled away and Wrath stilled. I considered it for a moment, forgiving him and moving forward just to get my memories. Would it be worth trusting him again?

"I will give you one more chance, Hermes. You burn me again and I will have your head on a spike."

I turned on my heel to go back to the party and he grabbed me again. I turned to him and he spoke to me softly.

"Do you want them now?"

I was frozen in place. There was that silence again. It was thick and filled with promises. I had a chance to recover everything I had lost. I wondered what could have been taken from me. He stood there quietly, allowing me the time to consider whether I was ready. I pulled away from him, averting my eyes.

"No. Not yet." I wasn't.

"Very well, Kora. You let me know when and I will be there."

Footsteps echoed towards the hall we had slipped into. We both looked up as Hypnos approached. His eyes slid from Hermes to me. Concern laced his brown eyes as they fell to mine. He shot a warning toward the red-haired God before turning back to me.

"Are you ok, Kora?"

I nodded slowly. "I'm fine. Hermes was just going to enjoy the party."

Hermes took the hint and slipped past us, flashing Hypnos a bright smile as he left. I watched him duck around the corner toward the music. When I turned my attention back to Hypnos he was staring at me, hurt shining in his eyes.

"Kora, I'm sorry…" I took a step towards him and his voice trailed off.

"You don't have to apologize, Hypnos. It's nothing."

"I don't want to ruin our friendship."

"It won't. It didn't." I placed my hand on his arm, smiling up at him faintly.

A harsh laugh cut through the silence. We turned to see Minthe, slinking towards us. She had a vicious smile on her face.

"If it isn't the love birds again."

I felt Hypnos stiffen under my hand. Minthe was quickly burning through every drop of patience I had. Wrath pushed against me, fighting to take control. She was eager to quench her thirst for blood and Minthe was the perfect victim.

"Minthe, I vaguely remember a conversation you and I had recently. If I recall correctly it involved your blood covering my hands."

She scowled at me before continuing on to the ball. My eyes followed her until she disappeared around the corner. I looked at Hypnos again. He had a wary look in his eyes. I shrugged nonchalantly.

"Be careful with her," he warned. "She's trouble."

"So am I."

We held each other's stare, his face full of worry, mine full of anger. I wondered if he would still feel the same about me if he knew how badly my hands itched to take her life. I doubted it. I brushed the thought aside. I had been gone far too long from the party and Hades no doubt had noticed my absence.

"We should get back," I mumbled as I stepped past Hypnos.

"Try to enjoy yourself tonight. We can worry about the future tomorrow."

I turned back towards him. He was right. I had been looking forward to a night of ease, free from worry and lies. I smiled, turning away from him again. As my heels clicked along the marble floor I called to him over my shoulder.

"You should do the same."

THIRTY-SIX

I stepped into the dining hall and my eyes slid around the room. The music had grown louder and more full of life. Everyone had gathered closely, and a God I did not know stood there with them. He was not quite as tall as the other Gods and his face and mannerisms made him seem much younger. He wore a white button-down, slightly open at the top, and brown trousers. Chestnut curls sat messily atop his head. Everyone burst out in laughter at something I could not hear.

I approached slowly, feeling like I was imposing myself on the conversation. His big, brown eyes lifted to mine as he sipped from a cup of wine, and then they widened.

"Kora!" My eyebrows shot up as I forced an uncomfortable smile. "The woman I've been dying to meet."

The crowd of Gods parted for him. He walked up to me and swept himself into a dramatic bow. My forced smile became genuine. I glanced at Hades who shot me an apologetic look.

"Where are my manners?" The young looking God grabbed me and pulled me into a hug. "So pleased to meet you!"

"The pleasure is mine," I replied, patting his back.

Hades placed a hand on the God's shoulder and he released me.

"Kora," The God of the Dead interjected. "This is my nephew, Dionysus."

"Bastard nephew," Dionysus corrected with a wink. "My father gets around."

A blush crept across my face and I laughed softly. Every God that Hades had invited to the ball had been so openly kind and welcoming. It was more than I could have hoped for.

"Hells below, Dionysus. Don't call him father." Ares looked more than annoyed.

Hades leaned in, mumbling softly to me, as Ares and Dionysus flew into a playful argument.

"They're half brothers."

"I never would have guessed," I teased. I saw a sparkle in his eyes as the joke left my lips.

"Drink! Tonight is quite the night to celebrate. My uncle never hosts anything fun. We're lucky if he shows up to Olympus long enough to attend the council."

Dionysus shoved a cup of wine in my hand. I was fairly certain it was his own cup, but I lifted it to my lips nonetheless. My eyes darted to Hermes. He looked unbothered by the earlier conversation and was speaking in a light-hearted manner to Aphrodite. I turned in time to see Hypnos coming back into the room. He approached Hecate and Medusa. My eyes swept to Ares who was still in an argument with his half-brother. Then they fell on Hades, who had drifted away. He was talking to Minthe.

I watched as she laid her hand on his arm. He shrugged her off, not bothering to hide his blatant annoyance. It would be a lie to say I didn't feel slightly satisfied to see him recoil from her touch. I told myself it wasn't jealousy. I told myself it was just my hatred for the Nymph. I told myself it would have been different if it was anyone else.

"Would it?"

Of course. I have no reason to feel jealous.

"Yet you do. Don't forget, Kora; I feel everything you feel. I can sense the lust burning inside of you."

I didn't bother to respond to her. There was no point, I knew that she just liked to goad me.

"I speak the truth and you know it."

My eyes slid back to Hades. Minthe was talking to him still, but his red eyes were not on her. They were on me. It was not the Nymph who held his attention. It was me. I watched as he raked his eyes down my body. My cheeks burned red. I had just decided to interrupt them when Dionysus called my name. I whirled around to face him as he sauntered up to me and extended his arm.

"May I have a dance?"

I quickly abandoned my idea and took his hand. It would lead to nothing good to intrude on their conversation anyway. I let the God and the music suck me in. He led me out to the clearing in the middle of the room and pulled me close. I tried desperately to follow along to his dance but stumbled. My face flushed and I bit the inside of my cheek. My eyes darted around to see if anyone had noticed my misstep. I had never been taught how to properly dance before. Ares and Aphrodite had made it look incredibly easy when I had watched them earlier in the night.

"Can I confess something to you, Kora?"

I furrowed my brows and nodded. "Of course."

"I was shocked when Ares told me that our uncle had brought a Goddess to the Underworld. Even more shocked to learn it was the daughter of Demeter. I assume by now you've heard about the prophecy from The Fates?"

"I know of it, yes."

"We all thought Demeter had hidden you away for good. We never thought he would actually find you. I look forward to the wedding, though! How would you feel about me calling you auntie?"

My mind screeched to a halt. I could no longer hear the music, or the words coming out of his moving mouth. My pounding heart drowned everything else out. I blinked, trying to process what he had said to me.

"What?" My voice was barely audible.

"I said you should wear black to the wedding. It makes your eyes pop."

"No… Before that."

He must have seen the shock on my face. He stopped dancing and his hands dropped to his side.

"You said you knew!" he whispered.

"I knew there was a prophecy that foretold my coming here. I assumed that meant as an underling!"

He groaned quietly. "Oh, I'm going to be in so much trouble."

My mind was reeling. Hades, no doubt, knew the details of the prophecy and he had kept it from me. Oh, the strife he could have saved us both if only he had been honest. A pang of betrayal hit me as I wondered if anyone else knew. I felt like a fool.

My stomach dropped. My scheming would cause an even greater mess than I thought. I would have to call everything off. Strike a new deal with The Furies. Or somehow manage to convince Hades that they could be trusted loose in the Underworld. Did I really want that, though? To tie myself to him for all eternity? My head was full of conflict.

Later, I would deal with it later.

"Just forget that you said anything, Dionysus. I'll not say a word."

He sighed heavily in relief. "Oh, thank you!"

"Excuse me?"

I turned to see Ares standing beside me. His eyes burned into mine. He had shed his embroidered jacket and unbuttoned his shirt nearly halfway. His breath smelled of whiskey.

"Get lost, Dionysus. My turn."

His half-brother bowed lowly to me and then hurried off to jump into conversation with Hermes and Aphrodite. I watched as he left and then my eyes slid back to Ares. He was looking at me like he could see straight into my mind again.

I held my hand out to him and he took it and swept me into a dance. It was easier to follow his movements than it had been with Dionysus. He danced slower and led me along with more expertise. Or perhaps I was just too distracted by the impending chaos from my newfound knowledge to notice my mistakes.

"Tell me, Kora. Why do you feel such anger when you look at the River Nymph?"

I hated that he could feel my emotions. It made me feel exposed. Naked. There was no point in lying to him about it, he would know. I glanced at Minthe, who was still trying her best to hold a conversation with Hades. My anger bubbled again.

"I just hate her."

"Why?"

My eyes flicked up to his. I didn't like the way he was pushing me. I tried to pull my hands free from his and he brought me in closer, sweeping me across the floor again. He kept his attention on only me. I would not get away without giving him an answer.

"She's snide."

"You're jealous."

"I'm not jealous!"

He smiled down at me. "Better keep your voice down or he will hear."

I glanced over my shoulder to Hades, who was now watching us dance. Minthe had slinked off somewhere else. I turned my eyes back to Ares, tightening my grip on his arms.

"I'm not jealous," I repeated quietly.

"You can say that as many times as you want, Kora, but you are. I have felt many people's jealousy turn to anger. I know it when I see it."

I opened my mouth to argue with him, but I was cut off by the door bursting open. Everyone froze, the music stopped, and all of the laughter died out. A Goddess stepped into the room, gliding across the floor in a fluid motion. Her eyes burned with a vengeance that sent my skin crawling.

I had no idea who she was, and judging by the way the party halted completely, I wasn't sure I wanted to.

THIRTY-SEVEN

Everyone stood silently and unmoving. All eyes were on the Goddess as she swept into the room. Darkness radiated off of her. Several candles snuffed out as she passed them. Her long, dark red hair billowed behind her. Black ink lined her upper lids. She wore a skin-tight dress, it was as black as a crow. No jewelry adorned her neck or wrists. She was both beautiful and terrifying.

Her eyes slid around the room, locking onto each and every one of us. I tore my gaze away from her quickly, glancing around to see everyone else's reactions.

"Don't halt the festivities on my account." Her voice sliced through the air, her words as sharp as a knife.

Slowly everyone resumed their conversations and activities, though tension was still thick. Ares released me abruptly and stalked off to stand with Aphrodite. I watched him put his arm around her protectively and she sunk into his touch. Her presence alone had caused everyone to be on edge.

Hecate slipped up behind me, startling me, and whispered hurriedly in my ear. "That is Eris, Goddess of Discord and Strife. Steer clear of her if possible. If you cannot avoid it, speak clearly and offer only what you must."

No sooner had she uttered her warning and the Goddess of Discord's eyes met mine. I shifted where I stood, trying not to allow my nerves to show. Eris marched over to me, burning a hole in me with her blue eyes.

As she approached Hecate retreated. She stood far enough away to give Eris a moment of privacy with me, but close enough that she could assist me if things went awry. I realized when she was standing face to face with me that she was no taller than I was. Still, she had an intimidating aura to her.

"You must be—"

Hades was on us in an instant, cutting into the conversation. "Eris. How lovely of you to grace us with an appearance tonight."

She narrowed her eyes at him. "Hades. You can imagine my surprise when I learned of your soiree and I wasn't invited."

There was no warmth in his eyes as he smiled at her. My eyes darted between them. They looked as though they might rip each other to shreds. My instincts screamed for me to flee, to run as fast as I could and not look back. But Wrath… Wrath kept my feet planted where I stood.

"My apologies," Hades said coldly. "Allow me to take you to get some refreshments."

She held up her hand, her black nails filed to a sharp point. She must have sensed him trying to steer her away from me just as clearly as I had. He was not good with subtleties. Her face was flat, anger lacing through her bright blue eyes like ice.

"No need. I was just introducing myself to our new addition here in the Underworld."

Hades clenched his jaw but made no move to insist. His red eyes flicked to me, a clear warning hanging there. I tried not to linger on him too long so as to not draw attention to it. She seemed on edge enough already. I turned back to her, steeling myself.

"I'm Kora. Nice to meet you."

"Kora…" She spoke my name like she was testing it on her tongue. "You're the daughter of Demeter, are you not?"

"Estranged, I suppose."

I cursed myself in my mind. Hecate had warned me not to say too much.

A simple 'yes' would have sufficed, I thought.

"I like her."

Of course, you do.

"I see. There are mumblings that you have been graced with very *interesting* powers by The Fates. I would love to speak privately. I want to hear all about it."

My stomach lurched and I fought the urge to be sick. I forced a tight smile, trying to appear as polite as possible.

"I'm not sure I would consider my green thumb to be particularly interesting."

Her lips pulled back into a smile, exposing a set of sharp canine teeth. She leaned into me, speaking in a nearly inaudible whisper. The hair on my arms stood on end.

"Come now, Goddess. Let us not play games. You are both life and death incarnate. I have waited countless years for someone like you to be born. And here you are, being served to me on a silver platter."

I pulled back to look at her. Her face was relaxed, her smile had turned soft. But her eyes… They had an eagerness that made me feel sick. I was a pawn in a game I didn't know I was playing.

Hades cleared his throat. "If you'll excuse us, I must steal Kora away."

Eris cut her eyes at him and grinned wickedly. The sight of it made bile rise to my throat.

"Making a habit of that, aren't you?"

Anger flared in his eyes as she fired her insult. I feared he might blast her with the dark flames he wielded. I could feel Wrath waiting in anticipation. She wanted the fight. I just wanted to know what Eris had planned.

He ignored her, grabbing my arm and leading me away without another word. I could feel her eyes on my back as I followed him from the party.

He pulled me along to a small sitting room away from everyone and closed the door. The music was faint in the background. He let go of my arm and stood with his back to me. I glanced around the room, not wanting to push him to speak if he was not ready. My eyes caught on lavish paintings that hung on the walls. Several lit candles burned enough light to see.

When he turned to look at me his face was lined with stress. I held his stare and anxiety built inside me. I wasn't sure if I was ready for whatever conversation was coming my way.

"I just wanted to tell you to be careful with Eris. She's unpredictable."

I grinned slightly, and the fear of confrontation ebbed away. "Well, you weren't exactly subtle out there. I'm sure she can surmise why you drug me away."

His eyes dropped to the floor before sliding back up to mine. There was something else. I could see it in his face. Perhaps Minthe had brought the issue with Hypnos to his attention. If he did indeed know the details of the prophecy then he would certainly not be pleased with that. I wasn't sure if I was more angry or embarrassed that I was walking around ignorant of the reason he brought me to the Underworld, while everyone else tiptoed around me. Surely they all knew.

"What else?"

He stood quietly, our eyes still locked. The longer he made me wait, the sicker I felt. The night was still young. I didn't want a fight between us to end it early.

"Aidoneus?"

His face softened as he heard his name on my tongue. I felt awful for using it. I knew I only did it to subdue his impending anger. It was manipulative and cruel. Two things I was seeing in myself more frequently.

"Yes. There is something else."

I noted the change in his tone, the way his lids became heavy. His eyes trailed down my body causing my face to heat and my heart to beat wildly.

"I didn't get a chance to tell you earlier; you look beautiful."

I glanced away. I couldn't look at him any longer. The hunger I saw in his eyes made my body ache. I wondered if the insatiable pull to him was a direct result of The Fates meddling. I hated feeling like I held no control. Not over my life, or my body. It was all the work of The Fates.

"Thank you."

"I hoped you would like the dress and jewelry I picked out."

I smiled at him and nodded. "It's all lovely. I appreciate it very much."

He stepped up to me and I craned my head back to look at him. I felt the blush creep up my neck and into my face. My breath hitched as he reached up to run his hand across my freckled cheek. His fingers were cool against my skin, sending a chill down my spine. Images from my dream flashed through my mind, making my legs weak. The seconds ticked away as we stayed there, eyes locked, his hand on my face.

My eyes dropped to his lips and my hands balled into fists at my sides. I was angry. I was angry for his lies, for the knowledge he kept hidden from me. I was angry at myself for doing the same to him. The game we had been playing in secret would cause us both to get hurt.

His fingers trailed down my neck and I sucked in a shallow breath, my eyes fluttering closed. I fought against the urge to grab him and kiss him.

When I opened my eyes again he was breathing rapidly, still staring at me intensely. I needed to get away. To tell him we should go back to the party. I needed to leave the room. I reached up to push him away, but my hands betrayed me. Instead, my fingers tightened around his arms.

"Please," I begged.

"Please?" he mused as he leaned in closer. "What do you want, Goddess?"

My words caught in my throat. *Please leave me alone*, I thought. But that wasn't what I wanted at all, was it? I wanted his lips on mine. I wanted his hands all over me. I wanted to know what he tasted like.

He cupped my face in both of his hands and brought his lips to mine softly. The touch sent lightning through my entire body. I would have sworn I heard it crackle and spark across my skin.

When he pulled away, and our eyes met again, the lightning turned into crashing waves. It was my power coursing through my veins, trying to find release somewhere. I felt his own power thrum against me in return. It was dark and calm compared to the urgency in my own. He ran one of his hands through my curls and laid the other flat against my back, pulling me closer.

    Instinctively my hands flew to the back of his head and our lips crashed together again.

THIRTY-EIGHT

The music of the party beyond us melted away and took with it all of my worries. The feeling of his skin against mine and the taste of whiskey on his tongue inundated all of my senses. My mind was a blur when he pulled away, trailing kisses down my neck.

    I huffed several ragged breaths, one hand tangling in his hair, the other gripping his arm tightly. He nipped my skin and a soft moan escaped my parted lips. My body burned like I was made of molten fire. My power rippled and pulsed against his, ark tendrils swirled around us like smoke.

    His hand moved from my back, sliding through the slit in my dress. He gripped my thigh, pulling my leg up to his hip. His fingers bit against my skin, making me gasp. He raised his lips back up to mine and I opened my mouth for his tongue. I ground myself against his hip, my body trembling from the friction. His hand slid further up my leg, cupping my ass roughly. He pushed me against his hip again as he took my bottom lip in his teeth.

    Our eyes locked and he froze inches from my face. Our ragged breathing mingled between us. I could see the panic in his eyes. Like he had crossed a line he hadn't meant to. My mind was unraveled, though, and all I could think about was the ache building between my legs. I didn't care about the consequences. I just wanted him to touch me, to kiss me again.

"I'm sorry," he mumbled.

Gently he released my leg, but he kept his other hand on my back. I might have fallen over had he not. My legs were still trembling and my body was weak. My fingers slid down his arm.

He kept his red eyes locked onto me as he spoke. "We should get back to the party."

I didn't want that. I didn't want that at all. I wanted time to stay frozen for us in that room, to avoid all of the mistakes we had both made. He made no move to leave, despite his words.

"I don't want to," I forced out softly.

I could see relief wash over him and his face relaxed. He took my face into his hands again and brushed a faint kiss against my lips. My hand slid down to his and guided him back to the slit in my dress. With our eyes never breaking away from each other he hoisted me up against his hip again. I ground myself against him, throwing my head back. He picked me up and I wrapped my legs around him. He carried me over to a long, cushioned seat and laid me down. I stared up at him as he hovered over me.

His eyes raked down my body and he slid his hand down my leg to remove my heeled shoe, then the other. His fingers ran back up my legs until they reached the top of my undergarments. He slowly pulled them off, never breaking his eyes from mine. He tossed them aside then leaned down to kiss me again. My whole body was shaking in anticipation. I had never wanted anything so badly in my life.

He moved to undo his trousers and I grabbed his hand. "Not yet…"

He smiled, then kissed my neck. I moaned softly, my hands roving over his back and arms. He moved from the cushioned seat, pulling me up with him, then swung my legs over the edge and knelt in front of me. His eyes flicked to mine as he gently opened my legs. I bit my lower lip and slid myself closer to the edge. He trailed soft kisses up the inside of my thighs. My hands lifted to my breasts, grabbing handfuls. His mouth found my core and I moaned loudly, the aching becoming too much to bear.

"Is this what you dreamed of?" His voice was husky and low.

There was no space in my mind for embarrassment as his tongue swirled around my bundle of nerves. I nodded feverishly, unable to speak. He slipped a finger deep inside me, then two. I cried out, unable to keep my voice quiet. He moaned against me, the vibration causing my legs to tremble. When he pulled his fingers out, my eyes flew open. My jaw dropped as he lifted his fingers to his lips and licked them clean.

He stood, pulling my shaking body up out of the seat. I helped him lift the dress over my head and it fell on the floor in a heap. I grabbed his face, bringing his lips back to mine. The taste of myself mixed with whiskey was enough to drive me crazy.

He broke away from me and laid down on the cushion. His hand took mine and he tugged me towards him. He guided my body to straddle his face and brought my hips down. I tossed my head back, another moan escaping my lips as he licked and sucked.

My body shook and my power crashed through me again. I could feel the earth rumbling beneath us, but I did not care. I ground myself against his mouth, riding his face. I gripped the arm of the seat as I felt myself draw near a climax. He undid his trousers and I glanced over my shoulder to see him pull his length out and start stroking it. My breath quickened and my walls fluttered. I rocked my hips faster.

His hands pushed against my hips, pulling me free from his face. I gasped loudly, my climax falling away. He smiled up at me, teasingly, and I frowned down at him. He turned my body around and then brought my core back down to his mouth. I looked down and saw how hard he was, a bead of cum formed at the tip. Slowly, I brought my face down and licked up the length of his cock, before taking the head into my mouth. He groaned against me and softly bucked his hips up. I sucked gently and then slid my mouth down farther, grinding myself against his face at the same time.

I bobbed my mouth up and down, finding a rhythm quickly. It wasn't long before we were both grinding into each other, moaning loudly. The ground shook again and his black smoke circulated around us. I felt my climax returning, and my movements became more frantic. It crashed over me like waves and I cried out loudly.

Nothing else around me existed anymore. It was only the two of us.

As my cries of pleasure and pulsing walls died down, he moved me from his face and turned my body back around again. He brought my dripping core towards his cock, not even bothering to remove his trousers or shirt. I lowered myself down, taking the tip in. I moaned softly as I slid further down his length, trying to adjust to his size. His fingers were digging into my hips as I started rocking against him.

He brought my lips to his and kissed me deeply. My walls clenched around him and he bucked upwards. I cried out against his mouth. He trailed his lips down my neck and chest to my breasts. He sucked my nipple in his mouth and cupped my ass in his hands, guiding my body up and down his cock. I whimpered as our bodies moved, feeling another wave preparing to crash over me.

We both cried out, reaching the edge at the same time. I felt his warm seed spilling inside me as he slammed himself into me one more time. I sat on top of him, breathing heavily. We locked eyes, both coming down from our highs. He pushed himself up, making sure to keep us locked together.

He looked down at the floor around us and smiled. I followed his eyes and saw the floor was cracked and split open. Dozens of paperwhite narcissus had sprung up and bloomed. He slid his attention back to me.

"Kora…"

My lips found his, cutting him off. I didn't want to hear whatever he had to say. I didn't want anything to spoil the complete ecstasy I was feeling. He ran his fingers through my hair and down my back. When I pulled away from him and our eyes met again, I realized exactly why I hated Minthe so much. Why everything she did and said angered me. Why Hades was enraged anytime he saw me with Hermes or Hypnos.

I slid off his lap, gathering up my dress. He stood after me, fixing his trousers and tucking his shirt back in. After I pulled the dress over my head I glanced around the flowered floor, trying to find my undergarments. Hades touched my arm lightly, and when I turned he had them in his other hand.

I reached for them and he pulled them away from me.

"I'll do it."

He knelt down in front of me and slid them up my legs. The sight of him on his knees in front of me had my heart hammering in my chest, it had my skin on fire once more. It also had guilt gnawing away at me from the inside.

After he had them in place, he stood up and our eyes met. He ran his thumb down my cheek. My stomach turned. That feeling crushed my chest and scared me to death. We had both made grave mistakes since I had been snatched from the upper world. We were walking a dangerous line, it felt like the edge of a knife at my foot. One wrong move and I would slip and end up hurt. We both would.

I had no idea how I was going to fix what I had done.

He leaned in and I let him brush his lips against mine. I closed my eyes, trying to forget everything but that moment. I would worry about everything else later.

Hades spoke softly, pulling me out of my worried mind. "I quite like the flowers here."

A smile spread across my face. "Perhaps I can redecorate the rest of the castle."

There was a gleam in his eyes that nearly brought me to tears. His smile was light and carefree. He looked happy.

He kissed my cheek and whispered quietly, "I would love that."

I took his outstretched hand, intertwining our fingers, and let him lead me back out to the party.

My mind was full of conflict and sorrow for what we could have been– if only we had been open with one another.

THIRTY-NINE

Music filled my ears and laughter brought the room to life. There were smiles on nearly every face there. I glanced up at Hades and he smiled down at me in turn. It was a soft smile. It was intimate. He was all I could smell, all I could taste. My body ached for more as our eyes met.

As much as I wanted to enjoy the feeling and the moment, my heart was still heavy with the secrets we both clutched to. Dread crept around inside of me at the thought of it all coming crashing down on us.

"Are you okay?" His voice was low, and full of concern.

I didn't want there to be things hidden between us. I wanted to tell him everything. But try as I might, I couldn't force the words out. Instead, I shot him a smile.

"Everything is great."

"Very well," he said as he brushed his thumb across the top of my hand.

My eyes drifted towards the party. To my friends, some old, some new. To my future. To the life I had been so scared to accept but was now ready to embrace entirely. It would be mine for as long as I lived.

So long as I mended the rift Hades had no idea was between us. I did not know him well, but there would be time for that. He was kind and opened his home and his life to me.

"Because The Fates made it so."

Wrath voiced my own thoughts; the fear that had been circling around inside of me. I worried he would grow tired of me. And there was Minthe. She would no doubt continue to try and upheave my life. I could not understand how he had let her live with him as long as he had.

"Do you want to dance?"

His question pulled me from my thoughts, drawing my attention back to him. Our eyes met and my heart fluttered. A smile spread across my face before I even realized it was happening.

"Yes," I whispered.

He pulled me out to the middle of the room, his touch gentle but firm. I glanced around as he swept me across the floor. Everyone had quieted their conversations and their undivided attention had settled on us. My skin started to crawl and my movements became hesitant. Their eyes were locked on us as we danced. I tried to follow his steps but found myself stumbling over him. It caused more embarrassment to flood me.

He leaned in slightly and spoke to me in a hushed voice. "You do not need to be nervous."

It was like he had read my thoughts. It must have been written on my face. I bit my lip and fought against the urge to slide my gaze across everyone who stood watching us. Instead, I kept myself focused on him, the way his red eyes bore into me caused my skin to warm.

"They're all staring."

"They stare because you look so utterly breathtaking, Kora."

My name on his tongue sent a shiver down my spine. My power pulsed against my will and I felt his own hum in response. It was as if our powers were intertwined, connected somehow. The work of The Fates, I assumed. They were rotten meddlers, sticking their fingers in the lives of others. I wanted to hate it.

But with his cool hands against mine and his eyes locked onto me, I could find no hate or contempt in my heart.

The song slowed to a stop and Hades lowered himself into a bow. Aphrodite approached us with a bright smile on her face. Her eyes gleamed in the candlelight. My own eyes drifted beyond her to Ares, who was in the middle of what seemed to be a heated discussion with Eris.

"They've never quite gotten along," she mused, pulling my attention back to her. "Perhaps a buffer, Hades?"

He opened his mouth as though he meant to decline her push for him to leave us. Aphrodite arched her brow at him and he shot me an apologetic look before excusing himself and marching off towards them. I watched him leave and then turned to her. She was smiling at me slyly.

"Is something wrong?"

"You," she said, leaning into me closely, "smell quite like Hades right now. Where did the two of you slip off to earlier?"

I could not conceal the heat in my face. "I..."

"You smell like sex," she continued. "Like lust. And love."

My entire body was set ablaze at her brash observation. I stumbled over myself, trying to get anything to come out. She laughed brightly and patted my shoulder.

"There is no shame in it, Kora. Embrace it. I can tell just as plainly that he loves you, too."

"Love is a strong word. I fear you are mistaken, Aphrodite. I cannot say that I have ever been in love before."

She pinned me with her eyes and hummed softly. "As you say, Kora."

Anxiety and guilt ripped through me violently. "It was very nice to speak with you. If you'll excuse me."

I turned on my heel and scurried away from her to the door. To outside. My chest burned with every inhale. My head was spinning. Air. I needed air. My vision started to blur and my breathing turned ragged. The music seemed to grow louder with every second and my head began pounding. I couldn't breathe.

I pushed the large door open and stepped outside. Frantically, I craned my head up, gulping in several large breaths to try and calm myself. The blanket of gray above me drew me out of my panic and settled me quickly. There was still a part of me that missed nights in the upper world. All of the stars and the moon. Still, the ashen sky had grown on me.

I heard the door open and close behind me and I turned to see who had followed me out. It was Eris. My stomach turned at the sight of her. Her predatory gaze made my anxiety bloom again. The Goddess of Discord.

"Kora." She said it politely, but there was still an edge to her voice.

"Hello, Eris."

We held each other's stares briefly, then she turned away. Her face was lined with tension. She stepped past me and stopped, looking up as I had been earlier. I knew I should heed Hecate's warning, but curiosity had always been my downfall.

"Something troubles you?" I asked.

Her sharp eyes slid back to me. "No. All is well."

I didn't believe her, I could taste her lie. It was not my place to pry, though. My mind drifted back to when she had first arrived. I stepped up beside her slowly.

"What did you mean? When you said you had been waiting for someone like me to be born?"

A smile crept across her face and I caught a flash of her pointed canine teeth.

"Someone with your potential, your powers. You are strong, Kora. Do you know what my domain is?"

I paused. "Discord."

"Yes, and strife. And you," she turned to face me head-on. "You will bring forth so much strife. It will be beautiful."

My heart dropped. Silence hung between us and another smile spread across her face. I stood frozen, lost in her words. Perhaps that was the reason The Fates had sent me below. To keep me from whatever Eris had foreseen that I could unleash.

"Goodnight, Kora. Until we meet again."

She vanished, leaving behind a scent that was distinctly burning wood and eucalyptus. And a nauseating dread that coiled in my stomach. My mind was reeling. My power of death and decay... I could not allow myself to use it in the way she so clearly believed that I would.

The door opened and closed again. I could not bring myself to look at whoever it was, I just wanted a few seconds of quiet and peace.

"Kora?"

It was Hypnos. I closed my eyes, fighting back tears. *Leave*, I thought. *Just go back inside.* His footsteps crunched softly as he approached.

"Are you well?"

I turned, finally, to face him. I could not begin to explain to him the tear I felt in my heart. Or the conflict raging in my head. I refused to allow The Fates, or anyone's desires for my power, to rule over my life.

"Fine." My voice was strained and I knew I was not hiding my emotions well.

He hesitated, considering whether to push the matter, then he averted his eyes. Tears rolled down my cheeks. I had been through more in the last couple of months than I had my whole life.

Without another word he stepped closer to me, resting his shoulder against mine. It was a simple gesture, but one that I needed. I leaned into him, keeping my chin high, and I wept. Silently and restrained, but I allowed myself to feel everything. Just for a moment.

I collected myself and wiped the tears from my face. "Thank you."

"Whatever you need, Kora. You have been there for me and I will be for you. Always."

I turned to him and smiled sadly. He stared at me, then raised his hand to brush his thumb across my cheek. He nodded once and looked back to the manor.

"We should get back."

So we turned and headed towards the party. When we stepped inside music echoed off the walls and filled the space. Gods still danced and laughed as the Nymphs and Satyrs drank and played their instruments. I felt better, more clear. It would all work out. I would end my schemes for the throne the next day, then everything would be fine.

Dionysus caught me by the arm, shoving a drink in my hand. "Drink, Kora! It is a good night!"

His voice was slurred and merry. My eyes shot to Hypnos, who stalked off towards Hecate, then drifted to Hades, who smiled widely at me. I disregarded the guilt that tried to eat away at me.

Later. I would deal with it later.

I tipped the cup back, the liquid warmed my throat and stomach. Just as I swallowed the last drop Dionysus was handing me another. Before I knew it my mind and body were fuzzy from the alcohol. I danced with every God there and even pulled several Satyrs and Nymphs onto the floor.

I allowed myself to forget all of my worries, even if it was just for one night.

FORTY

When I woke I was still drunk on wine and chocolate, a dull throbbing in my head. The night before came flooding back to me in a jumbled mess. All of the party guests, my conversations with Hypnos and Hermes. Meeting Eris. My time with Hades…

I rubbed my eyes and groaned. I never should have allowed that to happen. Within one night I successfully destroyed my entire plan for the Underworld. If only I had been privy to the entirety of the prophecy. I needed to find Hecate, to tell her the whole plan was off.

"Will you be satisfied sharing the throne?"

I would have to get her to speak with Hypnos and Hermes. I couldn't have them doing anything that would allow Hades to find out what I had been planning. And I didn't have time to visit them all myself.

"What if he doesn't give you any say in ruling?"

I continued ignoring Wrath's incessant commentary and drug myself out of bed. The room spun slightly around me. I had drunk far too much. I needed to figure out what to do about The Furies.

I bathed quickly and threw on a comfortable shirt and breeches. Between my throbbing head and Wrath's voice, I struggled to concentrate. I didn't bother brushing my hair, I tied it back and slipped from my room.

My footsteps were loud through the corridors and rooms as I trudged onward to leave the castle. Everything was spotless, which shocked me. After the party, I assumed the entire place would be wrecked. I didn't run into anyone on my way out. Everything was quiet.

Once outside I steadied myself, fighting off the nausea and headache from the wine. Hecate had told me to warn her before I used my power to jump from place to place, but I didn't have time to walk to her. I needed to get to her quickly. I hoped she would be able to advise me on what to do. As I reached for my power it grew and blasted through my body with a force I was not expecting. In a flash, I was standing in her kitchen.

I looked around quickly, my heart racing. I had actually done it. Her dogs leapt to their feet, growling at my sudden appearance. I watched as their faces relaxed and hackles laid back down once they realized who I was.

My eyes searched the space but Hecate was not in the kitchen. I ran frantically through the hut looking for her, but she was not anywhere inside. I stepped outside and still did not see her.

"I don't have time for this," I muttered. "Hecate! Hecate I need you! Where are you?!"

My scream echoed around me. Within seconds I felt her power drifting through the air. She appeared in a plume of black and purple smoke. Her hair was pulled back into a single, sloppy braid and her dress looked as though it had been slept in. She looked exhausted.

"Hells, Kora! What has happened for you to cause such an awful racket?"

I grabbed her arm. "We need to talk. Right now. It's urgent."

The annoyance left her face and she became serious. She took my hand in hers and led toward the door. "Let's go inside."

She ushered me back into her hut and went straight for her wood stove to brew tea. The dogs paced nervously around us. I pulled up a chair at the table and took a seat. My eyes briefly caught on the small weasel, she was sleeping peacefully on a large serving platter.

Hecate gestured toward me. "Don't wait for the tea to be done, jump right in."

I sat in silence, counting my shallow breaths. She turned from the stove to look at me. I could see the concern on her face. She had so eagerly agreed to side with me in my claim to rule, it was a slap in the face for me to come to her now with a change of heart. But I could not overthrow Hades. After all we had done, after the way he had looked at me…

I couldn't do that to him.

"There is no room for things like affection if we want to rule the Underworld." Wrath's words stung me.

"I'm calling it off."

Her brows shot up and her eyes widened. She did not speak. She turned back to the tea, pouring two cups full. The silence that hung between us was painful. I needed her to say something. Anything.

She brought the cups over and sat one down in front of me, then took her seat. Her eyes flicked up to mine as she sipped the bitter drink.

"What can I do to help? I assume I should discuss this with Hermes first, he's more apt to put his foot in his mouth."

Once again she had my back. No questions. I had done nothing to earn her unyielding loyalty to me.

"Aren't you going to ask why?"

"My dear... I do not need to ask why. I knew the moment the two of you met this would happen. I told you before; even the Gods cannot escape The Fates."

Her words only made me feel more ridiculous. I hadn't even considered that The Fates had meant for us to be together.

"Why didn't anyone tell me?" Betrayal burned in my eyes and tears threatened to fall.

"Would that knowledge have brought you to acceptance more quickly?"

My eyes dropped to the table. She was right. If I had known that was why he had taken me... I would have fought it. I covered my face with my hands, and my shoulders fell. My lungs burned as I inhaled deeply. There was no time to dwell on the past. I needed to fix things quickly. I lifted my face and looked at Hecate.

"Speak with Hermes, then Hypnos. I'll need to think of some way to placate The Furies."

She nodded solemnly. "Everything will be fine, Kora."

But everything did not feel fine. There was a sick feeling in my stomach ever since I had given myself to him at the party. Impending doom crushed me from the inside. We sat in silence, sipping our tea. I wanted to tell her everything.

"So, at the ball last night..." My voice trailed off.

"Yes?"

"I– well, we... Uhm. Hades and I..." My words trailed off slowly.

She sat up straight, slamming her cup down on the table. "Hells!" She paused. "It was *consensual*?"

"Yes! He didn't force me."

"Good. Sometimes men are cruel, Gods included. How are you feeling about it?"

"Good, I think. I just have this sinking feeling that he's going to find out about everything I did before and then he will hate me."

"He has no way of finding out." She paused again. "Are you *in love*?"

My face turned red. Love was a strong word. I had never loved anyone, not truly. I wasn't sure I even knew what it was supposed to feel like.

"I don't know."

"Well, there will be plenty of time to figure all of that out. As long as you're happy."

I tapped my fingers across the table. "Speaking of love, are you and Medusa?"

She choked on her tea. "That obvious, is it?"

"She seems lovely."

"She is. She is kind, even after everything she's been through. I admire her deeply."

"Do you love her?"

Her eyes met mine. "Yes. Though, had you asked me a few years ago I would have told you I did not. She slithered her way into my rotten heart despite my hesitance."

I considered her words. It gave me hope that perhaps one day I would know love without doubt. I just had to get past one very complicated obstacle first. An obstacle that could have been so easily avoided. I wondered how Hades felt about me. If he had the same reservations.

"I should probably get back. I should talk to him about last night."

"Indeed. Chin up, Kora. Rest and enjoy today. Make sure you're ready to practice tomorrow."

I rose from the table and she followed me outside. Words of reassurance repeated in my head over and over again as I pulled at my powers. I thought of the castle, of Hades. Blush covered my cheeks at the thought of seeing him again. We would make everything work somehow. We could start to really get to know one another and put all of the lies and secrets behind us. Move forward towards a future of change. We could make it work.

My power swirled around me, engulfing me entirely. I appeared just outside the door of the manor. Not quite where I had intended, but close. A smile bloomed on my face, I was proud of the progress I had made in such little time.

When I opened the door my stomach turned sour. The air inside was cold and rigid. My heart pounded in my chest as my eyes shot to the throne, where Hades sat.

Instantly, I knew something was wrong. My smile fell. He was glaring down at me, an icy rage in his eyes. My mind was racing as I stepped in and closed the door behind me. I told myself to breathe. I told myself everything would be ok. We could make it work.

"Aidoneus?"

He scoffed, shaking his head. "Don't call me that. Did you really think that you could sneak around behind my back and plot to take my throne without me learning of it?"

Fear and guilt flooded me, and I felt his anger radiating across the room towards me.

He had found out.

FORTY-ONE

I strode across the room towards him, my mind frantic to fix things, to explain what I had been thinking. He held up a hand, stopping me mere feet from the steps to the throne. There was a lump in my throat and my eyes stung with tears. I hated the way that he was looking at me.

"Aidoneus, please," I begged. "Let me explain."

"Explain? How can you justify such a wild act of betrayal? I trusted you, Kora."

His words were like a knife straight to my heart. It was guilt. Guilt was what caused his words to hurt me. Because what else could it have been?

"I didn't know! I didn't know about the prophecy. You snatched me away from my whole life to bring me here and you told me nothing!"

I flinched as soon as the words left my lips. I hadn't meant to shift the blame to him.

"He is to blame."

So are we.

"So are you," Wrath corrected.

"So your plot to overthrow me is *my* fault?" He shook his head.

"No. That's not what I meant. I only want you to see where I'm coming from. How things looked to me."

"I have been kind to you, Kora. And patient."

Another slice at me. I had no idea what I could say or do to fix it. I had been rash in my plotting. I had let Wrath whisper in my ear and soil who I was.

"Do not blame me."

"I know. You have... I– I was calling it all off."

His head tilted to the side, but somehow he just looked angrier. I swallowed thickly. I just wanted to take everything I had done back. I wanted another chance to start over.

"Since when?"

I paused. "What?"

"When did you decide to call it off?"

My heart sank. He would not like my answer. "Last night, after we snuck away from the party."

He stood, stalking over to me, burning into me with his red eyes. My heart was pounding, my power thrumming through me the closer he got. I could feel his power pulse in response to mine. He stepped up to me. The warmth from his body danced across my skin the way I remembered the sun once had. My hands twitched at my sides. I wanted to reach out and grab him, to beg him to forgive me.

"You will not beg."

I would do anything if it meant he didn't hate me.

"What changed?"

"What do you mean?" My words were barely a whisper.

"What changed for you last night?"

"I..."

Hecate's voice slipped back into my mind. *'Do you love him?'*

He waited, his eyes softening on me. I wanted to say it. But those words scared me. I wasn't sure I actually felt that way. I had no idea how to tell. And I was still trying to navigate who I was and what I wanted.

"I don't know."

His expression hardened. Was that disappointment there in his eyes? I wondered if I should have said it, even though I was uncertain. But the words would not come.

"When did you decide you wanted to take my throne?"

Deeper I sank into despair. His questions would only yield answers that would hurt him. We stared at each other as I struggled to speak. I didn't want to tell him. I didn't want to see more disappointment in his face. I could have thrown myself from a cliff at that moment.

"Kora."

I closed my eyes and inhaled, trying to calm my nerves and prepare for his anger. When I opened my eyes he was looking at me in a way that mirrored how I was feeling. Angry and hurt and sick.

"Not long after my arrival."

He frowned, I could see the pain in his eyes. I hated that I had hurt him.

"And what brought you to that decision?"

Every time he asked me another question I hated myself more. My face crumpled, and my eyes were pleading. I fought back tears. I didn't want to continue with the conversation anymore.

"Aidoneus."

"You wanted to explain," he snapped. "So explain."

I sighed, giving in. It didn't matter anymore. Any affection he might have had for me was surely gone. Any chance for us to rule together had crumbled away with all of my scheming.

"I saw the Underworld. It's bleak and desolate. The souls live–"

"The souls?" His eyes narrowed. "You went to see the shades? In The Furies territories?" There was both anger and worry in his voice.

"Yes," I said sternly. "They live their eternities in such a sad place, being tortured by Megaera and her sisters."

"You spoke to The Furies?"

"Of course I did! They're not happy either. Nor are the Gods who live here. Hecate resides in a hut, for Hell's sake. And Hypnos lives in a *cave*!"

"The Furies would have been put to death if it wasn't for me. And the Gods choose to live the way they do."

"Do they? I'm not saying you haven't tried, Hades. But I am saying that you have fallen short! You have been stagnant here. The souls need– they deserve– better. So do the Gods."

"And you think you could do better?" he spat.

I squared my shoulders. I struggled against Wrath, who had been growing and raging inside of me while I spoke.

"Yes! Yes, I do think I could run this place better. I can make this place beautiful–"

His laughter cut me off. "Oh, I have no doubt that you could. But it takes more than a few pretty flowers to rule, Kora."

"I could learn–"

"You could learn? From whom would you learn?"

My face burned red and I scowled. He was right, though.

"Stop interrupting me!"

"You're speaking nonsense. Do you even realize how naive you sound? You are young and inexperienced. You could never rule this place successfully!"

I recoiled, shame and guilt crashed over me. My eyes stung. He looked at the tears sliding down my cheeks and I thought I saw regret on his face. I was sure he thought they were from sadness but he was wrong. They were from anger.

"All your years and experience haven't mattered. You have failed everyone here!"

All of the sympathy left his face. He opened his mouth to speak and my power flared, shaking the entire castle.

"And," I continued, angrily. "You *did* bring me here against my will! And you have lied to me. You have withheld so many important matters, like the fit my mother is throwing above!"

His brows furrowed. "How did you–"

"And that *ridiculous* prophecy? Did you ever think I deserved to know? Maybe if you had been honest with me, I would have been honest with you!"

His face fell. I had struck a nerve. "Kora…"

"Who told you?" I demanded.

"What?"

"Who told you about what I was planning?"

He looked at me, clenching his jaw. He did not look like he wanted to tell me. Curiosity melded with my anger. I would find out one way or another.

"Does it matter?" he asked softly.

"It matters to me."

He paused, holding my stare. When he spoke the name I felt like a fool. I had fallen into her game and she had played me again. Wrath tried to rage against me. She wanted to destroy, to have her vengeance on the Nymph. But my heart fell, and suddenly I felt empty. I had no fight left in me. She had gotten her way.

"Minthe."

FORTY-TWO

The hopelessness spread through me like a blight. It rotted and strangled out all of the fire in my soul. My fervor had led me down a dark path, but Minthe… Minthe had been my end. All of my dreams for the Underworld were now out of reach. I had no reason to stay any longer. I would not be welcome at his side. I could not win a war he saw coming. And any chance we had together… It had decayed before my very eyes. When I finally spoke my voice was weak and trembling.

"Of course. Minthe has wanted me gone since I arrived."

"That is not fair and you know it. If she had come to me with some petty grievance we would not even be having a conversation. You were trying to remove me from my own realm."

I lifted my eyes to him. I knew he was right, but I also knew if Minthe did not feel the way she did about him she would not have told him. It *was* jealousy that ignited my hatred for her. And hers for me. It did not matter anymore. Anything I tried to accomplish moving forward would be fruitless. Still…

"She loves you." The words flew from my lips before I could stop them.

He narrowed his eyes. "I know."

Of course, he knew. She made no effort to hide it. But hearing him acknowledge it still stung me. I wasn't sure if a denial would have been any better, though. The Fates had been cruel to me. I ripped my eyes from his and glanced down at the marble floor. I was numb.

"Kora–"

I held my hand up and shut my eyes tightly. I did not want to hear him say anything else. I had felt enough. Wrath stirred around inside of me.

"Fix this, damn you!"

But I no longer cared to.

"I want to go home."

I shocked myself with the admittance. The Underworld had become my home. Things I hated when I first arrived had become comforting. I supposed if you stayed anywhere long enough you would get accustomed to it.

But I could not stay after all that had happened. I didn't belong below, anyway. I was the Goddess of Spring. The sun should be kissing my skin. I should have rich dirt beneath my nails. I should be above.

"Kora, you do not have to leave. You can stay here."

"We have worked too hard for you to run away now!"

My eyes flicked back to his. Desperation. That was what I saw in them. It tugged at my heart, threatening to break me. I shoved the feelings down, buried them.

"I cannot stay here."

"You can."

His voice was pleading and I did not understand why. How could he even consider me staying an option? He certainly did not understand how deeply that would hurt me. How it would slowly carve away at every piece of me.

"No. I cannot look at you every day and remember that night. I cannot see Minthe again."

"You are making a grave mistake, girl."

"Minthe will not say a word to you."

The constant back and forth between him and Wrath was driving me mad. There was a high-pitched ringing in my ear that told me an explosion was imminent if I did not get away somehow. I needed to leave.

"I know that she will not, because I won't give her the chance to. If I see her again I will kill her." It was not a threat. Just a fact.

His eyes widened with surprise. Silence fell between us. The seconds ticked by so painfully slow. The ringing subsided, replaced by the pounding of my pulse in my ears. My body was completely empty.

"Kora." He reached for my hand and I recoiled.

"Do not touch me."

He looked as though I had slapped his face. His hand dropped to his side.

"I want to go home," I repeated.

"This is your home."

"Listen to him, Kora!"

His insistence agitated me. How could he go about his days pretending as though nothing had happened? I would never be able to look at him the same. Every time our eyes met I would picture him underneath me and hear his moans of pleasure. We would never be able to go back to how we were before.

"This has never been and never will be my home!" My voice rang through the room and the ground rumbled. He flinched and his face fell.

"If you leave, the other Gods will find out and they will come for you."

"My mother, you mean? The one who hid me away to keep me safe from *you*?" I knew I shouldn't have said it, but I could not stop the words of pain coming from my mouth.

"There are things you are unaware of–"

"Because no one will tell me anything! You've all assured that I have been well kept in the dark."

"It has been for your own wellbeing."

"So you all keep saying."

He looked at me with what I knew was disappointment and shook his head. "If I send you back up then we are done."

"We are already done."

"You are walking into a den of vipers, Goddess. You are going to regret this decision, and when you do… Do not come crawling back to me."

"I would rather die!" I spat.

His face was flat, and he shook his head. "And then you would end up right back here forever. Try not to die."

He waved his hand and I felt his power flow through the room. My heart leapt and my stomach dropped. Black smoke swirled around me. Panic set in, though I held my ground firmly. He was actually sending me away. My heart and my Wrath screamed for me to stay, but I clamped my mouth shut. I could not stay, no matter how much I longed to. I kept my eyes glued to his as his power grew more tangible.

The sadness on his face would be burned into my mind forever.

"Goodbye, Goddess."

His words rang through my head like a bell as darkness swallowed me whole and the smell of iron and smoke surrounded me. Seconds later light broke through and my feet were back on solid ground again.

My eyes darted around, scanning my surroundings. I was in the woods. Familiar woods, not far from my village. The sun was so bright it burned my eyes and there was an abundance of smells. Dirt, grass, flowers… Birds sang from the trees above me. It overwhelmed my senses.

The wind blew and it was frigid, sending a chill over my whole body. I tried to remember how long I had been in the Underworld, what time of year it was. I had no idea. The constant gray and lack of day or night there had ensured I lost track of time.

The last bit of his scent scattered in the wind and I was alone. I would be fine. There was no other choice but for me to be fine. With a deep inhale I cleared my mind. My time in the Underworld had changed me, that much I could not deny. But it was time for me to find a new purpose, a new future. If I had to fight The Fates tooth and nail for the rest of my life, then that is just what I would do.

I started walking towards the village, my boots crunching over dried twigs and leaves. It must have been late winter, I must have just missed the snow. Spring would be coming soon, and no doubt the village could use my help with crops.

And if the Gods came for me, so be it. I would deal with them when they came. I was stronger than I once was. My power had been tamed and was easier for me to control.

But first, I needed to see my grandmother.

FORTY-THREE

"You have ruined everything we worked so hard to build." Her tone was sharp and accusatory.

It doesn't matter anymore. It's over.

I ducked under a branch, stepping carefully to avoid twisting my ankle on all of the loose rocks littering the ground. I placed my hand on the trunk of the tree as I passed, its bark was cold and rough against my palm.

"It does not have to be over. Call for him. Apologize."

He told me before I left not to call for him. He would not come, even if I did.

I pushed some brush down out of my way as I walked on. The thin, dry branches snapped apart at my touch. Everything was brittle and dead from the cold season.

"You do not know that. You saw the look in his eyes."

I inhaled deeply at the thought of his expression before I left. A sharp pain shot through my chest. It hurt to even breathe. *The cold*, I told myself.

Stop. I will not have this conversation with you any longer.

"But–"

"Enough!" My shout echoed through the trees causing birds to scatter. The sound of their wings was eerily loud as the rest of the woods went silent. That was it, I had truly lost my mind.

"*Have you?*" Her voice no longer sounded like it was coming from inside me.

I turned to see myself standing several feet away, black ichor leaking from my eyes. No. It was Wrath. I blinked, expecting her to vanish, but she did not. I reached up and rubbed my face. Still, she was there.

"*You are wasting your potential.*"

"I am so sick of you."

"*I am you.*"

I groaned loudly. I had hoped being back in the mortal realm would quiet her voice. Instead, she was even more tangible, making her harder to ignore. I would never be free of her.

"*What about all of your aspirations? All of your plans? Do the souls below truly mean so little to you?*" Her words were like a knife to my back.

"They are not my responsibility."

I started walking again, leaving her standing alone. I just wanted her to be quiet. To let me process all that had happened. She appeared in front of me, startling a gasp from my lips.

"*Why? Because you have deemed it so? The Fates–*"

"The Fates can find someone else to torment. I am over their games."

I walked on, passing through her. Her image rippled and dissipated like smoke. I knew she was not gone, though.

"Besides," I continued. "Even if I wanted to stay there, Hades would never share the realm. He would never allow me to make decisions and change things."

She appeared beside me, walking along with me. Her feet made no sound as she stepped. I kept my eyes straight ahead but I could feel her stare on me. It caused the hair on my arms to raise.

"You do not know that. He will forgive you, eventually."

"I do not care anymore."

"What about your friends? Hecate and Hypnos? What about The Furies?" Her words wounded me, and I winced before shaking my head and responding.

"I can see Hecate and Hypnos when they visit the upper world. The Furies will continue on as they always have."

"And what of your deal with Hermes?"

I stopped walking. Hermes. He would have to get over the abrupt ending to our deal. However, he had something that belonged to me. I considered for a moment whether I was truly ready to get back all of the memories I had lost. I wasn't sure, but it seemed like a good time to retrieve them. I might very well need them moving forward.

"That is not what I brought him up for."

I shot her a smile. "All the same, thank you for reminding me."

"You need to consider all of our options before you start making decisions."

"*My* options," I corrected, turning to her. "You are merely a fragment of my mind. You are me. Therefore they are my options."

She stood there, glaring at me. I felt a sliver of satisfaction from being able to use her own words against her.

"And my mind is made up. I am leaving the Underworld behind me. I shall retrieve my memories and move forward with my life. I will pave my own future. My own fate."

She paused. I realized then, staring into her inky black eyes, they were the same eyes that The Furies had. I wasn't sure how I hadn't noticed before.

"I do not like this."

"You do not have to."

I turned from her, checking my surroundings. I was still a little way off from the village. It was quiet, the perfect spot to call for Hermes. There would be no risk of any villagers spotting us. I opened my mouth to say his name and–

"No need. I'm already here."

I whirled around to see him standing there, dressed in robes. His red hair was a shaggy mess. He smiled, a mischievous sparkle in his eyes. Somehow he was always there when he needed to be.

"When did you make a habit of talking to yourself, Kora?"

FORTY-FOUR

Hermes stood across from me, his back resting against the trunk of a large oak tree. I had managed to keep my emotions wrangled thus far, but as I sat there on the cold ground I began to falter. Suddenly all of my feelings were rushing back to me. I was hurt, and sad. Things had not gone the way I had hoped at all.

"So, care to tell me what happened?"

I looked up at him. The lump in my throat made it difficult to speak. I took several shallow breaths and steadied myself. I knew Hermes would not accept silence as an answer.

"Hades discovered my plans."

His brows knitted together. "Hecate said you had called it off."

"I did. But I guess I was too late."

He stayed quiet. The silence allowed me to reflect and the more I did so, the more I was pained, so I forced myself to keep talking.

"I called it off because I… I think I have feelings for him. Not that it matters now." I wasn't sure why I was even bothering to tell Hermes that. He had hurt me, too.

"Did you tell him that?"

I cut my eyes at him. "No."

"So you decided to come back to the mortal realm?"

"I didn't have a choice."

Again, silence fell between us. He pushed himself off of the tree and walked over to me, taking a seat directly in front of me on the ground. His hazel eyes locked with mine and he smiled. It was a soft, kind smile.

"I assume you've made up your mind about your memories, so I'll not insult you by asking if you're sure."

I nodded. Between the lump in my throat and the nausea, I didn't dare speak. He lifted his hands and placed his fingers gently on my temples. They were warm against my skin, which had chilled from the frigid winter air. I had no idea what to expect from the memories, I was still terrified to regain them.

Before I had the chance to reconsider, a bright light flashed across my vision and pain erupted through my head. It was too late to change my mind.

***

I was looking down at a bowl of fruit on a table. They were all bright and perfectly ripened. I wiped tears from my face with my small hands. I was a child. A young neighbor had broken my favorite toy.

A familiar voice whispered to me. *"You should break one of her toys. She deserves it."*

Anger rippled through me. I ground my teeth and slammed my tiny fist on the table. Power coursed through me, darting towards the fruit. They turned brown and rotted within seconds. I stared, wide-eyed, then glanced down at my hands.

"Yes!"

"No, no, Kora."

I whirled around and saw, who I didn't know at the time was Hermes, shaking his head. I scurried down from my seat, backing away from him. I remembered the fear I had felt. I had no idea who he was. I worried I would be in trouble for what I had done.

"Who are you?"

"A friend," he said softly.

He knelt down to my level, smiling at me. There was something comforting about him. He beckoned me closer.

"You're not in trouble."

I took a few steps towards him. "My grandmother will be mad."

"No, she won't. Come here, Kora. I'll explain everything."

I walked up to him slowly. He placed his hand over my eyes and with a flash of light, I had forgotten it all.

***

More memories resurfaced, all of them similar situations as I aged through my life. Either accidental destruction, or rapid growth in my garden. I had been using my power my whole life, I just didn't remember. Each one ended with Hermes coming to suppress the memory.

Until... A much more recent one came back to me.

I was running through the woods, leaving Hecate's cabin. My mind was racing from the red-eyed man I had seen. Hades. As I burst into the village I saw someone walking. I stopped and turned to see Theo. The old man that had died. He saw me and raised his arm to motion me to him. Curiosity overcame me, and I approached him.

"Theo, what are you doing out so late?" I whispered. Not that I had room to talk, I was also out and about after I should have been.

"I was just going to your house, Kora. I need your help." It was late and neither of us wanted to wake the village, so he also spoke in hushed tones.

"What's wrong?"

"It's my horse. I think something is wrong with her."

I had no experience with horses, I was not sure why he needed *my* help. I was sure there was nothing I could possibly do.

"Can it not wait until morning?"

"Oh, I fear she won't make it to morning."

With a nervous glance over my shoulder, towards the red-eyed man in the woods, I followed Theo to his house. We did not speak as we walked, but he kept glancing back at me. I offered him a polite smile each time. I hoped there was nothing serious wrong. I was still unsure why he chose me instead of someone with more experience.

As we approached his home he turned to face me.

"Why don't you come in for a cup of tea, Kora?"

My mouth dried. Suddenly I felt very vulnerable. I had never really known Theo well, and I was now alone in the dark of night with him. I struggled between not being rude by declining his offer, and keeping myself safe.

"That is kind, Theo, but your horse…"

"She can wait a few moments. Please," he said as he opened his door. "I insist."

Nausea rolled through me and I felt light-headed. Every instinct I had told me to turn and run. That voice in my head was screaming at me.

"I'm not sure…"

"Very well. Come, the gate to the horse pasture is through my back door."

I felt like a trapped animal. I could see no way out. I envied the trapped animal at that moment, for they could chew off their own leg to escape. Against my better judgment, I flashed him a nervous smile and stepped inside.

Once inside he closed the door behind me. Instantly his demeanor changed. I could feel his nefarious intentions thick in the air. I should have listened to my instincts, to that Wrathful inner voice. He turned to me and smiled. It was sickening. My heart dropped.

"I've always thought you were such a beautiful young lady, Kora."

I took a small step back to the door.

"Thank you," I forced out. No amount of flattery would appease him, though. He had already decided what he wanted.

"Why don't you come rest in my bed for a while? It's so late."

Another step back.

"I really think I should be going, actually."

"What's the rush?"

Just one more step and I could grab the door.

"It's late, as you said."

My foot slid back and his eyes flicked to the door. I took the only opportunity I might be given and lunged for the knob. As my fingers closed around it he grabbed a fistful of my hair and yanked me back. My scalp screamed and I scrambled to get to my feet, but he dove on top of me. I struggled against him, he was much stronger than I had guessed he would be. Years of working the fields had served him well, unfortunately for me.

He fought against my clothes, trying to tear them from my body. His hands groped as he struggled against me. Our bodies collided with a table in the midst of our fight and a vase fell to the floor, shattering into pieces. Frantically, I reached for a shard of glass and swung it up towards his face. He blocked it with his arm, which was flayed open in one slice. He let out a cry of pain, allowing me to slip from under him.

I jumped to my feet and ripped the door open. I was mere feet outside when he grabbed me again and shoved me to the ground. I rolled to the side just as he dove at me again. He hit the ground with a thump. I was on my feet quicker than him. Our eyes locked and then his eyes dropped to my left hand. I was still clutching the large piece of glass.

"Now, Kora… Let's take a minute to calm down," he whispered.

But my mind was a blur of fear and Wrath. He nearly had me… Had nearly raped me. The realization made me sick.

"You lured me here."

"You seemed like you wanted it. I thought that's why you came with me."

"Excuses!" She screamed.

All of my rational thinking vanished. I was left with my fear and Wrath alone. Before I could even make sense of what I was doing, I tossed the glass aside and jumped on him. My fingers sunk deep into his throat, ripping it open before he could even scream. Blood sprayed, splattering across my arms and face. His eyes were wide with terror as he crumpled to the ground.

But I was not done.

My nails grew into thorny daggers, and I tore into him again. I shredded his chest and reached inside the cavity, tearing out his organs and throwing them aside. My hands gripped his ribcage and with a loud crunch and crack, I broke them apart. My gaze flicked to his face. His eyes were frozen open. Disgust and anger flooded me again. I grabbed his head and snapped his neck, turning it away from me.

Movement from the corner of my eye caught my attention, drawing me away from my savage mauling. A large mountain lion stood at the edge of the tree line. Her head hung low and her tail swung from side to side. Her golden eyes were locked onto Theo's destroyed and bloodied body and then they flicked up to me.

"Good. Let the animals devour him."

I looked down at Theo, at the carnage I had wrought, then down at my bloody hands. My anger melted away and panic set in. What had I done?

"You killed him."

No. No. No.

"Yes. He deserved it."

My whole body started shaking violently and sweat dripped down my face.

No. That was blood.

"Kora..."

I turned to see a man with a mop of red hair and bright hazel eyes, shock clear on his face. I shook my head, as though that could undo all I had just done.

"I didn't mean to..." Tears streamed down my face.

Hermes sprang into action. He rushed over and grabbed my arm, yanking me inside Theo's own home. He led me to the kitchen and pumped some water into the basin. He scrubbed my face and my arms clean of blood. My mind had shut down. I could no longer form thoughts or words. I didn't know who the man cleaning me was, and I didn't care. I would be burned at the stake for what I had done.

Once he had me clean he took my arm again. There was a flash of bright light and then we were standing in my room. I was in shock, the sudden change in scenery didn't even register. He sat me down at the edge of my bed and knelt in front of me. I stared past him, feeling completely numb.

"Kora, listen to me."

My eyes flicked up to his.

"You won't remember any of this, but I want you to know I am so sorry. I'm sorry I let this carry on so long. I'm telling Hades about you. You're too big for this mortal world. He will be good for you, and you for him."

I didn't understand anything he was saying to me. He placed his hand over my eyes and with a flash of blinding light the memory was taken from me.

FORTY-FIVE

I sat there in the dirt with tears pouring from my eyes. *I* had been the one that killed Theo. I had left him in the mess everyone had found him in the following morning. They had blamed a witch, a beast. But it was me.

And Hermes... Hermes had been protecting me all along. Had come to me throughout my life to keep me safe. At the behest of my mother, he had said. But I could see his affection for me in my memories. I had been so angry with him. I had thought about killing him. I had been wrong about him, though.

He reached out and brushed the tears from my cheeks. His fingers were warm against my skin. It pulled me from my thoughts and I glanced up at him. His hazel eyes were staring down at me, and the remorse I saw in his face brought my guilt deeper.

"I'm sorry I didn't tell you sooner." His voice cracked as he spoke.

"No!" I sobbed. "I'm sorry for all of the trouble I have caused you over the years."

He smiled sadly. "I have always known that you would be larger than life, Kora. You have never been trouble for me."

Another sob escaped my lips. He leaned forward and pulled me into his arms, letting me cry until I had no tears left. My weeping echoed through the woods around us, filling the silence. My body shook, and I clutched his robes as he held me. I cried for everything I had lost. My childhood, my mother, the life I could have had if I had been raised as a Goddess. The Underworld, the change I could have made there, the life I could have lived with Hades.

When I finally finished I sat back, glancing to the trees behind him, to the village beyond. I needed my grandmother. I needed to see her, to speak with her. My heart was so full of sorrow and grief, I needed one good thing.

"I suppose I couldn't talk you into returning to the Underworld now?"

I looked back at him. I wanted to say yes, to go running back to Hades. To go back to the place I had grown to love. I missed it there already. My time in the Underworld had shaped me in ways I had never imagined. But…

"I cannot go back. I need to go see my grandmother."

He nodded, accepting my decision without argument. "Very well, then. Should you need me, I will not be far."

With that he stood, casting his eyes down at me one last time. And then he vanished in his radiant light, leaving me alone in the woods. Once more I felt empty. Like a large piece of myself was missing. I stayed there, sat on the ground, for a long while. Until my legs cramped and my bones ached. My body was still shaking, from my nerves or the cold, I could not tell. My mind was a jumbled mess. I replayed my newly recovered memories over and over. Going through every detail of every one of them, making sure I did not miss a single thing. Making sure I had every moment memorized.

"*Are you going to sit here forever?*"

A deep sigh escaped my lips, my eyes drifted down to the earth beneath me. I ran my fingers through the thick rich soil and it caked under my nails. I found myself wishing it was iron instead.

I thought you didn't want to return to the village?

"I don't. Even more so now. Those mortals are all disgusting."

Not all of them. Not my grandmother.

I stood, brushing dirt from my legs. The wind blew and sent a chill deep into my body. I started walking towards the village, setting my mind on the task at hand. It was quiet. The birds had ceased their singing and there were no other signs of life around me. It was as though the world itself had stilled. Like I was the only living thing around. Leaves crunched loudly under my feet as I walked. It was unnerving.

Should I tell my grandmother who I really am? Do you think she will hate me?

Wrath paused. "Tell her or don't. I do not think it matters if you plan to live out your days cowering from the Gods, living your life as a mortal."

I sighed heavily. *You are so supportive.*

"Only when I feel you're making the right decisions. And for the record, I do not think you are making the right decision."

So I've gathered.

She was silent for a beat. I half thought she had retreated within me, finished with our conversation. But to my disdain, she spoke again.

"Hermes is right. You're too big for this world."

A soft chuckle escaped my lips. *I never thought I would hear you say those words.* 'Hermes is right'.

"I can give credit where it is due."

Now that I know what I am capable of, and I can control my powers, I think I'll do just fine among the mortals.

"You think?"

I did not respond to her because I had said exactly what I meant. And I could only hope I was right because I could not return below. I had ruined my chances with that already, and I knew Hades would never forgive me.

"You give in too easily. Have some backbone."

Will you stay quiet for five minutes, please?

"...I could, if you were not so absolutely infuriating."

I rolled my eyes and rubbed my head. She was going to make for a miserable walk through the woods. The eerie silence would have been more comforting than her neverending nagging in my ear.

"If I must be miserable, so will you."

You cannot possibly hate the village that much.

"You saw what Theo nearly did to you."

And Theo is dead.

"I am sure the others are no different than he was."

And in that respect, I hoped she was wrong. Or at the very least I never had to find out. I glanced around again, noting the silence once more. I still had not heard any birds or wildlife.

"It is winter."

But this felt different, it was too quiet. Too still. Suddenly, a screech broke the silence and my eyes shot to a branch above me. A single crow sat there, staring down at me. *One for sorrow*, I thought.

Anxiety coiled in my gut. Something was wrong. My steps quickened until I was running as fast as I could. The wind whipped my hair behind me and the cold air stung my face. I was nearly there. I pushed through the last of the brush and stepped into the village.

I saw people I knew bustling about, and chickens and sheep wandered around aimlessly. For a split second everything seemed right as it should be. Just as I had left it. I nearly huffed a sigh of relief. Nearly scolded myself for being so anxious over silly superstitions.

But the stench of death filled my nostrils. My eyes darted around. No one else seemed to even notice the smell.

Then my eyes fell on a corpse, a brown shawl still wrapped around her shoulders. My grandmother. Nausea turned my stomach and bile rose to my throat. A scream stuck in my chest, refusing to break free. The villagers were turning to look at me, finally noticing my arrival. But my eyes were glued to her. Or what was left of her.

She was dead. Her body had been mangled and broken. Her flesh was torn and rotting, covered in flies and maggots.

She was *dead*. Bones were clearly protruding and snapped. I could see obvious chunks missing, as though animals had been eating away at her over time.

She was dead. My mind tried to make sense of what I was seeing, what had happened. I couldn't understand why they had just left her there. Tears stung my eyes and horror completely overwhelmed me.

Gallus approached me slowly, his hands held up in front of him. "Kora," he said cautiously.

I turned to him with wild, unbridled rage-brimmed eyes. My power was bubbling over, pushing against the seams of my very being. It tore at me, trying to free itself. It wanted to blast through the village, decomposing everything in its path. It wanted destruction and vengeance.

It wanted death.

The earth beneath us trembled and shook. When I spoke my voice was calm and even, in contrast to the storm raging inside of me.

"What. Happened?"

FORTY-SIX

Wrath grows like a pomegranate tree. It starts off like a small seed, growing quietly beneath the surface, unbeknownst to those walking around it… Some would say Wrath alone is not sustainable enough to get you through life, but I beg to differ.

***

"What happened?!" I demanded louder.

His eyes were wide and I could smell a fear so deep it crippled him. His mouth opened and closed again as he searched for an explanation. Every second that passed in silence only caused my fury to flourish further. It grew into a tangled mess, threatening to ensnare and choke out all of the life in its path.

No. It was not a threat, it was a promise. A promise I was ready to allow it to fulfill.

"It was the work of the Gods. We couldn't stop it."

I had already guessed as much. The wounds inflicted on her were too similar to the ones I bestowed on Theo. But Theo had been a rotten man, plagued by his demented lust. My grandmother was a good woman.

Was. She had not deserved such a gruesome end. Guilt tried to smother out my anger. If I had not left her; if I had been at the village with her…

"You did not do this."

"And you left her there?" My voice cut through the air with a deadly calm.

"They told us to leave her there. Said if we moved her they would come back and do the same to us."

My eyes flashed with that feral rage again as I tore my eyes from her ruined, maggot-filled body back to Gallus. The smell of rotting flesh was nauseating. Every time I inhaled it burned my throat.

"What God was it? Who did this to her?"

Gallus shrunk into himself, taking a step back. "We don't know, Kora. We never saw their face."

"Find out who did this." Wrath whispered. *"Have your retribution."*

Someone would surely pay for the life that had been taken. I would make sure of that.

Again my power pulled at me, begging to be released into the world. It skittered through my veins like lightning, it burned like hot coals, it came in waves like an ocean. I fought to keep it contained within me, but it was too much.

My eyes drifted back to my poor grandmother. Had she been scared in her final moments? Or in pain?

Her words replayed in my mind.

'The Gods are vengeful and angry creatures. They do not like to be scorned or slighted.'

Gallus spoke again, drawing my attention back to him. "I'm sure you want to bury her, Kora. But–"

"Bury her?" I mused softly. "Bury her?!"

My voice became shrill and I felt myself tipping over an edge I would not be able to come back from. The image of her body was burned into my eyes and my mind. I would never *not* be able to see her like that.

My grandmother had been right; the Gods were vengeful and angry creatures. And *I* was a God.

"What I wanted," I said with a ruthless tone. "Was to come home to find my grandmother alive and well!"

He flinched away from me. The other villagers had stopped whatever mindless tasks they had been doing and they stood, watching me. I could taste their terror in the air. And it was delicious. I scanned them all like a hungry animal. They had no idea just how disgustingly weak they were compared to me. They were nothing more than bugs. And they had stood by while my grandmother was killed. A woman they had all known their whole lives. A respectable woman.

Theo's slimy smile flashed across my mind. I wondered how many others he had attempted to hurt, or worse. Who else in the village had done exactly as he had planned to do to me? I could not stand by and let people like that walk free in the world. People who would steal the innocence from young girls or leave a broken body strewn across the town square to rot.

I thought of Medusa and the way she had been punished for being a victim, the God who defiled her left to walk away without so much as a slap on the wrist.

"Kora?" My eyes flicked back to Gallus as he said my name weakly.

No. Indeed, I would not stand for it. I craned my head back to the sky. It was the most breathtaking shade of blue. The warmth of the sun seeped into my skin. I had missed the way it felt to be above. I felt stronger in the upper world. Like it fed my body exactly what it needed to be at the pentacle of its strength. My power crashed against me like a tidal wave, and I opened myself up to it completely. I let it consume every sliver of my being. It pounded against my bones and my muscles and flew through my veins.

My fingertips burned as my nails grew into sharp points. Black ichor leaked from my eyes, sliding down my cheeks. My back barked in pain, sending me doubling over. I could hear my flesh tearing open as a pair of large, leathery wings erupted. Wings exactly like The Furies had. The same I had looked at not long before with envy.

I stood tall, stretching them out around me. They were heavy and foreign, but my power coursed through them and I knew I could control them. I beat them against the air once. Twice. I felt incredible. I felt powerful.

Gasps and cries filled the air as my black eyes scanned the villagers. Several people screamed and fainted. A few fell to their knees, begging for their lives. I watched in contempt. They were people who had turned their noses up at me. People who had shunned me my whole life… Until they needed me. I could not help but wonder if my grandmother had also begged for her life. Had they heard her cries and stood by idly?

I took several careful steps towards Gallus, who was trembling. I inhaled deeply, breathing in the scent of his fear. He fell to his knees, looking up at me with wide eyes. Tears lined his cheeks. I knelt in front of him, inches from his face, and tilted my head to the side.

"Tell me Gallus; why did we forsake the Gods for so long?"

His lips trembled. The wails of the villagers filled my ears but my eyes were locked onto his. I waited patiently for his answer as he stared at me. I needed to hear him say it. When he finally spoke his voice cracked weakly.

"The Gods are evil."

I looked down at my clawed fingers, then beyond him to the crowd of people who had gathered. They held each other and sobbed. They were terrified. It filled me to the brim with satisfaction. They should be terrified.

I glanced back at Gallus. "Indeed."

In one fluid motion, I reached my arm out and dug my nails into his chest. Flesh and bone alike sliced apart until my hand was wrapped around his heart. Hot, sticky blood splattered across my face. I felt the rhythmic beating against my palm. It sputtered and struggled to pump. A single tear slid from his lifeless eye as I clenched my fist, crushing his heart in my hand. His body fell limp to the ground with a loud thump.

A bloodcurdling scream broke through the air and my predatory eyes snapped up to the woman. Her face was contorted with horror and she clutched her chest. Her whole body shook violently. Power blasted through me again, ravenous and angry. It swirled around me and then it engulfed me.

In an instant, I was in front of her. She barely had time to realize I was there before I ripped out her throat. Blood sprayed me again. The taste of copper coated my tongue. I shoved her body aside. It slammed into the earth loudly.

    I turned then to a group of villagers huddled together, as though that could save them from me. I raised my blood-stained hand and pointed at them. Death and decay spread across the ground, hurtling towards them quickly. It leeched life out of the ground as it pushed on. The dirt dried and cracked and the grass turned brown and brittle. It reached several goats first, and before my eyes they crumbled into dust. The people I had known most of my life tried to scramble away but my power was too fast. Their bodies were sapped of life, their flesh turned gray and dried out, and then they too were dust in the wind.

    Several other people made to run, drawing my attention to them next. I flexed the muscles in my newfound wings, beating them against the air as hard as I could. A breeze caught them and they heaved my body upwards to the sky.

    The wind blew against my curls as I darted towards them. My hair whipped around me, tangling into a mess. I grabbed one of them by the head and with one swift motion I snapped it clean from his shoulders. I moved on to the others, my claws ripped and shredded them to pieces.

    I was covered in blood and gore. My mind had hollowed out, the only thing I could think of was death and destruction. And vengeance. My power begged for more. It *needed* more. Screams continued to fill the air as I flew towards more people. I chased them all down, sweeping through their homes to drag them all into the street before I tore them apart.

    I did not stop until every last villager had been slaughtered. Wrath had been quiet during my rampage, leaving me to my revenge. My breath heaved as I inhaled and exhaled, filling the silence that now hung around me. Every muscle in my body ached and my heart pounded in my chest. My wings and claws receded, and the ichor dried along my cheeks. My legs trembled and gave way, and I allowed myself to drop to the ground.

My eyes drifted down to my blood-stained hands.

'You are a force of nature, Kora.'

I threw my head back and screamed up at the blue sky, shattering the silence that lingered heavily in the air. My scream turned into mournful sobs as my grief swallowed me. I would never again hear her voice. Never again would I come to her in search of words of comfort. She was gone.

My eyes drifted to the sea of blood and mangled corpses that I had left in my wake. I had killed them all. Men, women...The children. They were all dead. Charon would be busy. Tears slid down my face and mingled with blood that was not my own, and I felt regret for what I had done. Certainly, they did not all deserve to have their lives taken. I was supposed to be a Goddess of Spring, of life...

Wrath's voice echoed in my head, leaving me feeling void and desolate–

"There can be no life without death," she whispered.

And that is exactly what I was. What I had always been...

Death.

EPILOGUE

Drip. Drip. Drip.

I ran my fingers across the coarse stone floor, leaving a trail of blood in their wake. How long had I been locked away? I had lost track what seemed like forever ago. My eyes drifted slowly around the room. It was a cell, no matter how many times I had been told not to refer to it as such. The shackles on my wrists and ankles were undeniable proof that I was a prisoner.

Drip. Drip. Drip.

Wrath had been quiet since I was locked away. She, too, was confined. As were my powers. I had never been truly alone before, she had always been there. Again and again, I replayed the last moments before I was chained. I had counted every visible brick since the shackles were placed. I had counted my ragged breaths. I had counted my heartbeats.

Drip. Drip. Drip.

And that Gods awful *dripping*! I yanked against the chain, the clanking echoed through the empty room. Then that dreadful silence came again. I fought back tears as I leaned against the wall. How many years of my life would be spent chained?

'Until I can trust you to behave.' That was what I had been told.

Behave. As though I were a child or a dog. *Behave.* Like some mindless, subservient woman. No. No, that would not be me. I could not let myself break. I would get out. And when I did, I would slaughter them all. Death to every single person who stood by as I was stripped of my power and confined. I would not stop until their blood nourished the earth.

Drip. Drip. Drip.

I yanked the chain again. And again. And again. I pushed inward, searching for any sliver of power that might have been hiding deep inside of me somewhere. There was nothing...

Wrath? Wrath!

Alone. I was alone. I slammed my palm into the floor until blood splattered. I didn't care that it hurt. Everything hurt. I leaned back against the wall and let my mind drift off. To a peaceful place that I loved, one that was far away. A place with gray skies and iron earth. Exhaustion crept up to take me. I fell asleep to the thought of red eyes, the smell of smoke and iron, and...

Drip. Drip. Drip.

Acknowledgments

    Thank you, Rafael, for encouraging me to pick up yet another hobby, and for believing in me every step of the way. Thank you, Lily, for listening to me ramble about the world and characters I created and love so much. Thank you, Mom, for helping me brainstorm and offering advice to make me a better author. Thank you, Kayla, for being beside me while I worked through all of my plotting and scheming to get this book written. Thank you, Courtney, for your undying support and excitement for my journey while writing my first book.

    Thank you to Allison, Baylee, Ashton, and Matthew for reading my first draft and giving me feedback that helped The Ballad of Wrath and Death turn into the story I knew it could be. Thank you to all of my beta readers, but especially Thea, Bre and Kaitlyn! Thank you to all of my other family and friends who offered support along the way, I never could have done it without you all.

    And thank you to every person who may pick this book up and read it. I hope you enjoy the story and the characters as much as I did while I was writing it.

About the Author

H.T. Mejia has a passion for animals and has worked in Veterinary Medicine for many years. She is a food enthusiast, lover of all things fantasy, and she is fascinated with Greek Mythology. H.T. Mejia is the author of the new novel: The Ballad of Wrath and Death. She started her author journey at the beginning of 2024 and looks forward to completing book two in the duology soon.

Milton Keynes UK
Ingram Content Group UK Ltd.
UKHW022150111124
451073UK00008B/258